As the prehistoric evening turned to night, Cohen found what he had been looking for, cowering in some underbrush: large brown eyes, long, drawn-out face, and a lithe body covered in fur that, to the tyrannosaur's eyes, looked blue-brown.

A mammal. But not just any mammal. *Purgatorius,* the very first primate, known from Montana and Alberta from right at the end of the Cretaceous. A little guy, only about ten centimeters long, excluding its ratlike tail. Rare creatures, these days. Only a precious few.

The little furball could run quickly for its size, but a single step by the tyrannosaur equaled more than a hundred of the mammal's. There was no way it could escape.

The rex leaned in close, and Cohen saw the furball's face, the nearest thing there would be to a human face for another sixty million years. The animal's eyes went wide in terror.

Naked, raw fear.

Mammalian fear . . .

—from "Just Like Old Times" by Robert J. Sawyer

Magic Tales Anthologies
Edited by Jack Dann & Gardner Dozois

Edited by Terri Windling

DINOSAURS II

EDITED BY
JACK DANN & GARDNER DOZOIS

ACE BOOKS, NEW YORK

This book is an Ace original edition,
and has never been previously published.

DINOSAURS II

An Ace Book / published by arrangement with
the editors

PRINTING HISTORY
Ace edition / December 1995

Acknowledgment is made for permission to print the following material:

"The Big Splash," by L. Sprague de Camp, copyright © 1992 by Davis Publications, Inc.; first published in *Isaac Asimov's Science Fiction Magazine*, June 1992; reprinted by permission of the author.

"Just Like Old Times," by Robert J. Sawyer, copyright © 1993 by Robert J. Sawyer; first published in *On Spec*, Summer 1993; reprinted by permission of the author.

"The Virgin and the Dinosaur," by R. Garcia y Robertson, copyright © 1992 by Davis Publications, Inc.; first published in *Isaac Asimov's Science Fiction Magazine*, February 1992; reprinted by permission of the author.

"The Odd Old Bird," by Avram Davidson, copyright © 1989 by The Terminus Publishing Company, Inc.; first published in *Weird Tales*, Winter 1989; reprinted by permission of the author's estate and the author's agents, Owlswick Literary Agency.

"Bernie," by Ian McDowell, copyright © 1994 by Bantam Doubleday Dell Magazines; first published in *Asimov's Science Fiction*, August 1994; reprinted by permission of the author.

"Small Deer," by Clifford D. Simak, copyright © 1965 by Clifford D. Simak; first published in *Galaxy*, October 1965.

"Dinosaur Pliés," by R. V. Branham, copyright © 1989 by R. V. Branham; first published in *Midnight Graffiti* #4, Fall 1989; reprinted by permission of the author.

"Day of the Hunters," by Isaac Asimov, copyright © 1950 by Columbia Publications, Inc.; first published in *Future Fiction*, November 1950; reprinted by permission of the author's estate and the author's agents, Ralph M. Vicinanza, Ltd.

"Herding with the Hadrosaurs," by Michael Bishop, copyright © 1992 by Michael Bishop; first published in *The Ultimate Dinosaur* (Bantam Books); reprinted by permission of the author.

"Ontogeny Recapitulates Phylogeny," by R. Garcia y Robertson, copyright © 1990 by R. Garcia y Robertson; first published in *Pulphouse Eight* (Pulphouse); reprinted by permission of the author.

"Trembling Earth," by Allen Steele, copyright © 1990 by Davis Publications, Inc.; first published in *Isaac Asimov's Science Fiction Magazine*, November 1990; reprinted by permission of the author.

For
Bob Walters
—Dinosaur Man

ACKNOWLEDGMENTS

The editors would like to thank the following people for their help and support:

Susan Casper, Janeen Webb, Peter Nicholls, Janet Kagan, George Zebrowski, Bob Walters, Michael Swanwick, Ellen Datlow, Sheila Williams, Ian Randal Strock, Scott Towner, R. V. Branham, Robert J. Sawyer, all the folks on the Delphi and GEnie computer networks who offered suggestions, and special thanks to our own editors, Susan Allison and Ginjer Buchanan.

Contents

Preface

In the five years since we brought you *Dinosaurs!*, our first dinosaur anthology, almost everything that scientists then thought that they knew about dinosaurs has been challenged by *some*one, *some*where.

The theory, popular in the 1980s, that dinosaurs were hot-blooded, agile, fast-moving, socially interactive, and smart (itself an overthrow of a previous generation's theory that pictured dinosaurs as immense, lumbering, stupid, cold-blooded lizards who spent their solitary days submerged up to their necks in deep water to help them support their vast weight) has been challenged by some scientists (although probably the majority of experts believe that they were hot-blooded—or at least that some of them were). The theory that birds are the direct descendants of dinosaurs has been challenged (with at least one expert advancing the fiercely controversial theory that instead *dinosaurs* were the direct descendants of *birds*). The theory that all of the dinosaurs were killed off sixty-five million years ago by an immense asteroid impact at the end of the Cretaceous—one of the most widely accepted and talked-about scientific theories of the 1980s—has recently been challenged. Some scientists proposed the idea that the spread of disease germs from one continent to another, made possible by the development of connecting land-bridges between the continents, was the agent responsible for the extinction of the dinosaurs, who would have had no natural resistance to the new germs. Other groups of experts attributed the dinosaur-killing to a dramatic worsening of the climate at the end of the Cretaceous from vast, sun-blocking clouds of dust produced by a massive worldwide upsurge in volcanic activity, rather than to vast, sun-blocking clouds of dust kicked up by a huge asteroid impact. Some heretics even suggested that a few dinosaurs may have lingered on in Australia long after they were extinct in other areas of the world, past the sacrosanct "Cretaceous Barrier"—the famous layer of iridium in the rock—that is supposed to mark the end of their days.

No, there is no agreement among the experts. In fact, it seems that the controversies grow *more* heated rather than less so, the more that is written about dinosaurs—and more *is* written every day, a swelling tide of verbiage in scientific journals, popular science magazines, newspapers, and even in the tabloids.

One thing that hasn't changed in the last five years is the public's fascination with dinosaurs. In fact, they're probably *more* fascinated now, as depictions of dinosaurs spill over into the movies (with *Jurassic Park* becoming the second highest grossing film of all time, and a thundering horde of sequels and imitations soon to follow), and onto our television screens, to say nothing of a flood of novels, comic books, children's picture books, computer games, arcade games, posters, art books, coffee mugs, milk cartons, T-shirts, and so on. Dinosaurs even serve as children's toys, peek out from computer screen-savers, and act as animated pitchmen on television commercials. In fact, in a rush to cash in on "dino madness," entrepreneurs have put likenesses of dinosaurs on just about everything on which it is possible to *put* them, including underwear and condoms.

We can't be too self-righteous about this, of course, since the book that you hold in your hands is, obviously, also calculated to cash in on the craze . . . but, we hope, in a way at least a little less cynical and more useful than some designer who slaps glow-in-the-dark dinosaurs on socks. For one thing, although these stories were written as entertainment, reading them may actually also teach you something as well, in a more enjoyable way than studying a dry textbook, or even watching Walter Cronkite pontificate about Apatasauruses on television while badly animated stop-motion models hop jerkily around the screen. Because, until someone invents a working time-machine, the best way to experience dinosaurs in all their intricacy and diversity, to feel the thrill of wonder and awe as you come face-to-face with these fabulous monsters, to marvel at their terrible immensity, to smell their deep musk and feel the ground tremble underfoot and hear them bellow, to see their gleaming eyes turn slowly toward you . . . or to know, with a shock of recognition, what it was like to be a dinosaur, to rend the steaming flesh of your prey, or to be so rended . . . or to know what it is like to sleep in the rock for millions of years . . . or to know what the world would have been like if the dinosaurs had never died, or if they lived again . . . is to see them through the inner eye of the imagination, the way that you'll encounter them in the pages of a good science fiction story . . . stories such as the ones we've gathered for you here.

So open the pages of this book, and enjoy the dinosaurs you'll find within. (But be careful! Watch out that they don't step on you . . .)

The Big Splash
by
L. Sprague de Camp

L. Sprague de Camp is a seminal figure, one whose career spans almost the entire development of modern fantasy and SF. For the fantasy magazine Unknown *in the late 1930s, he helped create a whole new modern style of fantasy writing—funny, whimsical, and irreverent—of which he is still the most prominent practitioner. His most famous books include* Lest Darkness Fall, The Complete Enchanter *(with Fletcher Pratt), and* Rogue Queen. *His short fiction has been collected in* A Gun for Dinosaur, The Purple Pterodactyls, *and* The Best of L. Sprague de Camp, *among many other collections. His most recent books include a novel written in collaboration with his wife, writer Catherine Crook de Camp,* The Pixilated Peeress, *and, of special interest to the readers of this anthology, a collection of his tales about Reginald Rivers's time-traveling adventures,* Rivers in Time.*

The story that follows is one of those adventures, a direct sequel to de Camp's famous story "A Gun for Dinosaur." This one takes Reginald Rivers and a band of intrepid scientists back through time to observe the mysterious cosmic catastrophe that wiped out the majority of all living things at the end of the Cretaceous. As Reggie soon discovers, though, the problem is not to observe it so closely that you become extinct yourself . . .

* * *

What was my closest call, Mr. Burgess? Let's see. There was the time that drongo Courtney James woke up a sleeping tyrannosaur by shooting a gun over its head. . . . But if you really want to know, on these time safaris we haven't had so much trouble from the animals as from the people, and we haven't had so much grief from the people as we have from natural forces. Like that time we ran into Enyo. No, not Ohio, Enyo. That's what those scientific blokes call the K-T Event. Somebody named it Enyo after some Greek goddess of destruction.

Ta, don't mind if I have another.

The K-T Event? That's what killed off all the dinosaurs; pterosaurs, plesiosaurs, etcetera at the end of the Cretaceous. So Rivers and Aiyar, Time Safaris, took a couple of scientists to the edge of the Event, hoping it would not kill us off along with the ornithopods. And it nearly bloody well did. If Bruce Cohen, the chamber wallah, had been a second sooner or later with the doors, Aljira only knows what—

Who's Aljira? That's the head god of one of the tribes of Abos—excuse me, Native Australians—in the outback. You see, down-under we have lots of wowsers, worse than your Puritans here in America. If they hear you say "By God!" they raise a stink. So I long ago got into the habit of swearing by Aljira to avoid arguments.

But to get back. The scientists had been arguing for half a century over the nature of the K-T Event. Some said a comet or a planetoid hit the Earth; others, that one or more of those big super-volcanoes, like the one that made your Yellowstone Park, cut loose with an eruption that blanketed the Earth with ash and smoke.

When Professor Prochaska, here in St. Louis, got his time chamber working right, and the Raja and I made a going thing of Rivers and Aiyar, a couple of big universities thought to settle the question by sending a pair of their biggest brains back in time for a firsthand look at the Event. One came from Harvard and one from Yale, since no other unis could have afforded the rates.

The man from Harvard was a paleontologist, George Romero of the Museum of Comparative Zoology; a short, plump, middle-aged fellow with sparse gray hair. The other was a geologist, Sterling Featherstone of Yale, a bit younger; a tall, angular, black-haired bloke of the kind they call "raw-boned." Imagine a younger Abraham Lincoln without his whiskers and you've got the idea.

This pair came into the office together and broke the news. I had a pretty full schedule lined up, but in one slot I had only two cash customers ticketed: Clarence Todd, a trophy hunter, and Jon O'Connor, an artist. If you're wondering why an artist should be keen to go back to the Mesozoic—or how an artist could afford the fare—he had a contract with that museum in San Francisco to paint Cretaceous scenes from life. They paid his way.

"You understand," said Romero, "that we shall also have to have an astronomer. We need him to keep watching the sky, in hope of calculating when Enyo will hit."

"Who's Enyo?" I said.

"That's our name for the planetoid whose fall caused the K-T Event—"

"He means," said Featherstone, "*if,* as he believes, the Event was the impact of an extraterrestrial body. I'm a supercaldera man myself."

"Has anybody seen this body circling the sun?" I said. "They keep track of a lot of asteroids with their telescopes."

"Of course not!" said Romero. "The impact vaporized it."

"Silly of me. Have you picked your astronomer?"

"Yes," said Romero. "If it's okay with you, it'll be Einar Haupt of Cal Tech."

"I shall want to meet Mr. or Doctor Haupt," I said. "We always like to judge our sahibs before we take them on. A crook choice can cause serious trouble later, as we've found to our sorrow. Right, Raja?"

"Absolutely," said the Raja—that is, Chandra Aiyar. I call him "Raja" because he's actually the hereditary lord of some place in India called Janpur. If he went back there now and tried to assert hereditary claims, the locals would probably throw things at him. I gather the last reigning Raja of Janpur, before the Republic, wasn't universally beloved.

Dr. Haupt turned out to be a big, beefy fellow, almost my size, with red hair and whiskers. He needed the beef to lug his instrument: a superscientific combination of telescope, transit, and radar set, all over knobs and lenses. By means of the radar he could get a quick reading on the distance of anything this side of Mars.

The first complication popped up when I talked to Beauregard Black, our camp boss, about the trip. The problem was that, since the Event was likely to be a bloody catastrophe for everything around, we had to have the chamber stay with us the whole time we were there leading up to the Event, so we could make a quick getaway. There's no telephone line to Present, so you can ring up and yell:

"Come and get us, quick!"

Bruce Cohen, who ran the chamber, said that that was okay with him as long as he was paid his regular rate. In fact, he said, he was glad of a chance for a good look at one of these primeval landscapes he'd been ferrying people to. So far he'd only had brief glimpses when he opened the chamber doors for the time travelers to hop out and later back in.

When we explained this to Beauregard, he said he had to talk to the rest of the crew, the helpers and herders and Ming the cook. Next day he came back to say in effect: sorry, mate, no dice. The sahibs and I could go back and sit on a log to watch the end of the Mesozoic world, but to him and the others that was taking too much of a chance. He said:

"Mr. Rivers, I don't know how fast we'd have to skedaddle; but it would sure be a lot faster than the usual way, with at least two trips in the chamber. With the jacks, it'd take at least three. And we jest ain't gonna stand around watchin' the world go up in smoke waiting for the chamber to come back for the next load."

"We're not taking the asses," I said. "Since we don't know the exact time of the Event, we shan't dare go far enough from the landing site to call for moving the camp. So the crew will be smaller."

Beauregard shook his head. "Jeez, I'm sorry, Mr. Rivers; but I'm afraid we jest ain't gonna. I've talked with the other boys, and we all agree. We got families and that kind of thing."

The Raja and I tried to argue Beauregard round, but we might as well have tried to knock over a mammoth with a flyswatter. I suppose I could have fired him and the others for breach of contract; but I doubted I should ever again find such a bonzer camp boss. We'd been on several *safariin* together, so I knew Beauregard pretty well. Not having our regular helpers would rather leave us up a gum tree. It's not the sort of expedition on which you could rely on casual, untrained help. To push off with such a crew would be asking for disaster.

And so it turned out, when I discussed the problem with our five sahibs. The scientists complained that all the pitching and striking camp, cooking and cleaning up, etcetera, wouldn't leave them time for their scientific work. O'Connor complained that it wouldn't leave him time for his art. But the loudest complaints came from Todd, who was one of these little, Napoleonic types who tries to make up for his physical stature by a prickly, aggressive attitude.

"If this safari doesn't have the things it was advertised as having," he said, "I'm damned if I'll go along on it. I won't be able to get in a decent hunt if I've got to fuck around collecting firewood and all that nonsense. I'll expect my deposit back, too."

Later, when the Raja and I were alone, he said: "I believe I see a way out, Reggie." Back down-under nobody calls me "Reggie." There, it's "Reg." But the Raja had been through one of those English-style educations and picked up some pommy habits. Americans on these jaunts hear him and copy him; so to them I'm "Reggie," too. I don't mind; life is full enough of real problems without stewing over trifles. The Raja explained:

"Suppose Mr. Black and his crew come back to pre-K-T with us, set up camp, and then go back to Present. Then let Mr. Cohen bring the chamber back to pre-K-T and stay there. When time comes to leave, we shan't strike camp in our usual environmentally careful way; just heave the small, valuable items like guns and instruments into the chamber and leave the tents, camp chairs, and so on where they are. The universities won't like the cost of wasting that stuff, but we shall simply tell them this is the only way the job can be done."

That's how it was decided. The sahibs still grumbled; but their protests were muffled when Ming decided to come along for the whole stretch, so at least they wouldn't have to cook and wash dishes. He explained:

"Mr. Rivers, some day I'll have my own restaurant, and I'll advertise myself as the world's greatest cook for dinosaurs and other extinct animals. You shoot 'em, I'll cook 'em. Besides, I want to try out that new set of kitchen hardware you bought for this time trip."

The first problem, Mr. Burgess, was in setting down the transition chamber at the right time—within a convenient interval before the Event, but not so far ahead that we should grow old while waiting for it. The dating for rocks from the time of the formation had narrowed down the time of the onset of the Event to about a year and a half. They were pretty sure it began in 65,971,453 B.C. or the year following. They couldn't get any closer, and certainly it was bloody marvelous to be able to pin it down to one part in tens of millions.

Neither would it do to overshoot our mark and land in the midst of the Event, which might cause the chamber and us inside it to go *poof*. It would also be unsatisfactory to land after it was over. If that happened, we could witness the aftereffects but we should not be able to tell what caused them. This was, after all, the main purpose of the project.

So we agreed that Cohen should pilot the chamber to somewhere in the low sixty-six millions, and then we should bring it forward in time by jumps of ten years, with Haupt setting up his instrument at each step to try for a dekko at Enyo—that is, assuming this asteroid or comet really existed. As we neared the date of the Event, we should shorten the jumps, first to a month each and then to a day.

The next question was, would the time we chose to settle in provide us with a suitable landing area? The chamber moves back and forth in past time but stays at the same latitude and longitude, and as the centuries fly past the land changes beneath you. For a part of the Cretaceous, the area around St. Louis, Missouri, was under an arm of the Kansas Sea, and the chamber's not equipped for landing in water. At other times, this spot might be the side of a cliff, or a mucky swamp where the passengers couldn't leave the chamber. This chamber has telescoping legs that allow it some latitude in terrain, but only within limits.

Since we couldn't move the chamber horizontally over the Earth's surface, we had to learn what we could from the sites we stopped at, whatever these turned out to be. The scientists—those who believe in an extraterrestrial Enyo, that is—had various ideas as to where it hit. The largest vote was for some place in the Caribbean Sea or the adjacent Yucatan peninsula. Others held out for India, and one group argued that the impact had caused the Bering Sea.

There was no sense in fetching the entire crew and equipment back with us each time. Each step required Haupt to sit up all night with his face glued to his eyepiece, while he twiddled knobs and either the Raja or I stood behind him ready to shoot any carnosaur that thought we smelled edible.

As things turned out, no carnosaurs came near us during a couple of score of these all-night vigils. As an astronomer, Haupt was used to these odd sleeping hours; but the Raja and I found them a bit—ah—taxing. We did see a lot of plant eaters, always much the more numerous in any fauna. Mostly smaller species of hypsilophodonts and hadrosaurids, they merely looked us over and waddled away, as if to say they didn't know what sort of creatures we were but didn't care to take chances on us.

I tell you, those months of popping in and out of the late Cretaceous and standing guard over Haupt while he fiddled with his instrument were just plain bloody hard, tedious work. Half the time, when we opened the chamber door, there'd be an overcast or rain. Then we should have to button up the chamber and go on to another day, better for Haupt's seeing.

One night, after his usual hours at the eyepiece, Haupt said: "Don't get your hopes up, Reggie; but I think I may have something."

"You mean you've got this Enyo in your sights at last?"

"It looks that way. Something at about twice lunar distance is headed our way."

"When's it going to hit, and where?" I asked. I'm afraid I let the excitement show in my voice.

"Can't tell yet," said Haupt. "Let me finish my observations. When we get back to Present, I'll have a stack of records for the boys to crunch in their computers. Want a look?"

I looked, but all I could see in the crosshairs was a little spot of light, like another star. "How do you know that's it?" I asked.

"The radar gives the distance, now about eight-hundred-thousand kilometers, and also tells us it's fast approaching. If we had a real star at that distance, we'd all be fried to grease spots in no time."

"Could this be a near miss?"

"I doubt it. Its bearing is close to constant, which means we and it are on a collision course. Even if it's not aimed for a bull's eye, Earth's gravity will partly correct that."

"How soon will it arrive?"

He shrugged. "Have to let the number-crunchers chew on my results. As a rough guess, I'd say three or four days."

"Stone the crows! That gives us bloody little time to get the reception committee in place. We'd better be off like a bride's nightie to fetch our people, if O'Connor's to have time for his paintings and Todd for his hunt."

I admit that Haupt's words gave me a bit of a shiver. I felt the way a fly must feel when it sees the swatter on its way down, and it's too late to take off—if you can imagine an intelligent fly.

So Bruce Cohen took us back to Present and, yawning from being up all night, I rounded up the gang. When I had explained Haupt's findings, Romero said to Featherstone: "Ha, Sterling! So much for your supercaldera theory!"

"Not at all, George," said Featherstone. "If this thing hit, the impact would send the grandfather of all earthquakes roaring around the globe. Then any supercalderas in a stressed condition might be touched off in eruptions, which otherwise might not happen for thousands of years. A few of those would have a more global effect than just the one impact of Enyo."

"Hm, we shall see," said Romero. "Reggie, how would it be for us to sit out the whole sequence, to try to detect by instrument whether any such eruptions occurred right after the impact?"

"According to what you scientific blokes tell me," I said, "the impact will send out a shock wave that will kill everything bigger than an insect and set fire to anything combustible, at least over the hemisphere in which the impact takes place. If you want to try it, you'll have to sign forms releasing us of any responsibility if we go back to Present leaving you alone with your instruments. Myself, I wouldn't dare try it; my wife would kill me for taking foolish chances."

Beauregard and his boys loaded the equipment into the chamber, and in we piled. O'Connor complained he'd forgot his sheath knife, but we didn't have time for him to go back for it.

The morning after Haupt's all-night vigil that discovered Enyo, Cohen took the whole party back to midday of that same day. I let several hours elapse between the time Haupt and I left the Cretaceous and the time we returned to it, for safety's sake. It wouldn't do to try to occupy the same time slot twice, since that would create a paradox. Can't have that sort of thing in a well-run universe, so the space-time forces snatch you back to Present and blow you to bits in the process.

The place we set down the chamber was about as good as we could have asked for. We were on the shoulder of a hill looking off to southeastward. There wasn't much vegetation on the shoulder, just some scrubby cedars and one big tree like the bombax I used to see in India. On the edge of the shoulder and on down the slope grew some stilt-rooted pandanus trees or screw pines. If we cut down a couple of these, we should have a clear view to the south and southeast; in other words, straight at the area where the blokes who favored a Caribbean or Yucatecan impact thought it would fall. On a clear day, Featherstone claimed he could see an arm of the sea on the horizon; but I doubt that. In any case, if the Caribbean bods were right, the thing hit at least two thousand kilometers distant. That was quite close enough for me.

Below the hill, the country was flat and, from what I could see through my glasses, swampy, with a dense forest cover. My American sahibs agreed that the trees were mostly a kind of bald cypress, like the one they knew from their own time.

I ought to know more about such things; but there's a limit to what you can cram into one mind. It's hard enough to master the fauna and flora of one area—say, within a hundred-meter radius of St. Louis—for one geological period. When you try to cover the biotas of a couple of hundred million years, it gets bloody hopeless.

As usual, the Raja and I jumped out of the chamber first, with our big guns ready, in case something hostile were out there to receive us. All we saw was a flock of black-and-white birds, which flew up out of a tree. They looked like normal present-day birds, like your American mockingbird. I couldn't see whether they had teeth in their beaks, as some birds from this time have.

While the crew were setting up the camp, I told O'Connor: "You'd better get on with your painting, Jon. Don't go away from the camp farther than shouting distance—say, fifty meters—and stay in sight."

So off went O'Connor with his load of canvases, paints, and accessories. He was the youngest of our sahibs, with the shaggy-artist look. If he'd been cleaned up and given a proper haircut, he'd have been movie-actor handsome. Otherwise he seemed a mild, obliging sort of young man, if a bit vague about non-artistic matters.

Then up bustled little Mr. Todd, saying: "Look here, Reggie, with so little time, I ought to start my hunt right now."

"Sorry, but we can't," I said. "The Raja and I are tied up with setting up the camp. In an hour or so, one or the other of us ought to be able to take you on a little recco."

"But," says he, "I want to go now, while the daylight lasts! If you can't come along, I'll go by myself!"

"Now, Clarence," I said, "you agreed in writing that you'd follow your guides' orders. It won't kill you to wait a bit. When that Thing gets closer, we shall all have to stay close to camp, to be able to board the chamber in seconds."

"You let O'Connor go off by himself!"

"Only to a distance of fifty meters, so we can watch each other. That distance wouldn't do you any good for hunting."

He turned away, grumping, and I went back to siting the tents and the galley. When that was done and the crew were filing back into the chamber, I asked Haupt:

"Is there any indication yet what part of the Earth that Thing will strike?"

"Give me another night, and I can make at least an educated guess. The distance of Enyo and its present velocity, with a correction for the acceleration by the Earth's gravity, will tell us when it will arrive; and knowledge of the time tells us which side of the Earth will be turned toward—"

He and I both jumped at the thunderous bang of Todd's

heavy rifle. I looked around the camp but saw no sign of him. I yelled at the Raja:

"Did you see that bloke leave the camp?"

"No," said Aiyar. "I was working with Ming on the supplies."

I was so angry at Todd that I was damned if I'd go crashing off in the outback looking for him, although I had a pretty good idea of where the shot came from. So the Raja and I spent the next half-hour waving off Cohen and the crew in the chamber and getting our sahibs settled.

By then it was near sundown. O'Connor straggled in, loaded with canvases, stands, palette, paints, and a camera. The Raja and I agreed it was time for our evening's spot of lubricant, so I called time. We were sitting round drinking our tot of whiskey. (I'm pretty strict about how much I allow per person. I've seen what can happen when someone goes over his limit on grog.) O'Connor showed off his sketches and talked a streak about *reculement* and other artistic matters that went over my head.

We all turned round as Todd came staggering up the slope. He was covered with blood, and for a bad second I thought he'd lost a chewing contest with a theropod. But he seemed cheerful, with his big-game rifle in one hand and his other arm around his trophy. This was the head of one of the smaller sauropods, the ones that look like a gigantic snake threaded through the body of an elephant. I think this was an *Alamosaurus;* there were still a few sauropods around at the end of the Cretaceous, though nothing like so conspicuous as they were in the late Jurassic. Todd had the head and almost two meters of the animal's neck balanced on his shoulder like a drooping log.

I never advise my sahibs to shoot sauropods. It's not at all sporting, any way you look at it. They're harmless creatures if you leave them alone, pretty stupid even by dinosaur standards. I don't mean that dinosaurs are extraordinarily stupid, any more than modern crocs and other reptiles. They have a set of serviceable instincts, which see them through most of the crises of their lives; and they can actually learn, though not so quickly as any mammal.

All the sauropods do, however, is eat, eat, eat anything green they can reach with those long necks. Some are bigger than people thought anything could be and still walk on dry land. But it seems the limiting factor is not the strength of their legs but how much greenery they can gulp down and process in those mighty guts in any one day.

They can survive a lot of gunfire, too. Todd was lucky to have got one in the heart with his first shot. And if you kill one, what have you got? Just that silly little head on that long stalk of a neck.

None of that had stopped Todd. "See?" he said, grinning ear-to-ear. "I got my trophy, and all by myself. Hacked off the head with my machete, and here it is."

"How far down the slope were you when you shot it?" I asked.

He waved. "Maybe two-thirds of the way down, just inside that timberline of bald cypress, where the trees are stunted and scattered."

"And you left the carcass there?"

"Sure! Did you expect me to haul ten tons of dinosaur up that slope? Where's the salt to preserve it with?"

"You bloody idiot!" I said. We get all kinds on these time safaris, but the buggers who cause the most grief are those out to prove their manhood. I went on: "Don't you know the smell will draw carnivorous dinosaurs like flies? They'll be having a grand carrion party before the night is over. That's all right so long as they stay round the carcass; but what's likelier is that a big one will chase off a smaller. Then the smaller, not to be done out of its tucker, will wander up here looking for more—us."

"Scared, eh?" he sneered.

"Why, you ratbag—" I began. Things were making up to a first-class row, when the Raja took hold of Todd's arm and led him aside, saying: "Now look, Mr. Todd, if we start off with a mutiny, we might as well all get back in the chamber and return to Present . . ."

They passed out of my hearing; but the upshot was that Aiyar calmed Todd down to the point where, looking crestfallen, he came back to me and mumbled something about hoping nothing bad would come of his impulsiveness. The Raja found him the preserving materials while Ming got our tea—what you fellows call "dinner."

On a normal time safari, I take the sahibs out on the first full day to hunt fresh meat; that gives us the protein we shall need for scrambling around a rough landscape and also to judge which of the time travelers is to be trusted with a loaded gun. In the Mesozoic, that means one of the smaller herbivorous dinosaurs, like a bonehead or a thescelosaur. This time our stay was to be so brief that it didn't seem worthwhile. We had enough food from Present to do us. Besides, Todd seemed the only one keen on hunting.

As I had predicted, the theropods gathered round the carcass of Todd's sauropod down the slope. We could hear their grunts and bellows as they sorted themselves out into a pecking order; but there was so much meat there that they didn't have to compete for it. Anyway, none came up to the shoulder of the hill where we were camped.

When the sun came up next morning, the last of the theropods had gorged itself until it could barely waddle, and little by little they all wandered off into the cypress swamp. Looking through the glasses I could see a set of bare ribs sticking up.

I suggested there was still a fair amount of meat left on the carcass, so we had better keep our guard up against theropod visitors. We don't get the famous *Tyrannosaurus* around our site at this particular time, but those we do get include an *Albertosaurus* big enough to make a snack of you.

Einar Haupt was up most of the night stargazing. After

breakfast, he came up with a little pocket-sized computer, saying:

"Reggie, I think I've got Enyo's arrival nailed down. According to my instruments' figures, it'll hit about dawn the day after tomorrow, and pretty certainly on this side of the planet."

"Can you fix the place of impact any closer than that?" I asked.

"Nope. If we were back in Present, my fellow astronomers could dope it out; but we're not."

That gave me an idea of what those blokes must have felt in the two big wars, when they were in a city the enemy was going to bomb. You might comfort yourself with the thought that there was a good chance the bombs wouldn't hit you; but it would be a lot nicer if they didn't fall at all.

"In other words," I said, "we may expect the lady in a little less than two complete revolutions of this bloody planet?"

"That's right." I hadn't said "forty-eight hours" because at that time the Earth rotated a bit faster than it does now, so the hours—I mean the twenty-fourths of one revolution— were shorter. This complicates our efforts to run a safari on schedule, since the sahibs' watches don't conform to the movements of the sun. I've thought of having special watches and clocks made; but the Raja and I decided the expense would be out of proportion to the benefits. Such timepieces would have to be adaptable to the planet's angular velocity for all the times back to the pre-Cambrian.

It was building up to a sticky-hot day. Sterling Featherstone wandered by, saying: "Have you seen George around, Reggie? There's a geological question I want to discuss with him."

No, I hadn't seen Romero; and a search of the camp failed to turn him up. Oh, lord, I thought: don't tell me another of these coves has gone walkabout by himself! It wouldn't have much surprised me with O'Connor, who seemed a vague, dreamy sort—but not George Romero, a brisk, no-nonsense field scientist. I once thought scientists of all people were supposed to have better sense, but I find that's not necessarily so.

I made the round of the camp, questioning everyone as to what had become of George Romero. At last Todd told me:

"He said something, half an hour ago, about taking a little walk to watch the local fauna undisturbed by our presence. I'm sure he hasn't gone far."

The Raja saw I was about to blow my top over the matter. He said, "Calm down, Reggie; I'll go hunting for—"

Then a disturbance interrupted. Around the bend of the hill came George Romero, doing a fair turn of speed in spite of being short and middle-aged. Right behind him ran a steno, trying to get close enough to flesh its fangs in his back.

A steno? That's short for *Stenonychosaurus,* one of the saurornithoids of this period. We call them "stenos" because people find *Stenonychosaurus* hard to remember. They're smaller flesh-eaters. One weighs around fifty kilos—in other words, as much as a smallish human being. They have a slim running shape, and when moving they come up about to your navel, with the head and tail sticking out horizontally. When they rear up, they can look you in the eye. They're normally harmless, since their prey is little things like lizards, birds, and the mammals of those times, all of which looked much like rats and mice.

But here this bloke was chasing our scientist with obvious hostile intent. Romero ran through the camp and headed for the time chamber, which stood on a slight rise on the edge with its doors open.

I jumped for the Raja's and my tent and came out with my heavy rifle, in time to see Romero dive in the doors of the chamber. Cohen was in the chamber, making adjustments, and I heard a startled yell from him. Then the doors slammed shut in the steno's face.

The reptile went splat against the steel doors and backed off, shaking its head as if in wonder at human technology. It looked about, seeming to realize for the first time that it had blundered into territory off-limits to dinosaurs.

I hesitated to shoot, lest I hit somebody or something in the camp. The Raja came out with his gun, but he paused likewise. Then the steno set off at a dead run, out of the camp and around the curve of the hill from which it had chased Romero. In a few seconds it was out of sight.

By banging on the chamber door, we persuaded Cohen to open up. Romero, still breathing hard, came out looking like a lad caught with his hand in the lolly jar. He apologized all over the place: I had seemed too busy to bother, and he took only a little stroll, etcetera. Meanwhile Cohen locked the chamber doors behind him in a marked manner.

"But," I said to Romero, "What on earth did you do to rile up that steno? Normally they leave us alone, since we're much too big to serve as their normal prey."

"It was this way," he said. "I walked quietly around the hill till the camp was just out of sight. There was a pair of these stenos on a little flat place, doing a kind of dance. So I watched. One just stood, while the other went through what looked like the calisthenics I do when I get up in the morning. It did deep-knee bends, squatting down and rising up again; then it stayed up but bowed down and touched its head to the ground, over and over. Then it went back to squatting and rising.

"I figured out that this was a mating dance, and the one doing the setting-up exercises was the male, hoping to get the female into a receptive mood. It seemed to be working, because the male extruded that great long hook-shaped hemipenis—or rather, he extruded the half of it on the side toward the female. Then he grabbed the female with his foreclaws, hoisted one leg over her hindquarters, and started feeling around her underside with this organ to find the point of entry.

"I couldn't resist the temptation to shoot a few frames on my camera. Whether the tiny click of the shutter aroused the male, or the motion of my arm, I don't know. But he suddenly stared at me, let go of the female, and withdrew his hook inside him. He uttered a kind of caw, like a crow, and started for me. Not being armed, I ran for it."

The Raja and I had the same thought, and we both burst out laughing. "Sport, he thought you were a rival, who wanted to screw his mate," I said. "Naturally, no right-thinking bull steno is going to stand for that!"

The whole camp had a good laugh over the incident. But then our spirits sank as the clouds formed huge anvils, with lightning and thunder. By the time for tucker, rain was coming down in buckets.

It kept up the whole night. Maybe theropods gathered again round the sauropod carcass to resume their feast; but the storm made so much noise we couldn't have heard them. The next day was more of the same, all day.

"Lousy luck," said Featherstone. "If we can't see the results of the impact from a distance, we don't dare hang around until it happens. The shock wave might catch us unawares and smear us."

Haupt said: "There may be enough light from Enyo to warn us as it makes its final plunge, even through the cloud cover."

"How about the big wave?" asked Romero. "If that Thing lands in water, it'll kick up the grandfather of all tsunamis. You know what they say: If you're at the beach and see a tsunami coming, it's already too late to save your life."

"Unless," said Featherstone, "you had a fast motor vehicle and floored the gas away from the beach."

"And if," said Romero, "the road wasn't jammed with other people trying to do the same thing. But how about *this* tsunami?"

"Don't worry," said Haupt. "One might wash inland over flat country for a few kilometers—maybe ten or twenty—but we're at least a hundred kilometers from any sea. The speed—"

"How do you know," interrupted Todd, "that we're a

hundred kilometers from the sea, when we haven't a map of the area for this period?"

Haupt answered with the forced patience of a school-ma'am with a backward pupil. "Because if it were closer, we could see it plainly from this altitude. The speed of the wave would be only a fraction of that of sound, which is a little over 330 meters per second, and which is also the speed of the shock wave."

I held up a hand to quiet the argument and said: "Listen, please. We shall get up hours before the expected impact. Then we shall load into the chamber all the stuff we plan to take back with us and stand by the doors, ready to leap in the minute you blokes see a flash in the sky. We shan't wait for any shock wave but take off for Present instantly."

So it was decided; but as things turned out, that scenario did not prove necessary. During a day of rain, I had to listen to Todd's complaints over not getting a second hunt, and O'Connor's complaints over not being able to paint more pictures, as if I were somehow responsible for the weather.

The evening before the Event, the rain tapered off and the clouds broke up. We loaded into the chamber the stuff we were taking back, like Todd's sauropod head and O'Connor's pictures. Ming hauled a bag full of our new kitchen utensils; he wasn't going to sacrifice them if he could help it.

When we got up before dawn, we had a clear, deep-blue sky overhead, in which the stars were going out one by one as the glow of the coming sunrise brightened in the east.

"Where's Enyo?" I asked Haupt.

"She'll be up any minute," he said. "The Earth has to turn more toward her—ah, there she comes! Call your gang together!"

Rising from the southeastern horizon, which was still a pretty dark blue, came another spot of light, somewhat resembling the planet Venus at her maximum brightness. I

stared at it but could not see any relative motion between
Enyo and the few stars still visible.

"Is she going to make it?" I asked Haupt. "She doesn't
seem to be getting anywhere."

"She's moving, but too slowly to make out with the bare
eyeball," he said. After we had stood for a while, jittering
and thinking—at least I was thinking—whether it wouldn't
have been smarter to have used robot instruments instead of
human observers, Haupt said: "Look carefully, now. She's
visibly declining toward the horizon."

I looked; and sure enough, the spot had moved. Down it
went, at first as slowly as the minute hand of a clock, then
faster.

"There she goes!" cried Haupt.

The spot disappeared below the horizon, but almost at
once a glow sprang up in the southeast. The glow of the
coming sunrise in the east was already quite bright, but it
was as if two suns were rising at the same time, almost a
right angle apart. The normal sunrise went on at its usual
leisurely pace; but the other one brightened much faster.
Then there was a perfect blaze of light from south-by-east.
I shan't say it was brighter than a million suns; but for a few
seconds it made the true rising sun in the east look like a
mere candle.

"Look at the horizon," said Romero. "I think the people
who bet on Windward Passage are going to lose. The
bearing indicates Yucatan."

The bright light faded, but then followed something the
like of which I had never seen. A kind of illuminated dome
thrust up over the horizon. This thing went up and up,
becoming the top of a vast single column. It was of mixed
colors, mostly red. Along the top it was a dark red, with a
kind of ragged appearance, as if made of a million separate
jets of steam or water or lava. Further down the column,
the color brightened to a brilliant yellow at the base, and
little blue flashes of lightning played all over the surface of
the whole fantastic thing. Romero said:

"What's the azimuth of that, Einar?"

Haupt squinted and made an adjustment, with his eye to the lens. "Eighty-four—no, eighty-five degrees."

"That would be the east coast of Yucatan," said Romero.

I asked Haupt: "Why haven't we heard anything?"

He said: "What do you expect? That's about two thousand kilometers from here, so it'll take at least twenty minutes for the sound and the shock wave to get here."

I looked at my watch and said: "Twenty minutes, and we must all be in the chamber and buttoned up. Has anybody any last-minute thing he wants to do?"

The column continued to rise, although more slowly, and the colors darkened and faded a bit. It reminded me of a flick I once saw, showing the explosion of the American H-bomb on some poor little island in the Pacific. This was something like that, but on a vastly greater scale.

"Fifteen minutes!" I said. "Are you ready to let us in, Bruce?"

"Yep," said Cohen.

"I'll hold the door when he opens it," said the Raja.

"Ten minutes!"

A band of darkness appeared above the horizon and seemed to be creeping closer.

"Dust, smoke, and water vapor, I think," said Featherstone.

Change crept over the cypress-swamp plain before us. It started at the limits of vision and came swiftly closer. The change was the turning of the whole forest into a vast bonfire. The trees along the leading edge of the change blazed up in bright yellow and orange and then were hidden by a colossal cloud of black smoke, while the next nearer line of forest blazed up likewise.

"There's our shock wave," said Featherstone.

"Five minutes!" I said. "Into the chamber, all of you! Fast!"

We ran to the chamber, to find Cohen and the Raja on hands and knees in front of the closed doors.

"What in God's name?" I cried.

"Bruce dropped his keys," said the Raja. "Don't anybody disturb the soil!"

They hunted and hunted, sweeping their hands over the ground. The time couldn't have been more than seconds, but to me it seemed hours. I thought the dawnlight was already dimmed by the onrushing cloud of smoke, but that may have been my imagination.

"Let me," said Todd. He produced an electric torch, which he played back and forth over the ground. Just as it looked hopeless, Cohen yelled: "Got 'em!" and pounced.

At any rate, Todd had proved himself something more than a mere pain in the arse. Cohen got the door open the quickest I'd ever seen, and we piled in. I counted noses as they went by and said:

"Where's O'Connor? Oh, *Jon!* Where the bloody hell are you?"

"Coming," said O'Connor, walking in a leisurely manner from the tents towards the chamber, with a framed square of canvas under his arm. "Forgot this sketch," he explained.

"*Run,* God damn it!" I yelled.

At last I got him safely inside and then myself. Bruce Cohen, at the controls, had his hand out to the door-closing lever, when another shadow fell across the doorway. I was sure all my sahibs were in. Several set up a yell as the newcomer leaped in with more agility than any mere human being could command.

Cohen hesitated, then frantically pulled the lever. The doors slammed shut. The newcomer uttered a squawk, because the closing doors had snipped off the last centimeter or two of the point of its long tail. It was in fact a steno, like the one that had chased George Romero into the chamber two days before.

"Take her to Present!" I shouted at Cohen, who was already working his controls.

There was a motion of the chamber that was not just

going through time; it was a physical movement in the late Cretaceous.

"Earthquake!" cried Featherstone.

By then Cohen had us well on the time-travel route. The lights dimmed, and everybody felt the horrid vertigo and vibration and nausea. I looked toward our stowaway, huddled in a corner of the chamber near the door. What the hell should we do with it? To fire a shot in those close quarters would be suicide. On the other hand, to leave our people at the mercy of a Mesozoic carnivore . . .

"He seems unaggressive, Reggie," said the Raja. "Must have remembered the chamber from the day before yesterday and, when he saw his world going up in smoke, figured that this was the safest place for him. They're considered bright as reptiles—oh, oh!"

The nausea affected the *Stenonychosaurus* so that it puked up its last meal on the floor of the chamber. Bruce Cohen, when he saw, did some of the fanciest swearing I've ever heard. Made the most eloquent bushie seem like a schoolma'am.

The Raja was right about the steno's being smarter than most reptiles. Some museum coves reason that if it hadn't been for Enyo, the dinosaurs might still be going strong, and the steno's descendants might have evolved into the reptilian equivalent of mankind.

"If we leave him alone," said the Raja, "he'll probably do likewise to us. He must have been more frightened by the Event than by us. Lots of zoos would love a live dinosaur. The museum that tried to bring back eggs had no luck; they didn't hatch. I'll see if he'll let me bandage his tail; you know me and animals."

"By God!" said Romero. "I do believe he's my sometime rival for the affections of that female. Has the same scar on his muzzle. The poor girl will have been killed by the shock wave."

"Too bad we couldn't bring the pair back," said Featherstone, "and breed them."

I said: "If you museum blokes will produce the money to fetch a pair, you'll find Rivers and Aiyar ready to talk business."

And that, Mr. Burgess, is the story of my closest call. It's like being shot at and missed. Makes you feel good at the time and gives you a story to dine out on; but on the whole you'd rather not take that kind of chance again. No more for me, thanks. My wife's due to pick me up. Ta-ta!

Just Like Old Times
by
Robert J. Sawyer

Canadian writer Robert J. Sawyer is the author of five science fiction novels, a dozen short stories in magazines such as Analog, Amazing, *and Canada's* On Spec, *five hour-long documentaries about the SF genre, and over two hundred nonfiction pieces. His first novel,* Golden Fleece, *won Canada's Aurora Award for Best SF Novel of 1990–1991. His other novels include the "Quintaglio" trilogy,* Far-Seer, Fossil Hunter, *and* Foreigner. *His most recent book is the novel* End of an Era. *(All four of the last-mentioned novels are, in one way or another, about dinosaurs—making Sawyer one of the most prolific writers on the subject in modern SF.) He lives in Thornhill, Ontario, with his wife and "hundreds of plastic dinosaur models."*

Let the punishment fit the crime! An object all sublime! And yet—there just may be unforeseen consequences of doing that . . .

* * *

The transference went smoothly, like a scalpel slicing into skin.

Cohen was simultaneously excited and disappointed. He was thrilled to be here—perhaps the judge was right, perhaps this was where he really belonged. But the gleaming edge was taken off that thrill because it wasn't accompanied by the usual physiological signs of excitement: no sweaty palms, no racing heart, no rapid breathing. Oh, there was a heartbeat, to be sure, thundering in the background, but it wasn't Cohen's.

It was the dinosaur's.

Everything was the dinosaur's: Cohen saw the world now through tyrannosaur eyes.

The colors seemed all wrong. Surely plant leaves must be

25

the same chlorophyll green here in the Mesozoic, but the dinosaur saw them as navy blue. The sky was lavender; the dirt underfoot ash gray.

Old bones had different cones, thought Cohen. Well, he could get used to it. After all, he had no choice. He would finish his life as an observer inside this tyrannosaur's mind. He'd see what the beast saw, hear what it heard, feel what it felt. He wouldn't be able to control its movements, they had said, but he would be able to experience every sensation.

The rex was marching forward.

Cohen hoped blood would still look red.

It wouldn't be the same if it wasn't red.

"And what, Ms. Cohen, did your husband say before he left your house on the night in question?"

"He said he was going out to hunt humans. But I thought he was making a joke."

"No interpretations, please, Ms. Cohen. Just repeat for the court as precisely as you remember it, exactly what your husband said."

"He said, 'I'm going out to hunt humans.'"

"Thank you, Ms. Cohen. That concludes the Crown's case, my lady."

The needlepoint on the wall of the Honorable Madam Justice Amanda Hoskins' chambers had been made for her by her husband. It was one of her favorite verses from *The Mikado*, and as she was preparing sentencing she would often look up and reread the words:

> My object all sublime
> I shall achieve in time—
> To let the punishment fit the crime—
> The punishment fit the crime.

This was a difficult case, a horrible case. Judge Hoskins continued to think.

• • •

It wasn't just colors that were wrong. The view from inside the tyrannosaur's skull was different in other ways, too.

The tyrannosaur had only partial stereoscopic vision. There was an area in the center of Cohen's field of view that showed true depth perception. But because the beast was somewhat wall-eyed, it had a much wider panorama than normal for a human, a kind of saurian Cinemascope covering 270 degrees.

The wide-angle view panned back and forth as the tyrannosaur scanned along the horizon.

Scanning for prey.

Scanning for something to kill.

The Calgary Herald, Thursday, October 16, 2042, hard copy edition: "Serial killer Rudolph Cohen, 43, was sentenced to death yesterday.

"Formerly a prominent member of the Alberta College of Physicians and Surgeons, Dr. Cohen was convicted in August of thirty-seven counts of first-degree murder.

"In chilling testimony, Cohen had admitted, without any signs of remorse, to having terrorized each of his victims for hours before slitting their throats with surgical implements.

"This is the first time in eighty years that the death penalty has been ordered in this country.

"In passing sentence, Madam Justice Amanda Hoskins observed that Cohen was 'the most cold-blooded and brutal killer to have stalked Canada's prairies since *Tyrannosaurus rex . . .*'"

From behind a stand of dawn redwoods about ten meters away, a second tyrannosaur appeared. Cohen suspected tyrannosaurs might be fiercely territorial, since each animal would require huge amounts of meat. He wondered if the beast he was in would attack the other individual.

His dinosaur tilted its head to look at the second rex, which was standing in profile. But as it did so, almost all of the dino's mental picture dissolved into a white void, as if when concentrating on details the beast's tiny brain simply lost track of the big picture.

At first Cohen thought his rex was looking at the other dinosaur's head, but soon the top of the other's skull, the tip of its muzzle and the back of its powerful neck faded away into snowy nothingness. All that was left was a picture of the throat. Good, thought Cohen. One shearing bite there could kill the animal.

The skin of the other's throat appeared gray-green and the throat itself was smooth. Maddeningly, Cohen's rex did not attack. Rather, it simply swiveled its head and looked out at the horizon again.

In a flash of insight, Cohen realized what had happened. Other kids in his neighborhood had had pet dogs or cats. He'd had lizards and snakes—cold-blooded carnivores, a fact to which expert psychological witnesses had attached great weight. Some kinds of male lizards had dewlap sacs hanging from their necks. The rex he was in—a male, the Tyrrell paleontologists had believed—had looked at this other one and seen that she was smooth-throated and therefore a female. Something to be mated with, perhaps, rather than to attack.

Perhaps they would mate soon. Cohen had never orgasmed except during the act of killing. He wondered what it would feel like.

"We spent a billion dollars developing time travel, and now you tell me the system is useless?"

"Well—"

"That is what you're saying, isn't it, Professor? That chronotransference has no practical applications?"

"Not exactly, Minister. The system *does* work. We can project a human being's consciousness back in time, superimposing his or her mind over that of someone who lived in the past."

"With no way to sever the link. *Wonderful.*"

"That's not true. The link severs automatically."

"Right. When the historical person you've transferred consciousness into dies, the link is broken."

"Precisely."

"And then the person from our time whose consciousness you've transferred back dies as well."

"I admit that's an unfortunate consequence of linking two brains so closely."

"So I'm right! This whole damn chronotransference thing is useless."

"Oh, not at all, Minister. In fact, I think I've got the perfect application for it."

The rex marched along. Although Cohen's attention had first been arrested by the beast's vision, he slowly became aware of its other senses, too. He could hear the sounds of the rex's footfalls, of twigs and vegetation being crushed, of birds or pterosaurs singing, and, underneath it all, the relentless drone of insects. Still, all the sounds were dull and low; the rex's simple ears were incapable of picking up high-pitched noises, and what sounds they did detect were discerned without richness. Cohen knew the late Cretaceous must have been a symphony of varied tones, but it was as if he was listening to it through earmuffs.

The rex continued along, still searching. Cohen became aware of several more impressions of the world both inside and out, including hot afternoon sun beating down on him and a hungry gnawing in the beast's belly.

Food.

It was the closest thing to a coherent thought that he'd yet detected from the animal, a mental picture of bolts of meat going down its gullet.

Food.

The Social Services Preservation Act of 2022: Canada is built upon the principle of the Social Safety Net, a series of entitlements and programs designed to ensure a high standard of living for every citizen. However, ever-increasing life expectancies coupled with constant lowering of the mandatory retirement age have placed an untenable burden on our social-welfare system and, in particular, its corner-stone program of universal health care. With most taxpayers ceasing to work at the age of 45, and with average Canadians living to be 94 (males) or 97 (females), the system is in danger of complete collapse. Accordingly, all social programs will henceforth be available only to those below the age of 60, with one exception: all Canadians, regardless of age, may take advantage, at no charge to themselves, of government-sponsored euthanasia through chronotransference.

There! Up ahead! Something moving! Big, whatever it was: an indistinct outline only intermittently visible behind a small knot of fir trees.

A quadruped of sort, its back to him/it/them.

Ah, there. Turning now. Peripheral vision dissolving into albino nothingness as the rex concentrated on the head.

Three horns.

Triceratops.

Glorious! Cohen had spent hours as a boy poring over books about dinosaurs, looking for scenes of carnage. No battles were better than those in which Tyrannosaurus rex squared off against Triceratops, a four-footed Mesozoic tank with a trio of horns projecting from its face and a shield of bone rising from the back of its skull to protect the neck.

And yet, the rex marched on.

No, thought Cohen. Turn, damn you! Turn and attack!

Cohen remembered when it had all begun, that fateful day so many years ago, so many years from now. It should have been a routine operation. The patient had supposedly been prepped properly. Cohen brought his scalpel down toward the abdomen, then, with a steady hand, sliced into the skin.

The patient gasped. It had been a *wonderful* sound, a beautiful sound.

Not enough gas. The anesthetist hurried to make an adjustment.

Cohen knew he had to hear that sound again. He had to.

The tyrannosaur continued forward. Cohen couldn't see its legs, but he could feel them moving. Left, right, up, down.

Attack, you bastard!

Left.

Attack!

Right.

Go after it!

Up.

Go after the triceratops.

Dow—

The beast hesitated, its left leg still in the air, balancing briefly on one foot.

Attack!

Attack!

And then, at last, the rex changed course. The triceratops appeared in the three-dimensional central part of the tyrannosaur's field of view, like a target at the end of a gun sight.

"Welcome to the Chronotransference Institute. If I can just see your government benefits card, please? Yup, there's always a last time for everything, heh heh. Now, I'm sure you want an exciting death. The problem is finding somebody interesting who hasn't been used yet. See, we can only ever superimpose one mind onto a given historical personage. All the really obvious ones have been done already, I'm afraid. We still get about a dozen calls a week asking for Jack Kennedy, but he was one of the first to go, so to speak. If I may make a suggestion, though, we've got thousands of Roman legion officers cataloged. Those tend to be very satisfying deaths. How about a nice something from the Gallic Wars?"

•   •   •

The triceratops looked up, its giant head lifting from the wide flat gunnera leaves it had been chewing on. Now that the rex had focused on the plant-eater, it seemed to commit itself.

The tyrannosaur charged.

The hornface was sideways to the rex. It began to turn, to bring its armored head to bear.

The horizon bounced wildly as the rex ran. Cohen could hear the thing's heart thundering loudly, rapidly, a barrage of muscular gunfire.

The triceratops, still completing its turn, opened its parrotlike beak, but no sound came out.

Giant strides closed the distance between the two animals. Cohen felt the rex's jaws opening wide, wider still, mandibles popping from their sockets.

The jaws slammed shut on the hornface's back, over the shoulders. Cohen saw two of the rex's own teeth fly into view, knocked out by the impact.

The taste of hot blood, surging out of the wound . . .

The rex pulled back for another bite.

The triceratops finally got its head swung around. It surged forward, the long spear over its left eye piercing the rex's leg . . .

Pain. Exquisite, beautiful pain.

The rex roared. Cohen heard it twice, once reverberating within the animal's own skull, a second time echoing back from distant hills. A flock of silver-furred pterosaurs took to the air. Cohen saw them fade from view as the dinosaur's simple mind shut them out of the display. Irrelevant distractions.

The triceratops pulled back, the horn withdrawing from the rex's flesh.

Blood, Cohen was delighted to see, still looked red.

"If Judge Hoskins had ordered the electric chair," said Axworthy, Cohen's lawyer, "we could have fought that on

Charter grounds. Cruel and unusual punishment, and all that. But she's authorized full access to the chronotransference euthanasia program for you." Axworthy paused. "She said, bluntly, that she simply wants you dead."

"How thoughtful of her," said Cohen.

Axworthy ignored that. "I'm sure I can get you anything you want," he said. "Who would you like to be transferred into?"

"Not who," said Cohen. "What."

"I beg your pardon?"

"That damned judge said I was the most cold-blooded killer to stalk the Alberta landscape since *Tyrannosaurus rex*." Cohen shook his head. "The idiot. Doesn't she know dinosaurs were warm-blooded? Anyway, that's what I want. I want to be transferred into a *T. rex*."

"You're kidding."

"Kidding is not my forte. John. *Killing* is. I want to know which was better at it, me or the rex."

"I don't even know if they can do that kind of thing," said Axworthy.

"Find out, damn you. What the hell am I paying you for?"

The rex danced to the side, moving with surprising agility for a creature of its bulk, and once again it brought its terrible jaws down on the ceratopsian's shoulder. The plant-eater was hemorrhaging at an incredible rate, as though a thousand sacrifices had been performed on the altar of its back.

The triceratops tried to lunge forward, but it was weakening quickly. The tyrannosaur, crafty in its own way despite its trifling intellect, simply retreated a dozen giant paces. The hornface took one tentative step toward it, and then another, and, with great and ponderous effort, one more. But then the dinosaurian tank teetered and, eyelids slowly closing, collapsed on its side. Cohen was briefly startled, then thrilled, to hear it fall to the ground with a *splash*—he hadn't realized just how much blood had poured out of the great rent the rex had made in the beast's back.

The tyrannosaur moved in, lifting its left leg up and then smashing it down on the triceratops' belly, the three sharp toe claws tearing open the thing's abdomen, entrails spilling out into the harsh sunlight. Cohen thought the rex would let out a victorious roar, but it didn't. It simply dipped its muzzle into the body cavity, and methodically began yanking out chunks of flesh.

Cohen was disappointed. The battle of the dinosaurs had been fun, the killing had been well engineered, and there had certainly been enough blood, but there was no *terror*. No sense that the triceratops had been quivering with fear, no begging for mercy. No feeling of power, of control. Just dumb, mindless brutes moving in ways preprogrammed by their genes.

It wasn't enough. Not nearly enough.

Judge Hoskins looked across the desk in her chambers at the lawyer.

"A tyrannosaurus, Mr. Axworthy? I was speaking figuratively."

"I understand that, my lady, but it was an appropriate observation, don't you think? I've contacted the Chronotransference people, who say they can do it, if they have a rex specimen to work from. They have to back-propagate from actual physical material in order to get a temporal fix."

Judge Hoskins was as unimpressed by scientific babble as she was by legal jargon. "Make your point, Mr. Axworthy."

"I called the Royal Tyrrell Museum of Paleontology in Drumheller and asked them about the tyrannosaurus fossils available worldwide. Turns out there's only a handful of complete skeletons, but they were able to provide me with an annotated list, giving as much information as they could about the individual probable causes of death." He slid a thin plastic printout sheet across the judge's wide desk.

"Leave this with me, counsel. I'll get back to you."

Axworthy left, and Hoskins scanned the brief list. She then leaned back in her leather chair and began to read the needlepoint on her wall for the thousandth time:

> My object all sublime
> I shall achieve in time—

She read that line again, her lips moving slightly as she subvocalized the words: "I shall achieve *in time* . . ."

The judge turned back to the list of tyrannosaur finds. Ah, that one. Yes, that would be perfect. She pushed a button on her phone. "David, see if you can find Mr. Axworthy for me."

There had been a very unusual aspect to the triceratops kill—an aspect that intrigued Cohen. Chronotransference had been performed countless times; it was one of the most popular forms of euthanasia. Sometimes the transferee's original body would give an ongoing commentary about what was going on, as if talking during sleep. It was clear from what they said that transferees couldn't exert any control over the bodies they were transferred into.

Indeed, the physicists had claimed any control was impossible. Chronotransference worked precisely because the transferee could exert no influence, and therefore was simply observing things that had already been observed. Since no new observations were being made, no quantum-mechanical distortions occurred. After all, said the physicists, if one could exert control, one could change the past. And that was impossible.

And yet, when Cohen had willed the rex to alter its course, it eventually had done so.

Could it be that the rex had so little brains that Cohen's thoughts *could* control the beast?

Madness. The ramifications were incredible.

Still . . .

He had to know if it was true. The rex was torpid, flopped on its belly, gorged on ceratopsian meat. It seemed prepared to lie here for a long time to come, enjoying the early evening breeze.

Get up, thought Cohen. *Get up, damn you!*

Nothing. No response.

Get up!

The rex's lower jaw was resting on the ground. Its upper jaw was lifted high, its mouth wide open. Tiny pterosaurs were flitting in and out of the open maw, their long needlelike beaks apparently yanking gobbets of hornface flesh from between the rex's curved teeth.

Get up, thought Cohen again. *Get up!*

The rex stirred.

Up!

The tyrannosaur used its tiny forelimbs to keep its torso from sliding forward as it pushed with its powerful legs until it was standing.

Forward, thought Cohen. *Forward!*

The beast's body felt different. Its belly was full to bursting.

Forward!

With ponderous steps, the rex began to march.

It was wonderful. To be in control again! Cohen felt the old thrill of the hunt.

And he knew exactly what he was looking for.

"Judge Hoskins says okay," said Axworthy. "She's authorized for you to be transferred into that new *T. rex* they've got right here in Alberta at the Tyrrell. It's a young adult, they say. Judging by the way the skeleton was found, the rex died falling, probably into a fissure. Both legs and the back were broken, but the skeleton remained almost completely articulated, suggesting that scavengers couldn't get at it. Unfortunately, the chronotransference people say that back-propagating that far into the past they can only plug you in a few hours before the accident occurred. But you'll get your wish: you're going to die as a tyrannosaur. Oh, and here are the books you asked for: a complete library on

Cretaceous flora and fauna. You should have time to get through it all; the chronotransference people will need a couple of weeks to set up."

As the prehistoric evening turned to night, Cohen found what he had been looking for, cowering in some underbrush: large brown eyes, long, drawn-out face, and a lithe body covered in fur that, to the tyrannosaur's eyes, looked blue-brown.

A mammal. But not just any mammal. *Purgatorius*, the very first primate, known from Montana and Alberta from right at the end of the Cretaceous. A little guy, only about ten centimeters long, excluding its ratlike tail. Rare creatures, these days. Only a precious few.

The little furball could run quickly for its size, but a single step by the tyrannosaur equaled more than a hundred of the mammal's. There was no way it could escape.

The rex leaned in close, and Cohen saw the furball's face, the nearest thing there would be to a human face for another sixty million years. The animal's eyes went wide in terror.

Naked, raw fear.

Mammalian fear.

Cohen saw the creature scream.

Heard it scream.

It was beautiful.

The rex moved its gaping jaws in toward the little mammal, drawing in breath with such force that it sucked the creature into its maw. Normally the rex would swallow its meals whole, but Cohen prevented the beast from doing that. Instead, he simply had it stand still, with the little primate running around, terrified, inside the great cavern of the dinosaur's mouth, banging into the giant teeth and great fleshy walls, and skittering over the massive, dry tongue.

Cohen savored the terrified squealing. He wallowed in the sensation of the animal, mad with fear, moving inside that living prison.

And at last, with a great, glorious release, Cohen put the

animal out of its misery, allowing the rex to swallow it, the furball tickling as it slid down the giant's throat.

It was just like old times.

Just like hunting humans.

And then a wonderful thought occurred to Cohen. Why, if he killed enough of these little screaming balls of fur, they wouldn't have any descendants. There wouldn't ever be any *Homo sapiens*. In a very real sense, Cohen realized he *was* hunting humans—every single human being who would ever exist.

Of course, a few hours wouldn't be enough time to kill many of them. Judge Hoskins no doubt thought it was wonderfully poetic justice, or she wouldn't have allowed the transfer: sending him back to fall into the pit, damned.

Stupid judge. Why, now that he could control the beast, there was no way he was going to let it die young. He'd just—

There it was. The fissure, a long gash in the earth, with a crumbling edge. Damn, it *was* hard to see. The shadows cast by neighboring trees made a confusing gridwork on the ground that obscured the ragged opening. No wonder the dull-witted rex had missed seeing it until it was too late.

But not this time.

Turn left, thought Cohen.

Left.

His rex obeyed.

He'd avoid this particular area in future, just to be on the safe side. Besides, there was plenty of territory to cover. Fortunately, this was a young rex—a juvenile. There would be decades in which to continue his very special hunt. Cohen was sure that Axworthy knew his stuff: once it became apparent that the link had lasted longer than a few hours, he'd keep any attempt to pull the plug tied up in the courts for years.

Cohen felt the old pressure building in himself, and in the rex. The tyrannosaur marched on.

This was *better* than old times, he thought. Much better. Hunting all of humanity.

The release would be *wonderful*.

He watched intently for any sign of movement in the underbrush.

The Virgin and the Dinosaur

by

R. Garcia y Robertson

*A relatively new writer, R. Garcia y Robertson made his first
sale in 1987, and since has become a frequent contributor
to* Asimov's Science Fiction *and* The Magazine of Fantasy
and Science Fiction, *as well as selling several stories to*
Amazing, Pulphouse, *and* Weird Tales. *His first novel,* The
Spiral Dance, *was published in 1991 to good critical
response. Upcoming are two new novels,* American Woman
and The Virgin and the Dinosaur, *and several of his recent
stories have been optioned for the movies. He was born in
Oakland, California, has a Ph.D. in the history of science
and technology and, before becoming a full-time writer,
taught those subjects at UCLA and Villanova. He lives in
Mt. Vernon, Washington.*

*In the vivid novella that follows, he takes us along with a
bumbling team of time-traveling documentary filmmakers
on location in the Upper Cretaceous, for an exciting and
action-packed romp through history, complete with zeppe-
lins, Sioux warriors,* haute cuisine, *sex, hurricanes, and lots
of dinosaurs, many of them hungry ones with great big
teeth . . .*

* * *

WELCOME to
Hell Creek, Montana
pop. 2

Toothed and feathered proto-birds scurried on clawed wings
into the upper branches; the screen of Mesozoic ferns and
flowering trees parted. Jake Bento watched a tall, red-haired
young woman step naked into the clearing—she moved

41

from the shoulders and waist; bare athletic legs bunching, then releasing with each step.

At that point-instant, Jake had Time by the tail. Five minutes before, he had navigated the Hell Creek portal perfectly, acing the coveted First Run with *no nasty shocks*. Microamps in his middle ear beat out an ancient victory anthem, "Light My Fire" by the Doors.

"Isn't it won-der-ful?" Peg rose on her toes, stretching in the steamy Montana air. Beads of sweat ran down between her breasts, across the swell of her belly, to gleam in her red triangle of pubic hair.

Jake had bent down to do a reactor check. When he'd looked up, Peg had shucked blanket coat, buckskins, and moccasins. He grinned in appreciation. "Welcome to the *fucking* Mesozoic."

His mix of Universal and English puzzled Peg. Jake tuned down the Doors, reprogramming for full Universal. "Yes, undoubtedly essential. Premium quality."

"You make it sound like a meat substitute. What does *'fucking'* mean?" Peg picked up the awe and reverence Jake packed into the English obscenity.

"A verbal noun, indicating affection." He dodged around the strict definition. "Intense personal affection."

"Well, then this whole *fucking* world is ours." She swung her arms to indicate the ferns and dogwoods, the pool, the sky, the dry riverbed. Insects buzzed about.

Just like Adam and Eve. Jake thought it, but did not say it. The absolute wonder of hitting that first point-instant in a new place had faded. Jake lived at the leading edge of FTL. He was the one who had brought them here. Peg was the neophyte, a raw first-timer, picked for this run because she happened to be young, healthy, ambitious, and over-qualified—Biofile rated her a dinosaur-genius. Only a beginner would lay claim to an entire world-era just because humans had finally arrived.

Jake's job was to play trusty guide and willing man-servant—show *memsahib* the period, haul her gear, bring her back intact. Rendering physical and personal assistance, *as needed*. Easy enough. The sort of assignment Jake could thrive on. Thousands of skilled and dedicated stay-at-homes had worked, sweated, and sacrificed so that he could share this clearing, this whole planet, with a criminally graceful Ph.D. in paleontology. He *owed* it to them to have fun.

She followed his gaze, seeming to notice her body for the first time. "Sorry. My skin needed to breathe. It's so incredibly hot." Fahrenheit surface temperature had tripled since passing the portal. "You don't mind, do you? We are adults."

"Mind? Not in the smallest." Jake was wearing moccasins and fringed leggings, soft as gloves, and a cotton annuity shirt given to him by the River Crow, but he had nothing against nudity. Cretaceous Montana was made for it— mesothermic climate, no rude neighbors—none that cared anyway.

However, he noted an alarming wholesomeness in the way Peg said "adults." As if sex only took place between tipsy teenagers or incurable juveniles. There was no hard, fixed rule that team members had to fuck—but Jake expected it. With Peg, he put a priority on it. Five minutes into the job, she had shucked everything but her belly-button. Fabulous. But Peg probably just enjoyed the feel of warm air. The blending with nature. Her nudity was not meant for *him*.

"So, when do we sight dinosaurs." She swiveled on her toes like a dancer, trying to see over the foliage.

"Say what?" He slipped back into English, still capti-vated by smallish breasts and large dark nipples.

"Dinosaurs. Huge archosaurs. Dominant megafauna of this period. Where *are* they?"

"Give them a moment." Jake was moderately pleased *not* to have stepped out of the Hell Creek portal into the path of megafauna with big teeth and Bad Attitudes. A nonsignifi-cant worry—the Mesozoic was a huge place; the very size of dinosaurs meant that they were rare, rarer than elk or rhino in a nature park. Navigating the Hell Creek anomaly had been infinitely more chancy. Jake had a private horror of portal skips—of just vanishing, leaving no clues, no clothes, nothing but the anomaly that ate you. With a dinosaur, at least you *knew* you were being devoured.

So far, Upper Cretaceous Montana resembled pre-contact Australia. The pool he sat by might have been a South Kimberly billabong in the Dreamtime. Little creatures stirring the brush seemed no more dangerous than a goanna or a roo.

"Come look." Peg pushed aside a flowering branch. "We could have hit the wrong era—Lower Paleocene instead of the Uppermost Cretaceous. That would be devastating." Hell Creek was the last stop for dinosaurs; in an eye-blink of geologic time, the huge creatures would be gone.

Never doubting his navigation, Jake took the excuse to stand behind her, making concerned noises, inhaling her odor. Short copper curls tickled the nape of her neck. Sweat beaded at the base of her spine.

The landscape *was* dull. Dense vegetation hugged the dry riverbed. The flats beyond were open canopy plains, hotter than a skillet, covered with scrub pines and thorny berry bushes. Peg must have made the mistake of trying to explore; Jake noted thin fresh scratches on her creamy hip.

A thunderous buzzing shook the air. Streaking from the sand by the billabong, a vicious metal-blue insect homed straight for them. Peg leaped backward, twisting and slapping at the whirring horror. Jake's shoulder holster slid a flat neural stunner into his palm. He yelped, "Drop."

Peg flattened on the sandy bank, and he fanned the air above her. The flying devil fell like a lead slug onto the wet sand. Peg pounced on the downed insect, prying open the jaws.

"See here." She waved the stunned bug beneath Jake's nostrils. "Mandibles meant for dinosaur. Nothing in the Lowest Paleocene would take jaws like *that* to chew through."

He agreed. The saw-toothed dental work looked ferocious.

Peg tossed the insect aside.

By now, Jake knew the tone to take. Peg had worked herself into a paleontological frenzy just to get here. He had to impress her with his calm professionalism, feigned indifference, and rugged charm. A truly inspirational aspect of this expedition was that things did not have to happen all at once. He and Peg would share a campfire tonight, and breakfast tomorrow, tomorrow, and tomorrow. Sooner or later, they were sure to be wearing out the same sleeping bag. Cheered by that certainty, he hummed through the rest of his equipment check.

Jake ticked off each item twice. He had a fabulous memory—360 megabytes of RAM tucked in the compweb stretched atop his skull, along with his navmatrix and music files. A Crazy Dog Blackfoot once tried to lift Jake's hair—not for any personal reasons; just part of the usual hysteria accompanying a Crow attack. One look under Jake's scalp, and the Crazy Dog dropped his knife and ran, spooked by gleaming fiberoptics. At a kill-talk, Jake returned the knife. The Crazy Dog apologized. Swore he would never scalp another Wasichu.

Buckskins, dehydrated rations, shock-rifle, microstove, and lounge chairs were broken down, collapsed, and closest-packed to fit through the portal. The Hell Creek anomaly was newly opened, poorly mapped, generally a tight squeeze. The 12 megawatt mobile fusion reactor had been the most obstinate piece, harder to get through than everything else combined. People passed easily—too easily, becoming the victims of portal skips or spontaneous transmission. Metals and hardwired electronics were the worst. Only the length of stay and the ground to cover justified bringing the reactor. A herd of pack ponies would have been easier to fit through the portal, but who knew how oatburners would take to Mesozoic Asiamerica. For openers, there was no grass.

Check completed. Jake kicked the reactor, mentally

telling the gray 1.5 meter cube to get into mobile mode. With a whirr and click, the reactor sprouted four shiny legs, with white rings on the ends. The whirr became a softer hiss. The white rings inflated into four balloon tires. "Mobile" reactors were made to live up to the name.

Jake climbed to a perch atop the pack saddle, reaching down for Peg. "So, will you come a-waltzing Matilda with me?"

"Wat-zing Ma-tilta?" Peg looked up. She was crouched on one knee, squeezing gravelly mud through her fingers— half eager scientist, half wood nymph. "This *has* to be Hell Creek. Sediment's too dry and rocky for the Tullock formation." She brushed the dirt off.

Time Shock. Jake recognized symptoms of a mild attack. Peg was doubting the period, feeling the air and mud, proving to herself that this world was real. Well, it *was* real. It was *Earth*. Human population, two. But Home and civilization were sixty-five million years away, thirty times faster than a trip to the Andromeda galaxy at lightspeed.

"I'll show you dinosaurs. Promise." Jake knew they were bound to see the big beasts soon. He might as well claim credit now.

Her eyes lit. "Even sauropods? It's essential I see sauropods." Sauropods were the *big* boys: brontosaurs, titanosaurs, supersaurs, and ultrasaurs. Few had made it to the Upper Cretaceous—none were known in Hell Creek.

"Sure, sauropods." He extended his hand further. "Don't make 'em wait."

She took his offered hand, vaulting easily onto the saddle beside him.

Jake told the reactor, "Downstream." They lurched into motion, splashing through ponds and puddles, keeping to the lowest part of the bed, feeling for the main channel. Steep banks and ginkgo trees turned the wash into a green canyon topped by a blue ribbon of sky. Pneumatic tires left silent prints in the bare mud.

Upper Cretaceous Montana had a semi-tropic climate and

a swampy coastline; somewhere downstream was the shallow Midwestern Sea separating Asiamerica from Euramerica. For the last twenty million years, continents had been drifting apart. Montana was on the east coast of the supercontinent Asiamerica, a great arc connecting Mexico to Malaysia—taking in the northern Pacific Rim, China, Siberia, and Mongolia. The Urals were a far western archipelago.

Greenhouse gases filled the air. Water smelled alkaline, and Jake saw signs of chemical erosion—soils leached by acid rain. Sort of like the twenty-first century Old Style, without the overpopulation, money collapse, and stock market hysteria.

The young Mesozoic sun sank quickly. Jake unshipped his shock-rifle. Late afternoon was hunting time in hot climates. He boosted his hearing, tripping the microamps in his middle ear. The rustle of wind and leaves became a roar.

Craning his neck, he switched his corneal lenses from wide-angle to telescopic, searching for fine details. Nothing. No snapped twigs. No three-toed tracks. None of the shed teeth commonly found in Hell Creek rock. The absence of animals was eerie.

"I've seen fossil beds with more left than this," complained Peg, her forearm on his shoulder. Words boomed in his boosted ears.

He finished fitting the shock-rifle together—telescopic vision made each part seem huge as prefab sewer pipe.

She eyed the assembled rifle. "Nine out of ten animals in the Hell Creek formation are harmless herbivores. Chances are less than one in a hundred of meeting a really hungry carnivore. Are you worried?"

"Me? Never." He noted that Peg still talked in terms of sediment formations and fossil ratios, as if this were a bone hunt, not a living, breathing world. Trundling around a corner, they startled a wee furry fellow drinking from one of the ponds. It scampered for the undergrowth.

Peg leaped to the ground, recorder running. "Why didn't you stun it?"

"Because it was rabbit-sized and scared senseless." The shock-rifle was designed for dinosaurs, and would have blasted the tiny mammal's central nervous system straight out its eyeballs. "I don't expect it was dangerous."

"It was probably a protoungulate—closer to a horse than a rabbit." She fingered prints in the soft mud, and reviewed her recordings—a 3V image of the creature repeated the scurry for safety several times.

"But how am I supposed to *know*, if I don't get a look at its teeth?"

Jake knew all about the paleontologist's love affair with teeth. Teeth preserved well and told you a lot. Careers were launched by broken molars—and they were happy as dental hygienists to see a clean, complete set.

"Oh, *great*, some droppings!" Peg poked and sniffed through a pile of wet turds squeezed out by the terrified mammal. "A genuine browser; bet he had real grinders."

She climbed back aboard, patting the shock-rifle. "Stow the nuke. Your stunner would be more helpful."

Jake slipped out of his shoulder holster, twisted about, and fit the holster over Peg's bare shoulder. Her skin felt smooth and dry beneath his fingers. "Here, Annie Oakley, blaze away at the rodents, just don't hit me."

"Annie Oakley?"

"Friend of Sitting Bull's. I'll tell you about her some-day—maybe introduce you." When he was not on the warpath, Sitting Bull had a relaxed and amiable way with women, even Wasichu women, one of the reasons Jake admired the medicine man.

They did not see any more of the tiny horses-to-be. Jake spotted a foot-long tree rat, which Peg thought was a primitive possum. She could not be sure because she was slow with the stunner, not having the bioimplants to control the holster.

The streambed widened into a broad expanse of hardpan,

cracked into blocks by the heat, each block as flat and regular as a piece of old paving. Jake smelled the oily reek of a jungle river. He halted, spotting a reptilian tail stretching back from the bank. Black fisher-storks stalked about, stepping over the scaly tail.

"That's nothing." Peg dismissed the tail with a shake of her head. "An archosaur, but hardly a dinosaur."

Boosting up, Jake saw a dozen big crocodiles basking in the afternoon sun; five-meter eating machines—jaws, stomach, and a tail. (If you don't believe there are crocs in Montana, just ask the River Crow.) These weren't the gigantic dinosaur-eating crocodiles found in Texas, but *all* crocs were cunning, dangerous brutes who would outlive the dinosaurs. The nearest one looked maybe three times as long as Jake, and easily ten times as mean.

Peg put down her recorder. "It's so *nonessential*, seeing everything but dinosaurs."

"Relax." Jake hopped down, keeping an eye on the crocs. He did not expect any to come dashing over the hardpan, but it never paid to turn your back on the reptilian brain. Gripping Peg's waist, he swung her to the ground, feeling her skin, smelling her fragrance, forgetting all about the crocs amid the burst of flesh. Strange how her sweat didn't stink. "I'll show you more dinosaurs than you ever dreamed of."

She smiled, "Not likely. I've dreamed nothing *but* sauropods since being picked for this."

Pack saddle and equipment cases followed her onto the hardpan. Then Jake sent the reactor lumbering down to the river for a drink, trailing an anchor line.

The crocs looked up. One took a speculative snap at the big balloon tires. Jake sent it a jarring shock from the reactor's defense system. After that the crocs ignored the reactor. Too big to swallow and too tough to chew. They let the ungainly newcomer waddle into midstream and toss out a second anchor.

While the reactor drank, Jake laid out sleeping bags and

pink champagne, dragging in driftwood for a fire, telling the microstove to whip up dinner.

Peg was fetching in her stunner and shoulder holster, running about recording the sleepy crocs and the flowering trees, radiating megawatts of misplaced energy.

He watched her zoom in on the black fisher-storks that were stalking about the shallows like operatic vampires. The tall birds spread their wings before them, forming black feather capes, shading out surface glare. Ducking their heads inside the dark canopies, they would strike at fish, then step gingerly forward to find a new spot.

It took over two hours for the reactor to extract a half-ton of hydrogen from the river, pumping it into an elastic gas bag—the reactor opened as needed like an origami box. When the expanding envelope was sauropod-sized, fifty meters long and twenty meters tall, Jake told the reactor to reel itself back to the campsite. The newborn blimp drifted over to hang above him, blocking out the setting sun. He sprayed the skin with metallic sealant, covering everything but the line of vents along the top and the transparent windows on the cabin-space.

Dusk brought more brontosaurian insects. Peg retreated to the campsite, where Jake set up a sonic field to keep the bugs at bay. He popped the pink champagne, pouring them both glasses.

Peg sniffed her drink. "I don't use alcohol at work. There *is* alcohol in this, isn't there?"

You betcha. Alcohol was an archaic vice. If Peg was an inexperienced drinker, he hoped the champagne went straight to her inhibitions. "But we have a ship to christen." Jake nodded toward the new fifty-meter airship floating above them, gleaming red and gold in the sunset.

"Christen?" She was still dubious.

"Sure. In the old days, they launched an airship by having a woman toast the ship with champagne, giving her a name."

"Didn't the woman already have a name?"

"Yes, but she gave the *ship* a name as well—all ships are 'her' or 'she.'" Jake assumed Peg had never been aboard an airship. At Home, ships of any sort were a rarity. A person could work, live, play, even travel from Montana to Pluto, without ever entering a vehicle.

"Well, what shall I call it . . . I mean her?"

"I was thinking of *Challenger*. You know, after Professor Challenger and his Lost World—the great jungle plateau full of dinosaurs." He could see that she hadn't read Conan Doyle.

"Is that fiction?"

"Very much, but *we* are real. So why don't you name our ship?" Be a sport.

She took a deep sip, and smiled up at the dirigible. "I name you *Challenger*."

The little ritual had served its purpose—the bottle was open, Peg had loosened up. He made sure the glass in her hand stayed full. Next stop, the cozy fire.

Jake was not thigh-struck enough to light his romantic campfire right under thousands of cubic meters of explosive hydrogen. The stressed metal skin was *supposed* to stop sparks, leaks, lightning, and St. Elmo's Fire—but why chance spoiling the moment by being blown clear out of the Upper Cretaceous. He told the airship to go up a hundred meters. It hung in the last of the sunset, while Jake served up *risotto a la milanese*, with eggplant vinaigrette, and tofu szechwan in triple pepper sauce—simple safari fare.

As they ate, he heard crocs moving about by the river. Night birds cried. Things went thump and crunch in the brush. The Mesozoic night never seemed to get really quiet—too hot.

Jake cut his microamps, telling *Challenger* to watch for movement and illuminate the crocs. Then he settled in, shock-rifle on one side of him, Peg on the other.

Peg lay back against the pack saddle, fed and happy. She had put on a Crow gift shirt for dinner, fancier than

Jake's—fringed buckskin, beaded with porcupine quills—
but she left off the breechcloth and leather leggings.

Hitting the champagne, she gave his leg a playful whack,
trying out some of his English, "The *fucking* Mesozoic.
We're *here!* Aren't you amazed, excited, dumbfounded? Do
you even *believe* it?"

His leg stung from the slap. Champagne was making her
frisky. But Jake could take a bit of physical abuse from a
woman—administered in the right spirit. "Damn well *feels*
like we're here." He slid an arm around her waist.

Seeming not to notice his arm, she stared moodily into the
sizzling night. "All except for the dinosaurs."

Right, no damned dinosaurs. He refilled her glass with his
free arm, amused by her inebriated swings of mood.

Challenger beeped him. Crocs were moving down by the
water. None were coming his way. He went back to
admiring Peg's thigh and the dark hollow between her legs.

She smiled over her champagne. "I mean, aren't you
disappointed?"

"Not yet." His hand closed on the hem of her shirt,
pulling her closer. Curved flesh felt warm beneath the
buckskin. She had a gymnast's body, taut and muscled.

Peg relaxed into him, saying nothing, wearing a dreamy,
expectant look. A really *essential* look, one Time never
touched. Jake had seen that look in the kohl-darkened eyes
of one of Cleopatra's handmaids. He'd seen it shining across
a dung fire in a yurt on the Camelback Steppe, beside the
Sleeping Sands north of the Gobi. Jake had seen that exact
look in a half-dozen centuries, on three habitable planets.
Thank goodness it always meant the same thing. He and Peg
were a millimeter away from foreplay.

Challenger beeped him again.

Jake checked the crocs—no change. Turning back, he
found Peg's red-haired head resting on his shoulder, waiting, eyes wide, lips parted. Her freckled face looked near
perfect in the firelight. He leaned in to kiss her, sliding his
hand under her hip for leverage.

Peg squealed, leaped up, lost balance, and sat back bare-assed on his hand, breathing hard and muttering, "Oh my, oh my . . ."

Staring at them from across the fire was a great, round yellow eye. The eye was set in a huge bony head, silhouetted by the night—half in shadow, half in light. Above the eye stood a horn as long as Jake was tall.

Triceratops. No 3V imaging, no mounted skeleton, no Feelie stimulation did the dinosaur justice. Imagine a four-legged beast, big as a bull elephant, with an armored head, three tremendous horns, and a terrible cutting beak. Picture this behemoth appearing out of blackness, without warning, when you are sitting by a night fire in a strange place, half-foxed on champagne, your hand stuck under someone else's butt. Jake was paralyzed.

And there were *more* of them. Immense six-ton bodies appeared on either side of the first, more wicked heads and horns. Hundreds were filling the dark wash, pushing toward the river.

Peg lunged forward to grab a recorder. Her tanned rear eclipsed the triceratops in front of Jake—but all thought of taking advantage of Peg had vanished. He yelled for *Challenger* to reel herself down the anchor line.

The ship did not come half fast enough. Clutching his shock-rifle, Jake watched powerful jaws crunch ginkgo and magnolia like broccoli. Were it not for his fire, the fleshy avalanche would have trod Peg and him into the hardpan. It could still happen. The dinosaurs being pushed toward the fire acted dangerously agitated. A sneeze now might start a stampede.

Challenger's balloon tires touched down atop the anchor grapple. Flames cast dancing shadows on the dirigible's hull. Jake had forgotten the fire. He pictured half a ton of hydrogen gas exploding like a bomb in the midst of a triceratops herd—with him beneath it. The first Mesozoic expedition would be finished well ahead of schedule.

In a fever to get aloft, he heaved equipment into the cabin

atop the reactor. Then he turned to Peg. She was sitting on her haunches, easy-as-you-please, panning the recorder, *totally* absorbed by the milling herd. He grabbed hold of the shoulder fringe on her Crow gift shirt, screaming, "Get aboard."

Peg's eyes shone clear and excited. "We found them!"

"Right, and this is too dangerous by half." Unshipping the nylon ladder, he shoved it into her hands.

Reluctantly, she stowed her recorder, climbing the ladder. Armored heads crowded closer. Any moment a horn might puncture the thin plasti-metal gas bag, releasing a torrent of flammable hydrogen. Jake dropped the shock-rifle, planted his hand on Peg's bottom, and shoved. "Put a wiggle on it!"

As he pushed Peg into the cabin Jake yelled to *Challenger*, "Up one hundred meters."

They shot skyward. Jake clung to the last rungs of the twisting ladder, watching the campfire shrink to a spark, surrounded by the shadowy backs and heads of the herd. Fumbling above the sea of spikes, he got a foot on the bottom rung, and swung back and forth, full of fright and exhilaration, ninety-odd meters above the hardpan. Perfectly safe as long as he did not let go.

"Aren't you coming up?" inquired a sweet intoxicated voice from above.

Without a word, Jake climbed the swaying ladder, tumbling into the lounge—the middle part of the cabin, with large entrance windows at either end—collapsing on the nonslip floor.

Peg hopped over him, full of alcoholic enthusiasm, trying to record from both ends of the lounge at once. Every so often, she ran over and shook him, with a bit of breathless news. "There are *hundreds* down there!"

A moment later she'd be back. "Make that *thousands*!"

Giggling hysterically, she tugged at him, "Come on, you have to *see* it." She had all the running lights on, illuminating the herd below.

"And juveniles. *Fucking* juveniles, moving with the

herd." Then she would bound off again to lean out a window, only her legs and bottom in the cabin.

Jake had busted himself to pass the portal, find water, set up camp, get *Challenger* ready, start a fire, serve dinner, and seduce Peg. The moment he had her tipsy and in his arms, he'd been nearly trampled, dangled from a soaring airship, and come closer than he needed to being blown apart. All on a head full of champagne.

He decided he hadn't a hope of calming Peg down and sliding her into a double sleeping bag. Finding his bag and kit, he crawled off to the privacy of a barren stateroom, cursing all thousand triceratopses for their *pre-coitus interruptis*.

T. Rex

Dawnlight angled in the stateroom window. Jake lay curled atop his sleeping bag, hammered by a vicious hangover. He'd forgotten how deadly sweet champagne was the next day. Peg padded back and forth in the lounge. Had she slept at all? Probably not. Groping about, he found his medikit, telling it to take away the pain. His head cleared. He felt not just better, but *good*. Last night's prize fiasco faded into a few not unfunny episodes; today had to be near perfect— just to balance the statistics. Cheered by that gambler's fallacy, he went to find Peg.

She was still wearing the fringed Crow shirt—her tired face full of heartless enthusiasm. "Have you *seen* them yet? They are ten times as thrilling by day!"

Easing back on the angle of attack, Jake gave her a professional greeting, and found the microstove, telling it to conjure up *café au lait*. He took a steaming cup into the cabin's glassed-in nose to gauge the day.

The day *was* magnificent. The fore and aft ends of the cabin area were completely transparent. Light and power poured through windows and floor. Jake sat amid blue limitless sky filled with towering white anvilheads. Green-brown flood plain snaked beneath him, coiling round islands of red earth. Mountains thrust up in the distance. He had his microamps pound out "Dawn Symphony."

The triceratops herd was truly awesome. Huge tawny bodies took up both sides of the river; moving, drinking, chewing up the greenery. Crocs had shifted to midstream to keep from being trampled.

He told the navcomputer to turn off the running lights, blazing uselessly in the daylight. Peg followed him into the glassed-in nose, constantly recording, shooting through the deck at their feet. "How long before we can get this ship moving?"

"Bored with dinosaurs already?" Jake noted dark circles under her bright eyes.

She waved in the direction the triceratops herd had come from. "It's essential to test the theory that carnivores will be trailing the herd."

He turned down "Dawn Symphony." Unwashed, circles under her eyes, wearing only a badly wrinkled buckskin shirt—Peg was every bit as stunning as he remembered. Of course, she *was* the only woman on the planet, the only one in all creation, for that matter, which accounted for at least 10 percent of her attraction. "I hate to move ship in this condition."

"What's wrong with it?" She glanced at the pristine galley and empty chartroom located behind the forward windows.

"Nothing's in place. Everything's piled where I tossed it last night. Lounge looks like a crash site." *Challenger's* cabin was designed to give them breathing room. Lounge, galley, and chartroom formed a common area amidships. Twin staterooms aft were enclosed and independent. Fore and aft galleries gave each person a place to be alone with the vast landscape.

Peg agreed. Before he could finish his coffee, she was clearing up the litter in the lounge and inflating collapsible furniture, hips bending and swaying as she worked. He decided she was not only a nerveless idiot with no sense of self-preservation, but also a shamelessly cheerful worker. Jake had no good reason to grouse. She finished off with yoga, moving to an inner music that needed no microamps. Her whole body sang. Peg was impossibly supple—chaste and naked at the same time.

Reeling *Challenger* down to the campsite, Jake hopped out for a final visit. Ashes formed a black scar on the dry wash, surrounded by bits and pieces left behind in the panic. A whole case of dehydrated paté had been mashed into the hardpan. The champagne bottle and glasses were ground to fine dust. Beside them was the gleaming stock of the shock-rifle. The rest of the weapon was gone, carried away between some thoughtless triceratops' toes.

An absolutely *fine* thing to forget! He had set the gun down in order to shove Peg up the ladder. Now they had *nothing* fit to take down a dinosaur. "Shock-rifle—missing," would raise a red flag in his report. Any weapon lost "out of period" was a headache. Debriefing would want *details*. He needed a better explanation than being caught in drunken panic with his hand on his partner's butt. Happily, debriefing was months away. A suitable explanation would turn up. Without a shock-rifle, he could easily be killed—then the problem would have solved itself.

Jake turned to piloting, something he fancied he did well. Compweb and navmatrix made *Challenger* an add-on to his central nervous system. Machinery leaped to his least command. Vague curiosity produced immediate data on buoyancy and windspeed. He released the anchor grapple, feeling the snap. *Challenger* rose silently upward. The reactor extended twin propellers. They were airborne.

Turning west, Jake climbed in huge steps toward the highlands, feeling the ship's balance as though the keel were a giant teeter-totter—anticipating trim changes, bracing for turns—flying a few tons heavy to maintain altitude aerodynamically instead of aerostatically. He relished the sense of control, and welcomed the challenge of translating Peg's instructions into something *Challenger* comprehended.

"Over there."

"Bearing two-nine-zero."

"A little to the left."

"Port five degrees."

"Closer."

"Down twenty meters."

He had Peg so pleased that she was running to the microstove to fetch him croissants and coffee, though the galley work was technically Jake's. As he suspected, Peg would put up with almost anything filed under WORK. Like many people who get good at what they do, she was eager to learn and not afraid to sweat. All he needed to do was to slip "sex" into her job description, then she would bang away with her customary enthusiastic efficiency. Coffee and croissants were a start.

The uplands were flat, rolling country—drier than a bottle of fine wine. Carbon lines in Hell Creek rock showed these high plains suffered from flash fires. Farther west, Jake could make out the wavy blue line of the proto-Rockies, a massive cordillera; young, vibrant, with gnarled valleys and active volcanoes. Mountain chains were the true *terra incognita* of the Mesozoic, mist-shrouded and mysterious—leaving no fossil record, they could be home to anything; unsuspected species, outrageous monsters, alien civilizations. Compared to the Rockies, Hell Creek was comfortably familiar.

"There it *is*!" Peg pounded his shoulder, stabbing the air with her finger.

Jake looked down. Nothing showed below but sandhills, clay pan, and steep gullies, held together by conifer stands and primitive broadleaf trees. He had seen several tanklike ankylosaurs and a herd of bipedal boneheads—but no sign of the carnivores Peg claimed were shadowing the herds. He descended, flushing out a flock of yellow-brown ornitho-

mimids that looked and ran like ostriches. Suddenly, at the
end of Peg's finger, there was *T. Rex.*

Jake had always pictured the brute striding along, jaws
agape, striking terror among decent law-abiding dinosaurs—
but this one seemed to be asleep, sprawled on its side. Jake
did a low pass and pirouette. Stretched out, the tyrannosaur
was over thirteen meters long—nearly three times as big as
the crocs that had worried him yesterday. The tyrant king
did not even look up.

"We have to land." Peg was already half out the window.
He suspected she wouldn't really feel she was *there* until
she shared the ground with this great beast. So he dropped
a grapple and anchor line, telling *Challenger* to reel herself
down, keeping the ship "light," ready for a fast take-off.
Then he slipped on his stunner holster, following Peg out the
window.

Glare off the sandstone kicked in polarizers on his
corneal lenses. The sleeping tyrannosaur had stood out like
a small hill from the air, but the ground was a maze of dry
wadis and cutbanks, divided by tall lanes of scrub and pines.
Twenty meters, and they could no longer see the tyrannosaur, or the dead ground between them and the airship. If *T.
Rex* decided to wake and stalk about, the carnosaur could
appear anywhere. Jake's stunner felt like a flyswatter tucked
under his armpit.

They came on the beast abruptly. One moment, the
tyrannosaur was "somewhere over there." A minute later,
Jake was nose to nose with the napping monster, its
enormous bulk half-hidden by a shallow wash. Mottled
black-and-tan coloring broke up the big beast's outline. Jake
got an uncomfortably close view of great shearing jaws and
saw-edged teeth. The boxy flat-sided head alone was bigger
than he was, reeking of half-eaten meat.

Peg went down on one knee, recording, while Jake kept
nervous watch. *Challenger* was not near enough to warn
him if another carnosaur popped out of a neighboring gully.

"Look at the ropes of muscle in those cheek bulges!"

Peg was clearly in awe of the nasty creature. "I wish it would open its mouth; we'd get a better view of the teeth and interior attachments."

The tyrannosaur opened one eye, looking right at Peg.

"He knows we're talking about him," Jake whispered.

"Don't be a worrier. See that blood smeared on the premaxillaries? Probably sleeping off a kill. I doubt if we look much like a meal to him."

"Mere *hors d'oeuvres.*" The ogre could down them like a pair of oysters, and the gore on its fangs was not reassuring.

"You *are* the nervous type, aren't you?"

"Not necessarily so." Every epoch had its burdens to bear. The fourteenth century had the Black Death; the twentieth had world wars and commercial TV. The bane of Jake's time and place was that people like Peg were too protected.

"This isn't a 3V or stimulation—everything here is *real*. Including *him*. Screw up, and no one's going to drag you out of that gullet."

The bony muscular head lifted up, turning snout and teeth toward them, stretching its powerful neck. Jake nearly jumped out of his leggings.

"Don't startle it." Peg held his stunner holster, keeping the gun from leaping out. Jake stopped breathing, staring at the tyrannosaur's evil grin.

The beast settled back, resting its chin nearer to them, seemingly more comfortable. The huge eye shut, shaded by its horny socket.

Just as Jake thought it was all over, Peg put down her recorder. She took two purposeful steps, leaned forward, and touched the horrible toothed head lightly on the snout.

The tyrannosaur snorted, nearly giving Jake a seizure.

Walking back over thorny wadis, under an unblinking sun, Peg explained, "That creature has no natural enemies, nothing to fear or defend against. If you are not afraid, or appetizing, you have nothing to fear from it."

He didn't argue. Maybe Peg was right; maybe she was

merely insane. Either way Jake was not about to run back and pat *T. Rex* on the nose.

He settled for picking up a shed tooth, notched with wear and larger than his hand. The cutting edges had fine bevels, like a jeweler's saw.

In the scorching air of noon, Hell Creek lived up to its name. Even Peg wound down under the incandescent heat. Shocked at the way Peg wilted, Jake realized she probably had not rested in a day and a half. Feeling a flood of concern and fondness that was less than two-thirds lust, Jake took *Challenger* aloft, so that she could sleep in the swaying air-conditioned cabin.

The shimmering landscape cooled. Jake woke from his own noon sleep fresh enough to tackle tyrannosaurs—exactly what Peg intended. "Can you take me back to the river? To see how these carnivores handle the triceratops herd."

The navmatrix in his compweb let Jake retrace his every movement, never allowing him to get lost. Releasing the anchor grapple, he gave *Challenger* full port rudder, flying with up elevator, letting the terrain fall away beneath them.

Peg kept urging him, "Closer." Which meant venting hydrogen to get right down at the cypress tops.

The glassed-in forward gallery looked out on green-tan countryside, cut by a vast loop of the red mud river channel. Jake saw bathing triceratopses, big crocs, and duckbilled hadrosaurs. Farther off, the river branched out into flat delta country, a collage of blue bayous and cypress swamps. In the far, far distance, his boosted eyesight made out a blue horizon line merging with the sky—the Middle American Sea, a shallow arm of ocean filling the Mississippi valley, connecting the Gulf of Mexico to Hudson's Bay.

"Here come the carnivores." Peg pointed to the right. Jake applied starboard rudder and down elevator.

Sneaking along a deep creekbed was a smallish, longlegged tyrannosaurid, about the size of a walking killer whale. Peg identified the skulker, "*Albertosaurus megagracilis*—a stalker and sprinter. It'll hang about the herds trying to pick off a straggler or juvenile."

From a secure height, Jake liked the little fellow. *A. megagracilis* was rust-colored with brown spots, more compact and graceful than the tyrannosaur Peg had played tag with, but also faster, hungrier, and a greater threat to humans.

Peg pulled on the leggings and moccasins that went with the Crow gift shirt, not bothering with the long, trailing breechcloth. The result was a short fringed minidress over hip-length leather. "I want to go down there, close to the herd. To cover the action from ground level."

Jake was not ready for another walk on the Mesozoic wild side. It was late afternoon. In the cooling half-light, carnivores were bound to be more active and dangerous.

"Oh, *you* can stay up here. We'll combine ground recordings with a wide-angle aerial sequence." She panned her recorder. "Here come more carnivores! A whole hunting pack!"

Jake looked the newcomers over; they were taller than *A. megagracilis*, chunkier too. Full-sized tyrannosaurids. A half-dozen black-and-tan boys (or gals) out to raise hell among the herbivores. They did not stalk the creekbeds, but ambled right toward the river, not caring who saw them coming.

Jake had seen this dance of death before, on the steppes of Central Asia, on the plains below Kilimanjaro. Carnivores approached casually from downwind. The herd edged slowly upwind to keep from being ambushed, maintaining a healthy separation. Neither hunter nor victim moved too quickly—neither wanted to exhaust their reserves. In the ultimate rush, a labored breath might make all the difference.

And Peg itched to be in the middle of it. Jake began to question the wisdom of picking an active young paleontologist who had never seen a battery of carnivore teeth outside of a fossil formation.

He set down on the leeward periphery of the herd, giving her a comlink to clip to her ear. "Take this *little fucker* with you."

"Little fucker?" English confused her again.

"Technical term. Just keep the link open."

Slipping the comlink into her ear, she swaggered off toward the brush, showing long sweeps of thigh between the slits in her shirt and the tops of her leggings. Jake hoped this was not his last look at her.

Fighting a crosswind, he kept *Challenger* positioned almost directly above Peg. *A. megagracilis* still worried Jake the most—but he had lost the cheetah-like stalker in the rough, and did not have time to hunt him up.

"How does it look? I have the herd in sight." Microamps made Peg sound like a flea in his ear.

"*A. megagracilis* is missing. Those big tyrannosaurs are moving in line ahead, a couple of kilometers downwind." Jake judged that the big ones were getting ready for a run in. The triceratopses thought so too. They were shifting their young into the herd center. Adults turned their horns toward the approaching carnivores, swiveling on their short front legs.

A game of bait and bluff began. Nature's ballet of death is never all-out battle. No carnosaur was going to charge into a hedge of horns. And no right-minded triceratops wanted to be separated from the retreating herd, singled out for slaughter. Heroism is not an herbivore survival trait.

"What's happening?" Stuck in the brush, Peg was missing everything. So much for being *on the scene*.

"Tyrannosaurs are fanning out, trying to turn a flank."

Defenseless duckbills scattered for the brush along the river.

"I'm heading over there."

"Don't get stepped on."

At that instant, something spooked the herd—maybe the flanking tactics, maybe the bolting duckbills. For whatever reason, the triceratopses got the wind up and thundered downriver, tyrannosaurs sprinting at their heels. Thousands of elephant-sized dinosaurs stampeded at top speed, heads down and tails up, sides heaving. Even larger tyrannosaurs dashed in among them, slashing and snarling, attempting to cut down a victim while running flat-out, meters ahead of the horns.

Death in the afternoon. Near-indescribable nightmare. The only thing Jake could compare it with was a breakneck Lakota buffalo hunt. The dust-covered tyrannosaurs reminded him of Crazy Horse and Company, whooping in to make their kills.

Only this time they missed. Perhaps the horns came too close or the herd broke too soon, maybe it was all a feint—for whatever reason, the carnivores rolled out and regrouped.

Peg missed it all. "I can see the dust raised by the herd, but where are the tyrannosaurs?"

"They rolled right, half a kilometer short of you." A good thing, too.

"I'm going to work my way up this dry wash, staying to leeward of the herd." The wash was a flood channel connecting two loops of the river, a shortcut that let Peg keep abreast of the frightened herd.

Jake acknowledged, dipping down to scout the wash, looking for that sneaky culprit *A. megagracilis*, but the fast little bastard might be anywhere by now.

A setting sun cast long, confusing shadows. Duckbills crouched like great frightened lizards in the greenery. The triceratops herd caught its collective breath. Rearmost adults turned, peering back into the dust, keeping a horned eye out for the pursuing tyrannosaur pack.

Challenger beeped him.

"Oh, I see them now!" Peg hooted with triumph. "Here they come!"

"Who? Where?" Jake turned back to her. His jaw fell. Both he and the herd had been fooled. Under cover of dust and half-light, the tyrannosaurs had wheeled, shifting from

line ahead to line abreast. Using Peg's shortcut, they were starting another run smack at the middle of the shaken herd, aiming to split it into two panicked segments.

Right in their path, Peg scrambled out of the wash, lying prone on the cutbank, her recorder running. Idiot luck had put her between the herd and the line of oncoming carnivores. Six frenzied tyrannosaurs rushed at her out of the twilight, teeth gleaming, tails straight, clawed feet chewing up the clay pan. For an awful instant, Jake saw her insanely refusing to move.

The wave of claws, teeth, and muscle swept over her, and her comlink went dead.

Seeing the Sauropod

Jake's job made him a generalist, but he did imagine himself a specialist on Time—Newtonian Time, post-Einsteinian Time, non-Euclidean Time. He had even yawned through an endless lecture by Plato on the subject. His navmatrix gave him a hyperlight time-sense that could carve days down to milliseconds or stretch them over millennia, never missing a click of the cosmic clock. The instant Peg disappeared beneath the charging carnivores, Jake started counting nanoseconds—screaming for *Challenger* to land.

He knew that what was left of Peg needed immediate life-support. A body *could* be regenerated. Bit by bit if need be. But nerve cells were slippery cases. As they died, they took with them the memories that made Peg who she was. Brain dead was dead.

He was out of the cabin before *Challenger* touched down, vaulting through a forward window, hitting the ground sprinting, medikit in hand.

Jake calculated he could have Peg on life-support in seconds. Minutes would put her at the portal. But on the far end of the portal, real medical care was still centuries off. There was no direct connection between the Uppermost Cretaceous and Home. At the other end of the Hell Creek anomaly, medicine was still in the business of killing patients—cut-and-stitch butchery done by buffoons in disease-ridden hospitals. Surgeons *paid by the limb* spent their odd hours denouncing public health and germ theory.

As he ran, his mind searched calmly for ways to push time back, to retrieve minutes, even seconds—to recapture the instant before this all happened. In theory, FTL made it possible to pull Peg out *before the tyrannosaurs hit her*. In well-traveled historical periods, STOP teams routinely performed impossible rescues.

Not here though, not now. The Hell Creek anomaly was too new, so poorly mapped that Peg had worried about being in the Paleocene instead of the Mesozoic. A STOP team could not count on hitting the right millenium, much less the right moment. But if he could get her through the portal to a historical period—a STOP team could be waiting. That was Peg's ticket to an autodoc.

Simultaneously, Jake cursed himself for letting Peg wander about guided only by her daft death wish. He was despicable, a fool, doing his job with a hard-on, so obsessed with bedding Peg he had given in to her suicidal whims.

Leaping over the crumpled lip of the wadi, he steeled himself for his first look at her. So much depended on what shape she was in. What he had to work with. What was *left*.

Peg was sitting calmly, covered with dirt, elbows propped on her knees, recording the disappearing tyrannosaurs. Jake hit badly, doing a perfect pratfall.

She turned, startled by his impact. "Are you hurt? It's good you brought a medikit."

Taking the kit from his nerveless fingers, she was all over him, checking for injuries, helping him sit up, making him feel twelve times worse. "Did you see the tyrannosaurids? That was a truly essential moment—they galloped right over me!"

He sat there, stunned, saying nothing—flooded with relief and anger, feeling all the guilt and rottenness turn to cold, hard fury.

"Feel better?" Her smile aimed at being helpful. "Could you look for my comlink? I think you landed on it. The *little fucker* flipped out in the fall."

Jake was wired to explode. But he to *work* with this brainless waif. He dug her comlink out of the dirt under him and slapped it into her palm, replying as diplomatically as possible, "If you are dead set on suicide, please do it on your *own* damn time, and have the decency to leave a note so mere bystanders won't be blamed."

Peg looked at him coolly. "Don't be anal. Ever since passing the portal, you have been in a testosterone frenzy—pawing me by the fire, bounding about saving me, making a farce out of a serious expedition."

He tried to argue, but her tone just turned huffy and academic. "Do you have *any* notion what the stride length of a tyrannosaur is?"

"*Damned* large, like the rest of him."

"Running flat-out—four to five meters. All I needed do was drop down, and they sailed right over me." Peg pointed to the first three-toed gouge, meters away in the middle of the streambed. One stride would have cleared a small ground car.

"Stop thinking with your gonads. I was never in any danger. Basic carnivore behavior says that no seven-ton carnosaur chasing a six-ton herbivore is going to stop to bother with a fifty-kilo person in its path."

She gave him a concerned look. "You are *so* edgy. It's a surprise FTL picked you for this."

Jake said nothing, knowing too well why he was here. FTL hadn't picked him—he had picked *Peg*, snapping up her and her Mesozoic project like a lovesick teen.

Cultural, academic, and entertainment institutions—as well as interested individuals—submitted field work proposals to FTL, which Faster Than Light filled at whim. Only STOP missions had instant priority. Cultural-scientific importance was meant to play some vague role in selection, but the real criterion was what veteran field agents thought they could accomplish. No one could be forced through a portal, and attrition was high, especially among first-timers. Field agents regularly succumbed to portal skips, excitable natives, and primitive medical beliefs. The stupid or gullible didn't last long. Trips that looked too dangerous, or too trivial, had no chance of happening.

Senior agents were free to argue for promising assignments, and Jake had his own system for scouting fresh projects. Locking himself in his Syrtis Major studio, he would order up a pot of coffee and a pipe of opium. Properly blasted, he would then have Biofile send him the open cases one at a time.

Everybody was there—the good, the ugly, and the merely impossible. People wanted a word with long dead relatives. . . . Psychics needed predictions tested. . . . A Ph.D. at Tehran U. wanted to shoot some Persian history in fourth century B.C. Mesopotamia. . . . SAVE THE CHRISTIAN MARTYRS had a long list of worthies they wanted plucked from the flames. THE JEWISH COMMITTEE TO EXPOSE THE SAINTS had an even *longer* list of worthies whose reputations they wanted blackened (and whom they wanted brought back to the future for trial). An *el grosso* Feelie mogul needed background for a porno mini-epic on the Marquis de Sade. *Then* came the cranks and the crazies. . . .

How to decide among so many admirable requests? Jake's opium-logged brain had not even tried. Peg and her Mesozoic proposal put everything else on hold. He must have replayed her proposal a dozen times, puffing on the opium pipe, getting every nuance of her voice, person, and presentation.

Her listings were incredible: Cuvier Fellow at the University of Paris at twenty-six . . . French, Latin, Classical Greek . . . swimming, yoga, aikido . . . Phi Beta Kappa, no criminal record . . . Reformed Vegetarian and practicing nudist. Endorsements by everyone from the World Paleontological Congress to the Teen Lesbians. A bright, well-balanced young professional, out to put her mark on the planet. Perfect. A field agent's prayer. Where could Jake go wrong?

The results had him doubting the wisdom of making crucial decisions while in an opium stupor. But even his sober brain had failed to see the flaws. Uppermost Mesozoic was a brand-new period—further back then ever before, a high-risk, high-opportunity assignment Jake could *not* pass on, not if he wanted to stay at the cutting edge. Whoever came back from the Upper Cretaceous would *own* FTL.

Unless he fucked up. FTL was infamously unforgiving. Faster Than Light had an army of active agents, and files filled with wanna-bees; its ingratitude was boundless. One bad bounce, and Jake was out. FTL trips were too troublesome and expensive for failure. If you screwed the pooch in some godawful corner of the past, the agency advised you to *marry* that pooch and learn to farm—for surely there was no point in coming back.

Sitting in the dogwood-shaded wash, listening to Peg explain what a dolt he was, Jake thought about how he *had* to succeed. Hell, he had to *excel*. Picking a crazed partner because you wanted to fuck her did not justify failure, not to FTL. He tried to decide what would work best with Peg, contrite apology or a vicious tongue-lashing.

Challenger beeped him.

With a bang and a crash, the brush parted. *A. megagracilis* burst out of the magnolias. Jake recognized the rust-brown spots and the cleaner, smaller, more gracile variation of the basic tyrannosaurid build. There was no way to measure stride length, but the carnivore was going at least twice as fast as Jake could.

Nerves shot, Jake suppressed a shriek, calling for his stunner. He thrust his hand into an empty armpit. No holster handed him a weapon. He had hopped out of *Challenger* carrying nothing more deadly than a medikit. If this long-legged tyrannosaurid had a toothache or a broken toe, Jake could handle it—otherwise, he was caught short.

Fifty meters upwind, a juvenile duckbill broke cover. Squawking in horror, the duckbill bolted from a four-legged crouch into biped flight. The two-ton dinosaur's green-and-black coloring, like old-fashioned camouflage, had made it nearly invisible among the ferns and dogwoods. Megagracilis must have smelled out the baby duckbill, because the tyrannosaurid showed no surprise, springing right for the spot where the duckbill emerged.

Seeing death coming, the terrified duckbill cut right. The tyrannosaurid cut even tighter, turning inside the bawling herbivore. They collided in a spray of dirt and gravel. Godzilla meets Baby Huey. Mercifully, it was quick.

Megagracilis got its jaws around the duckbill's neck, biting down. The duckbill's eyes bulged in terror. Slowly its thrashing subsided as A. *megagracilis* started to feed.

Jake sat rigid, so tense his muscles had set. Peg was right. To these terrible giants, two humans were a pair of odd bumps on the landscape. Insignificant bugs. While he and Peg argued, a game of eat and be eaten had gone on. Megagracilis had smelled out the hiding duckbill. The poor herbivore had watched death stalk closer, panicking at the last instant. Neither had paid the least attention to the humans. Very deflating.

A glance at Peg was even more deflating. She was on her feet, shooting each slice of flesh as it came off the duckbill. The look on her face was otherworldly, completely relaxed—not smiling, not happy, merely transported. By picking this young paleontologist, he had handed her the adventure of her life, an adventure at once astounding, romantic, professional, and damned near to orgasmic—an epic in which Jake himself was only a poorly written stanza, as necessary as the reactor, but certainly no more important.

Jake was just cynical enough to consider using that truth. He could point out to Peg that if it were not for *him*, then *she* would not be here. Jake was cynical enough to think it, but too proud to *say* it. He was not going to grovel.

He liked thinking of himself as witty, handsome, and as

brave as he needed to be. Peg put a strain on that self-esteem. So it was time to give his libido a rest. Maybe they would *not* make love, but they would *damn* well work together. No more loose adventuring, waiting for lightning to strike. *Gung Ho*, or no go. What he needed was a plan, something he could hold Peg to when she veered off on her next tangent.

Telling the navcomputer to illuminate the darkening wadi, he trotted back to the *Challenger*, slipped on his shoulder holster and ordered an Irish coffee from the microstove. Mug in hand, he walked back to the wash to watch *A. megagracilis* demolish dinner.

Coffee and whiskey had just the right bite for his mood, and he got back in time to witness a tail-lashing feeding frenzy. Two of the larger tyrannosaurids came strutting back from the bend in the river. Perhaps this pair had missed their kills. Perhaps the pack had had a falling-out. In any event, the big tyrannosaurids decided that a baby duckbill would do nicely. There was some snapping and snarling as *A. megagracilis* made a pretense of asserting property rights. The smaller carnivore was too quick to be hurt badly, but the outcome was never in doubt. The two tyrannosaurs settled down to a thieves' banquet. Megagracilis slunk off to hunt up another duckbill.

Jake saw a lesson in this. Megagracilis was a specialist, a speedy killer of small duckbills. Much as Jake admired its compact lines and well-honed technique, Jake was glad to be a generalist. The two tyrannosaurs were generalists—big enough to tackle a triceratops, but not too big to scavenge. Given enough time, generalists always won. Or so Jake hoped.

Peg, snub nose stuck in her view finder, was the specialist *par excellence*.

They walked back to *Challenger* together. Peg tossed her recorder on the chart table, propping moccasined feet beside it. "A totally essential day. I'm thrilled, famished, and exhausted—in about that order."

She produced a huge shed tooth, pushing it toward Jake. "For your collection." A peace offering. Dinosaurs shed their worn teeth, so tremendous canines weren't rare, but Peg seemed eager to make amends, to *be sociable*, despite a gritty weariness in the corners of her eyes.

Jake was touched. He served up mushroom moussaka and cabbage borscht, accompanied by a favorite Moselle. Outside, snapping bones added to the night noises as great crunching jaws broke up the last of the duckbill.

Peg nodded toward the darkening night, "Giant carnivores are nice enough, in their bloody fashion, but I still want to see sauropods."

Sauropods again. She had mentioned them the first day. Jake knew that these brontosaur-type, long-necked herbivores were the ultimate in dinosaurs—twenty to thirty meters long, weighing as much as a hundred tons.

Peg's sleepy eyes glowed. "Sauropods are essential to this expedition, essential to the extinction question. Essential to *everything*."

"We're unlikely to find them here in Hell Creek," he pointed out.

She shrugged, "FTL picked Hell Creek. *I* wanted to go straight to the Morrison Formation."

"Upper Cretaceous is as far as the anomaly goes." Jake smiled. Peg's overspecialization was showing; she was weak on Wormhole Theory. *Jake* was the one who had turned her original proposal into something workable. Morrison Formation was Late Jurassic, maybe eighty million years further back.

The Mesozoic was gigantic. He and Peg had only broken the surface. *T. Rex* was closer in time to human civilization than it was to brontosaurus and the Great Age of the Sauropods. Jake had brought them in as close as he dared to the mysterious KT boundary that marked the Cretaceous extinction, figuring that the end is never a bad place to start. Success here meant that they could look for other anomalies, going farther back, seeing more.

But Peg wanted to see it all *now*. "What we have here in Hell Creek is an explosion of new types: tyrannosaurids, triceratopses, boneheads, ankylosaurs, and advanced duck-bills. Evolution is fast-forward. But it's essential to know what is happening to older types as well, and sauropods are some of the oldest."

Jake admitted that he wasn't a paleontologist, but he swore he could *feel* the great extinction coming. Hell Creek dinosaurs looked healthy enough—at petting range, *T. Rex* was frighteningly impressive—but there was a frantic quality to dinosaur life he didn't see in the crocs and fisher-storks. The net connecting life to life hummed with tension.

"Sure, I've seen it too." Peg catalogued the symptoms: "Carnosaurs forced to squabble over kills. Triceratops herds surging across the landscape, searching for water and sustenance. Poor harassed duckbills unable to protect their offspring."

Jake put in his pitch for generalism. "Aside from the ostrich-types, there are no hordes of small dinosaurs. No tiny generalists waiting to take over if the big boys falter."

Peg shook her head. "The whole show is propped atop the food chain." One day something would hit the props hard—the crash would be tremendous. Even as they talked, world calamity hurtled through space-time toward Earth. "But that's why sauropods are so *basic*. They are well established herbivores, who have *already* survived numerous extinctions and cosmic collisions."

Jake liked the notion of a sauropod hunt. The long-necked herbivores were huge but relatively harmless, unless they stepped on you. Seeing a sauropod was such a sane ambition, compared to playing tag with tyrannosaurids. "So, where could we find large sauropods in the Uppermost Cretaceous?"

"Maybe in the Highlands; certainly in South America."

Enjoying her enthusiasm, Jake had *Challenger* project maps of fossil finds onto the chart table. The maps reminded him of the charts that pretended to describe nineteenth century Africa. Fossils formed where sediments were being laid down, so the maps showed coastlines, river deltas, floodplains, and the like. Continental interiors were great blank areas.

Peg dismissed the Euramerican sauropods, "So-called *titanosaurs*, they hardly live up to their name. Not much bigger than duckbills." Euramerican predators were also small to medium—megalosaurs and dryptosaurs. *T. Rex* would have roared through them like a lion at a poodle show. Much of Europe was just plain underwater. Eastern North America, Greenland, and Scandinavia were united into Euramerica—but Southern Europe was a string of semi-arid islands, some inhabited by dwarf dinosaurs a couple of meters long, quaint rather than impressive. Peg did not have time for evolutionary U-turns.

Jake suggested that they ride the prevailing westerlies south and east, at least as far as North Africa. The Sahara was supposed to be a green tropical expanse, connected to Euramerica by the Spanish Isles.

Peg shook her head. "West Africa will have more of those misnamed titanosaurs—bigger than the ones in Euramerica, but not by much. We can look in on them later, on our way to India." India was another huge blank spot, as mysterious as in the days before da Gama, thought to be terribly exotic—perhaps an island, perhaps attached to Africa.

She wanted to go straight to South America, even though it meant flying through the teeth of the megathermal, and the tropical storm belt. "There we are sure to see *real* sauropods."

Jake weighed the iffy weather, then agreed. He would cheerfully face a dozen tropical cyclones if he did not have to endure another tyrannosaur chase.

Feeling like they had finally arrived, he took *Challenger* aloft for the night. In his evening systems check, he noted Peg's recorder was drawing minimum power, on hold at the end of a file. She must have fallen asleep reviewing data.

Curious, he interfaced with the recorder through its power intake, telling his compweb to break any encryption. The recorder code was a simple digital transformation, keyed to Peg's birth date—putting PEG with BIRTHDAY brought the date out of memory. The deciphered image went straight to Jake's optical lobe.

He was surprised by a familiar purple-blue sky. White vapor streaked the ruddy horizon. The recording had to come from Home; the image was not from the Mesozoic. It was not even from Earth.

Frozen in the 3V foreground was a group of teenage girls—young, gawky, big-eyed—leaning on each other, tired and triumphant. They wore respirators and altitude suits, but had doffed their masks for the recording. Thin lips were blue from cold and lack of oxygen. They were on Mars, the western summit of *Olympus Mons*; Jake recognized the red ochre *Amazonis Planitia* in the background.

Olympus Summit was a typical tourist destination, but these weren't typical tourists. *They had climbed the sucker*, the biggest mountain on a habitable planet. You could see the incredible hike in the girls' faces.

And Peg was in the middle—very adult, very in charge. Of course. Teen Lesbians. She was probably a Pack Mother or something. Her proud look, backed by the Plain of Amazons, explained part of his problem.

Next morning they scouted the proto-Rockies, finding dense impenetrable forest. Peg thought the highlands might hold large sauropods. Jake did not disagree, "There might be ultrasaurs down there, or lost cities, or leprechauns, but the only way to know is to tether *Challenger* to a tree and blunder about on foot—two people and no shock-rifle. The sauropods of the Rockies will have to wait."

Bayou country came next; lower, swampier, opened by waterways. Jake played cajun tunes in his head, while Peg catalogued flora and fauna from the air. "Swamp cypress, cycads, tall stands of fir and pines . . ." They spotted a pack of small tyrannosaurids—*Albertosaurus lancensis*,

Peg thought, but she could not be sure without seeing teeth and other internal parts. Nothing remotely resembled a sauropod.

Then came the sea. Green-white shorebreak. Blue water. Reefs and atolls. *Challenger* descended to top off the water ballast and fill the hydrogen cells. Peg took sea water samples and swam nude inside a reef. Small-toothed shore birds wheeled above.

Leaving balmy Montana, they sailed south and east along the Dakota shoreline. Kansas was completely underwater. Peg sat on the transparent cabin deck, shooting straight down to the sandy sea bottom, picking out marine reptiles, twelve-to-sixteen meter plesiosaurs, long-necked versions of the Loch Ness monster. She still worked in the nude aboard ship—but that had become mere entertainment. Jake admired her yoga positions over breakfast, then relaxed into his role of flying chauffeur.

He swung far enough east to sight the Euramerican shore, seeing duckbills in the Alabama swamps. "Alabama Song" played in his head as he set a mental course for South America. He flew in bright sunshine alongside immense flocks of long-legged ducks, as big as flamingos.

This part of the trip was like coming home. Jake had learned airship technique in the twentieth century aboard the original *Graf Zeppelin*, working as a rigger for *Lufthansa* on the South America run—Frankfurt to Recife to Rio, then back to Germany by way of Seville. That was when Rio *was* Rio, not just another branch of Megapolis. He remembered fevered nights full of music, women, and *mardi gras*, with Nazi reichsmarks burning a hole in his pocket. Not a bad time and place—between the world wars and before the AIDS pandemic—unless you were poor, or perhaps a Jew. He rummaged through his music files for a samba, or maybe the Bolero.

By now they were in the megathermal, the fevered blanket circling the waist of the planet—a perpetual steam-bath with temperatures in the wet 100s. Everything was

sopping. Decks and bulkheads sweated. Pillows turned to
warm sponges. Buckskin came apart in soggy clumps. Jake
took to wearing only light cotton pants; anything more was
intolerable.

Approaching the equatorial trough, wind died to a whisper. Depressed by the heavy air of the doldrums, Jake
dumped ballast and headed farther out to sea, hoping that
the higher marine air would be cooler. A mere ribbon of
water separated South America from Asiamerica and Africa,
a seaway too small to be called the South Atlantic. The
fishlike shadow of the airship swam over the waves.

Weather radar noted convective turbulence, an easterly
wave of low pressure signaling a weak equatorial low.

Peg stood, recorder ready, anxious for her first glimpse of
South America and its sauropods. After tracking them
across two continents, her eagerness was easy to see. Jake
decided that as soon as they found a decent-sized sauropod,
he was going to hit on her again—catch her in a paleontological frenzy, and anything was possible.

Tall anvilheads reared before them, a fluffy colonnade
leading up to Olympus. High sea-surface temperatures
created warming unstable air masses. Typhoon weather,
with storm pillars ten kilometers high.

Seeing a gap, Jake shot for blue sky and blue water,
hoping to put the emerging storm cells behind him.

More white patches appeared ahead, boiling rags of mist
that swelled rapidly into cottony thunderheads, roots gray
with rain. Peg was disappointed to find the horizon clouding
up. "I cannot get a clear view of the coast."

Not surprising. Weather was closing in from all sides. The
barometer tumbled into freefall. For the first time, *Challenger* fought terrific headwinds. Rain splattered in the open
window; fat searing drops hit Jake in the face.

Shielding her eyes with her viewfinder, Peg announced,
"I see a black line to the south."

"That's the coast." He watched her turn to maximum

magnification. In this thickening storm, she had as much chance of sighting Rio as she did of seeing a sauropod.

"It isn't getting any closer."

Jake nodded. "This south-east headwind is a *bastard*. Maximum revolutions and ground speed is *falling*."

"Is that possible?"

"I would not have thought so an hour ago. But it's happening."

Challenger's twin propellers were churning at peak revolutions without gaining a meter. The headwind had topped 160 kilometers per hour. Strain on the ship was transmitted to Jake as a line of tension along his spine, humming from head to buttocks.

Peg complained that South America was slipping away. At last, she let her recorder fall. "It's gone. Nothing but gray skies and gray wave caps." They were being blown backward by gale-force winds.

Red Woman is the first woman. Like Coyote, she has always been with us, doing much that is bad and some that is good.
    Pretty Shield, Crow Medicine woman and
        wife to Goes Ahead, Custer's scout.

Red Woman

The storm seized them with astonishing speed. Inrushing winds immobilized *Challenger*. Radar reported ominous rings of cumulonimbus spreading through dense stratiform clouds—the signature of a truly intense cyclonic storm. A hurricane was being born around them.

Jake stole a glance at Peg. She did not look worried—nothing new there. As much as he admired her fine brain, Peg did not have the sense to be scared. Mesozoic weather was advertised as mild. At Home, cyclonic storms had long been tamed; satellites seeded them from orbit to remove energy as rain and limit crop damage. Aside from the unwary sailing buff, people simply avoided storms. No one except suicide cases went ballooning about in a typhoon.

But Jake had been through horrible blows before— rounding the Horn under hatches aboard a tea clipper, and clinging to the mast of a leaky Athenian coaster off Cape Matapan. He *knew* what it was like to have life hang at the whim of wind and sea. It was a lesson he did not need replayed.

Lightning scrawled across the sky, connecting thunderheads. A thermal tugged at the airship. Jake applied maximum down elevator, to keep *Challenger* below her pressure height. He did not want to vent hydrogen in a thunderstorm. The column of valved gas could act as a conductor, drawing lightning straight to the ship.

"There must be excess power in the reactor." Peg was still set on seeing the sauropods of South America.

"Sure, the props could rip the reactor right off the hull. Wouldn't help us much." They had to run before the storm. He reduced power on the port propeller, using starboard rudder to bring the airship about.

Challenger struggled to obey. Headwinds beat at the control surfaces. Staggered by the buffeting, *Challenger* was blown sideways, then leaped ahead like a sprinting sauropod. Ground speed zoomed from less than zero to several hundred kilometers per hour.

Peg observed the transition with calm interest. "Where are we headed now?"

"Most likely north by northwest." So near the center of the swirling cloud mass, winds shifted too rapidly to give a steady course.

Rain beat against the cabin, blotting out the sunlight. Windows closed. Interior lights winked on. Jake ordered a pot of coffee from the microstove. He started to pour, bracing himself against the heave of the storm.

Challenger shot upward, flinging hot coffee on Jake, Peg, and the surrounding bulkheads.

Yelling for more power and down elevator, Jake snagged

a window frame with one hand and Peg with the other, keeping her from flying through the galley into the lounge. The ship continued to rise, sucked up at a sickening angle.

Jammed against Peg, with only wet coffee between them, Jake felt compelled to make conversation. "We're caught in a convection cell!"

She nodded, eyes wide and staring.

Challenger started giving the altitude in hundred meter steps as they neared pressure height, "Eight hundred meters, nine hundred meters, a thousand . . ."

"At twelve hundred meters, we'll reach pressure height, and have to valve hydrogen, or the gas cells will rupture." His explanation sounded absurdly calm even to him.

"Pressure height," announced *Challenger*. "Butterfly valves opening."

Feeling hydrogen gush from the ship, Jake ordered down elevator. The stall alarm rang in his head, but still they kept rising, borne aloft by a rushing bubble of air.

". . . fifteen hundred meters, sixteen hundred meters . . ."

More hydrogen spewed into the storm.

". . . twenty-three hundred meters, twenty-four hundred meters, twenty-five hundred meters . . ."

They could defy gravity only so long. "Brace yourself." He held harder to Peg.

At more than twice its pressure height, the airship lurched to a stop. They teetered for several seconds. Then *Challenger* plunged into the boiling darkness.

"Dump ballast," Jake kept his lips tight, voicing the command in his head. Why show Peg how scared he was? Water ballast streamed from the ship. But now they were caught in a downdraft; deflating cells sucked air into the hull, offsetting the loss of water, threatening an oxyhydrogen explosion.

"Look, the ocean." Peg pointed. Rain-swept waves appeared as they plummeted through the bottom cloud layer. *Challenger* righted herself so close to the whitecaps that

Jake could see spray flying from the chop. She began to climb immediately.

Jake ordered added power and down elevator to counteract the climb. Each wild oscillation cost him both gas and ballast. The airship threatened to yo-yo until they lost all buoyancy and plunged into the sea.

Fresh water and hydrogen were all around him, but Jake had no notion of touching down to refill the tanks. Wind force had to be fearsome. He saw waterspouts, a conga line of twisters sweeping over the waves. Lightning struck the ship with alarming regularity.

A year or so before Jake shipped on the *Graf*, an American helium airship, the *Akron*, stronger and heavier than *Challenger*, touched down in seas milder than these. Three survivors were plucked from the Atlantic. Admiral Moffett and seventy-odd others went down with the ship, and so did a smaller airship sent to find them. Not enviable odds. And here there were no rescue ships. Jake didn't like their chances of flagging a ride on a passing plesiosaur.

Altitude figures started to tumble. Another wet downdraft had *Challenger* headed for the wavecaps.

"Prepare for ditch procedure," the airship advised in a disinterested monotone. "Your lounge chairs double as lift rafts."

Jake clutched the window frame, staring at Peg. "Maximum power. Up elevator." He could not see them riding out a typhoon in lounge chairs.

"Ditch procedure," repeated the ship. Emergency circuits had made their heartless calculations. "Warm water ditching. Remove excess clothing. Place your head between your knees."

Jake tuned *Challenger* out. He had played all his cards but one. Water ballast. Elevators. Reactor power. Still the rainswept sea was only meters away. Jake wanted to escape, but he'd have to settle for a stay of execution.

"Jettison reactor."

Propellers whirling, the reactor detached itself, plunging into the wavetops.

An almighty surge lifted them up. Lightened by the loss of the reactor, *Challenger* shot skyward, reeling off new altitude numbers. "Six hundred, seven hundred, eight hundred meters . . ."

"What happened?" Peg sounded like she'd fully expected to get wet.

"I dumped the reactor."

"Won't we need it later?"

"It was that or touch down in berserk seas." Compared to the reactor, provisions and inflated furniture did not mass enough to matter.

Challenger tore through her old pressure height, ". . . twelve hundred, thirteen hundred, fourteen hundred meters."

At over two thousand meters they leveled off. Wind speed fell. The nonslip deck felt firmer now that they were free ballooning, no longer fighting the storm.

Jake let go of Peg and the window, walking slowly over to the microstove. Ordering a light lunch, he took it into the lounge. Water beaded on the windows.

Peg followed him. "What now?"

"*Soufflé aux blancs d'oeufs*. And the last of that Moselle. No sense saving good wine for after the crash."

"Crash?"

"When the hurricane hits the coast of Asiamerica, we have to bring *Challenger* down." Unless they missed Asiamerica. He pictured them shooting the gap between the two continents, sailing out into the near-limitless Pacific. That would pretty much match his luck.

"How bad do you expect it to be?" Peg asked the question casually, as though it hardly involved her.

"Only been in one airship bang-up. Aboard the *Graf Zeppelin*, returning to Pernambuco from Rio, we hit a heavy tropical squall a hundred meters above the field. Drove us right down to the deck." Remembering that nauseating crunch made him shiver. "We lost a rudder and came down hard on some poor Brazilian's shanty. Rammed the chimney right into the *Graf*'s hull. Breakfast was cooking, so smoke and sparks poured over tons of hydrogen and fuel gas."

He shook his head thoughtfully. "We'd have been blown back to Frankfurt, but an on-the-ball mechanic leaped out of his gondola and dashed in the front door of the shack. He grabbed a pot of coffee off the stove and put out the fire." Zeppelin crews were the best, one reason Jake had trained with them.

Peg smiled at the story. Jake did not add that it was the sort of luck you could not count on twice. Over *café au lait*, he considered making a final stab at seducing Peg. But it would be only out of a sense of duty. The line he had been saving, *"look, I got you here,"* was now wildly inappropriate.

Night fell. They dozed in their respective armchairs, behind black rain-streaked windows.

Near to dawn, Jake awoke. Light showed in the east. Thunderheads towered over a stratiform cloud plain—not a day for yoga and "Dawn Symphony." Peg lay curled in her armchair, studying the cloudscape. "Did you ever *see* anything so lovely?" The cloud plain was flat as polished ivory.

Jake nodded to starboard. "First sign of land."

A speck hung in the false dawn. Boosted vision brought it into focus—long leathery wings, a sharp pointed head, and the compact body of a pterosaur.

Peg hopped out of her chair. *"Quetzalcoatlus."* Another non-dinosaur—merely a huge flying reptile, but sufficiently incredible, a living creature with the wingspan of a small aircraft.

The pterosaur flew in formation with the crippled airship, narrow pointed wings not even beating, staying aloft through sheer mastery of the elements. Jake's microamps played "Riders on the Storm." Listening to the Doors, looking into *Quetzalcoatlus'* wrinkled face, Jake felt the full eeriness of this other earth, where birds had teeth and huge reptiles had wings and beaks.

He also sensed the same evolutionary tension. The pterosaur was big, beautiful, and otherworldly, but fragile as well. Great size meant small numbers and overspecialization. If *Quetzalcoatlus* faltered, who would take its place? Not another pterosaur, because there *were* no others. Replacement would come from the flocks of tiny birds which were growing ever more numerous.

"But it's not a marine animal." Peg recorded and catalogued furiously.

"Exactly. We must be headed inland." Assuming the pterosaur knew its way home. "Perhaps it was blown out to sea by the storm."

"Something to put in the report," she declared. Her certainty amused him. Jake guessed that it was an even bet that he would never get to file on this run.

Ghostly landforms appeared on the chart table. He announced, "We're headed for the Texas coast." This late in the Cretaceous, the Lone Star State was just taking shape. Much of what would be coastal plain was still beneath the sea. The New Mexico highlands were steeper, not nearly so far inland.

In open-mouthed astonishment, he watched the coast's outline shift. *Storm surge.* Sea level was rising, submerging coastal islands, inundating lowlands. "This storm won't let go," Jake marveled at the flood. "Flats are filling up. There may be no place *to* land short of the highlands."

Dawn turned to day. The tempest whirled inland, losing velocity. Jake watched the tail end of the proto-Rockies poke up through the cloud plain. Black islands in a foamy white sea.

"Gorgeous." Peg was in rapture.

Jake scanned the mountain spine—no sign of a landing site. Ground speed was still formidable. Without power or aerodynamic control, *Challenger* would batter herself against the passes.

"Strap in." The crash rushing toward them shriveled hairs on his spine.

"But I can hardly see from that chair," Peg complained.

"We are going to hit badly." A wild understatement.

"Will being strapped down make a difference?"

"It might."

She shrugged, strapping the belt and harness across her body. It was plain that Peg did not plan to spend her last moments with her head between her knees. She meant to enjoy them. And record them. Her 3V was taking in everything.

Black pine tops broke through the clouds below; a high saddle lay dead ahead.

"Present course will terminate in three minutes." *Challenger* did not think they would make the saddle.

"Down five-hundred meters." No sense in staying up here. He had to find a landing spot, or all his maneuvering would only succeed in smearing them on the oncoming saddle. Pine tops grew larger. Jake's enhanced vision searched for a clearing.

Challenger gave a two-minute warning.

"Down fifty-meters." Conifer forest reached up to tear the guts out of the airship. Still no gap in the canopy.

"One minute."

No clearing. No opening of any sort. Jake had to choose between rocks and treetops.

"Release remaining hydrogen." He braced himself.

Pine tops leaped at him. A giant sequoia slammed against the cabin, snapping and shuddering. Plastic shattered on impact; shards exploded through the lounge. Thrown against his straps, Jake heard *Challenger* cracking like an aluminum eggshell.

Metal shrieked as the cabin tore free from the hull. Another plunge. A jerk and fall, followed by a rain of debris.

.Then silence, eerie in its completeness.

Alive enough to hurt, Jake hung face down in his straps,

tasting blood and vomit in the back of his mouth. His head
sang with pain.

Twisting about, he tried to look over at Peg. It was
blacker hanging in the tree tops than it had been in the
morning air above—the crushed and deflated hull formed a
silver canopy, blocking the light. Rain dripped in. Through
a screen of pine boughs he saw the back of her inflated
chair.

"Peg, are you there?"

"Where else would I be? Was that it?"

"Was *what* it?"

"Are we going to fall some more?"

"*Hell*, I hope not!" A stupendous hunk of pine was thrust
through the lounge into the chartroom; a meter more to port
and it would have speared him on the way. It was thicker
than Jake's waist, unlikely to break.

"Good." In a flurry of white limbs Peg unstrapped,
dropping down to the rear bulkhead which had become a
deck. She pushed aside the foliage. "What about you? Alive
or dead?"

"Alive, I think."

"Great." She helped undo his straps. "How do you feel?"

"Like *shit* hammered through a small hole." The Mesozoic was still tumbling. Would his legs work? Apparently.

They knelt together on the bulkhead, feeling for breaks.
First his limbs, then Peg's. Then they felt each other's
bodies. Soon they were just feeling, then stroking and
caressing. They kissed. His tongue still worked. "Sorry
about the blood."

"Oh, I don't mind." Peg had the Look. That same dreamy
half-smile he'd seen by the campfire in Hell Creek.

Fumbling to get his pants down, Jake could barely believe
they were *finally* going to fuck—in a shattered cabin,
halfway up a tree.

She watched him strip, showing almost clinical interest.
"You know, this is the wildest thing I have ever done."

"Not nearly." He kicked his pants off. "The wildest thing you ever did was to pat that tyrannosaur on the nose."

She laughed. "The second wildest, anyway."

"Wrong again. The second wildest was when you . . ." He pulled her to him. Seeing all those yoga positions had given him some great ideas.

"I mean I have never done anything like this before."

"Never made love atop a sequoia after ramming into a mountain? It won't be near so hard as it sounds." He slid his hand between her legs. Peg felt as good as he'd imagined.

"No, I mean I have never made love. Not to a *man*."

"Shit and damnation." His hand stopped. How could an attractive twenty-six-year-old not have had heterosex? "Why didn't you tell me?"

"I just did." She shrugged bare shoulders. "It makes this, you know, essential."

After sleeping half the night in a chair and caroming off a mountain, Jake was not sure how *essential* he could be. "Why didn't your sex therapist take care of this when you were a teenager?" Virginity had been cured ages ago.

"Sex therapy bored me. All those lectures on the joy of procreation."

"Right, I got the procreation lecture too." But it hadn't discouraged Jake from having heterosex—not completely at least. "So why are you starting now?"

"Because we *made* it. This is the *fucking* Mesozoic." She whacked her hand on his hip. "Besides, you saved my life. I owe you for that."

"Like *hell*. It's nothing but a plain everyday miracle we survived. You could just as well say I slammed you against a mountain, but didn't manage to kill you."

What a conversation to have with his hand in her crotch.

"Either way, you got me here." Peg wore an impish grin. Putting her hands on his cheeks, she kissed him again. "Ever since I was a girl hunting up fossils, I dreamed of coming here. I worked and bled until I was the best young Ph.D. in the field. But none of that mattered, until *you* picked me. Jake Bento did that. No one else."

"You knew that I picked you?"

"Of course." She caressed his chest with short graceful strokes.

"When you submit a proposal, it's *essential* to know who will judge it. If I can diagnose the personal life of a dead reptile from a shed tooth, I can certainly find out how FTL passes on its projects. To get here, I had to interest the right person."

"Me?"

"You, or someone like you. It was not hard to figure out what you'd want."

"I'll be *fucked*."

"First, we have to see how much I remember from comparative biology." Her hand slid between his hips. "So this is what the adult male organ feels like. I haven't held a penis since playing sex therapist in kindergarten. But that one was not so big and active."

Flattered, Jake felt himself respond.

"Oh look, an *erection*," she murmured. "This is fun!"

Her hips moved. Her breath came quicker. "You know, we could have done this that first night, after seeing the triceratops herd. But you crawled off to your cabin. I was too shy to go knocking on your door, making you think I was desperate."

Shy? At that point-instant, Jake knew it was never going to be easy with Peg. But there was no way he was going to stop—the woman was a prize, with more angles than a dodecahedron. He did his best to start slowly. It was her first time.

He'd barely got going, when her eyes went wide. "Oh my, the cabin's shaking."

"It only feels that way." Jake was hitting his stride.

"No," she insisted, sitting bolt upright at the risk of giving him a hernia. "The whole tree is moving."

Jake felt it too. The cabin shook like it was getting set to fall again.

Seizing her recorder, she squirmed over to the window. "Jake, come look, it's a sauropod!" She lay there, aiming the recorder. "An *Alamosaurus!* I can almost count the teeth."

Jake saw the beast's head from where he lay, framed by Peg and the window. It was stripping greenery off a pine branch with short cylindrical teeth. One eye looked in at him.

Peg was not returning anytime soon, so he crawled over to be with her. No denying it. Alamosaurus was tremendous, a titanosaur in more than name. The head wasn't much larger than a horse's, but it was attached to a great wrinkled neck reaching far down into the foliage. The sauropod had half its thirty-ton bulk in the air, holding the sequoia with huge forelimbs.

Like all dinosaurs, it had that ancient, lord-of-creation look. Of course, sauropods were old, unbelievably ancient. They had seen continents separate and seas dry up, turning to shale and sandstone. The little protolemurs in the trees would come down, lose their tails, learn to walk upright and to build star ships, but they still would not be as old as late Cretaceous sauropods.

Magnificent. Inspired by the sauropod, Jake ran his hands over Peg's hips, starting again where they had left off.

She set her recorder down, rolling over to face him, eyes gleaming. "Do it. But quietly. Don't disturb the dinosaur."

He cocked his head toward the pine boughs and inflated furniture. "We can be more private and comfortable."

"No," she shook her head violently. "I want to see the sauropod. It'll be absolutely essential. I've waited all my life for this."

Whatever gets you going. At least Jake did not have to worry about being essential. Alamosaurus had seen to that.

He salvaged every necessity they could realistically carry— medikits, microstove, sleeping bags, and some provisions—

using a winch and cables to lower them to the ground. Peg studied titanosaurs, tropical birds, small mammals, and the refinements of heterosex. Given the need for caution, and frequent fucking, it took Jake five days to get them down out of the tree.

Then they headed north, through the foothills of the proto-Rockies.

It took more than five months to walk back to Hell Creek, recording, collecting samples, sleeping in trees, living on whatever the medikits identified as edible. Jake could not imagine a more complete honeymoon.

Then it was over. They stood beside the same billabong they had begun at six months before, taking last looks at the Uppermost Cretaceous—Peg could barely stand to let it go.

Systems check was a snap. He hardly had any equipment left. The missing shock-rifle no longer stood out in his report; it was nearly swallowed by bigger calamities, showing that it never pays to worry early. He saw a feud ahead with FTL. He had lost the reactor. He had crashed *Challenger*. Worst of all, he had hardly done half the assignment. Aside from the duckbills of Alabama, they had recorded nothing outside of Asiamerica. South America, Africa, India, and Australia-Antarctica were as mysterious as ever. The only fuck-ups he had *not* committed were calling in a STOP team, or losing his client.

But after five months in the foothills of the Rockies, their recorders could not hold a byte more of data. They were carrying an incalculable treasure. Highland species. Scores of new genera. Gene samples. Tissue cultures. DNA scans. Humanity's first look at the Mesozoic.

Fuck it. If FTL did not treat them like returning heroes, they would start their *own* agency. Call it Time Tours. Clients would climb all over them.

And he had added nicely to his artifact collection, finding another shed tooth, and a huge *Quetzalcoatlus* claw. Peg wanted to bring an egg. But she would have had to sit on it all the way Home. The incubator chamber had gone down with the reactor, and they were headed into winter.

Sweating, bundled up in spare clothing, Peg was finally overdressed. Jake cleared his head for the most dangerous part of the return. Riding a tropical hurricane was nothing compared to doing the blind drunkard's walk through a newly opened portal.

He engaged his navmatrix. The billabong, the flowering trees, the proto-birds—everything vanished.

Space-time blew about him, a near infinite number of point-instants thrown together by the anomaly. This time he was not lugging the reactor. The compweb beneath his scalp produced just enough drag to act as an anchor. He searched for the faint stirrings in the vortex that pointed to the far end of the anomaly. Luckily, he had been through this portal once already. His navmatrix projected a wispy gold filament—the path he had made on his first passage.

Each correct movement made the next one easier. Each mistake meant a possible portal skip to an unintended point-instant, the vast majority of which were in intergalactic vacuum.

He did not know they had made it until he saw snow-covered badlands and felt the howling Montana wind. "Light My Fire" throbbed in his microamps.

Four Hunkpapa warriors were sitting waiting by a fire, wrapped in buffalo robes. Wearing fur caps and winter leggings made from Mackinaw blankets, they gave Jake and Peg the flinty looks that passed for Lakota greetings. Their names were Swift Cloud, Bear Ribs, High Bear, and Sitting Bull, the Medicine Man and Strong Heart Chief. With the Hunkpapas was a forlorn, light-skinned Assiniboin boy, called Little Hohe. Hohe was the Lakota name for Assiniboins. The Hunkpapas had killed Little Hohe's family, and were taking him home for adoption.

It was no longer the Mesozoic. Jake recognized the year Minniconjous called The Winter When Ten Crows Were Killed.

As Jake and Peg appeared out of the frigid air, Sitting Bull started to repack his redstone pipe—a sign that guests had arrived. "I see you, He-Who-Walks-Through-Winters."

"I see you, Sitting Bull." Jake knew sign language, and was fully programmed for Lakota. Peg had to make do with French.

"You have been gone long in the Spirit World, He-Who-Walks?"

Jake folded his legs and sat down across the fire from the Strong Heart Chief, settling naturally into a lotus pose Peg had taught him. "For me it has been six moons, maybe seven."

Sitting Bull's face crinkled up into a smile. "For us it has been only as long as it takes to light and smoke a pipe."

Jake made a sign that meant, "Marvelous are the ways of the Great Medicine." Lateral drift had deposited them a few minutes further along the time stream. Which was normal. You never came back to the exact same point-instant.

"Your Walking-Wagon did not come back with you," Sitting Bull observed.

"My Walking-Wagon went south." Jake smashed his hands together to describe the wreck of the reactor.

"It is good we have Hohe horses." Sitting Bull indicated a string of stolen ponies. He lit the pipe from the fire— offering a smoke to Grandmother Earth, Grandfather Sky, the Four Winds, and then to Jake.

Jake smoked, spreading out the gifts he had been gathering. Swift Cloud, Bear Ribs, and High Bear got shed tyrannosaurid teeth. He gave Sitting Bull the big *Quetzalcoatlus* claw. Little Hohe got only a few proto-bird feathers from Peg, but then, Sitting Bull had already given the boy his life.

Everyone was pleased by the presents from the Spirit World, saying they were *"Sha-sha,"* which meant, "Very red." Excellent. Sitting Bull added, "Will He-Who-Walks and Red Woman come back with us to the camp circle?"

"You betcha," Jake accepted. The Hunkpapa laughed

aloud. "You betcha," was Sitting Bull's favorite Americanism.

Jake helped Peg onto a stolen pony. The nearest nineteenth century portal was well to the south, but Sitting Bull's good will made them welcome in lodge circles as far as *Paha Sapa*, the Black Hills that sit at the Center of the World. He and Sitting Bull had always gotten on well, and seemed to be getting along even better now that Peg accompanied him. Sitting Bull liked to have striking women in camp, and had given Peg the name Red Woman—after his own first wife, who had also gone into the Spirit World.

Handing Peg her drag rope, Jake thought how remarkable Sitting Bull's taste in women was. Peg was *sha-sha*, very red, very excellent.

"We're in," he grinned. "Play our cards right, and Sitting Bull will throw us a wedding!" He-Who-Walks-Through-Winters and Red Woman rode off across the white landscape into the Winter When Ten Crows Were Killed.

All in all, Jake could not call it a bad run. . . .

The Odd Old Bird

by
Avram Davidson

For many years, the late Avram Davidson was one of the most eloquent and individual voices in SF and fantasy, and there were few writers in any literary field who could match his wit, erudition, or the stylish elegance of his prose. During his long career, Davidson won the Hugo, the Edgar, and the World Fantasy Award, and his short work was assembled in landmark collections such as The Best of Avram Davidson, Or All the Seas with Oysters, The Redward Edward Papers, *and* Collected Fantasies. *His novels include the renowned* The Phoenix and the Mirror, Masters of the Maze, Rogue Dragon, Peregrine: Primus, Rork!, Clash of Star Kings, *and* Vergil in Averno. *His most recent books are a novel in collaboration with Grania Davis,* Marco Polo and the Sleeping Beauty, *the marvelous collection* The Adventures of Doctor Eszterhazy *(one of the best collections of the decade), and a posthumously released collection of his erudite and witty essays,* Adventures in Unhistory.*

Here he gives us an affectionate, eccentric, and tasty look at a very odd old bird . . .

* * *

"But *why* a canal?"

"Cheaper, more, and better victuals."

"Oh."

Prince Roldran Vlox (to cut his titles quite short, and never mind about his being a Von Stuart y Fitz-Guelf) had "just dropped in" to talk to Doctor Engelbert Eszterhazy about the Proposed Canal connecting the Ister and the Danube . . . there were, in fact, several proposed canals and each one contained several sub-propositions: should it go right through the entirely Vlox-held Fens ("The Mud," it

was fondly called . . . "Roldry Mud," the prince sometimes called himself)? should it go rather to the right or
rather to the left? should it perhaps not go exactly "through"
them at all, but use their surplusage of waters for feeder
systems? and—or—on the one hand This, on the other
hand That—

"What's that new picture over on the wall, Engly?" Guest
asked suddenly. Host began to explain. "Ah," said Guest,
"one of those funny French knick-knacks, eh? Always got
some funny knick-knacks. . . . The British for sport, the
French for fun. . . ." Still the guestly eyes considered
the picture over on the wall. "That's a damned funny
picture . . . it's all funny little speckles. . . ."

"Why, Roldry, you are right. What good eyes you have."

Promptly: "Don't soil them by a lot of reading, is why.
Lots of chaps want to know about a book, 'Is it spicy?'
Some want to know, 'Is it got lots of facts?' What *I* want to
know is only, 'Has it got big print?' Shan't risk spoiling my
eyes and having to wear a monocle. One has to be a hunter,
first, you know." He made no further reference to the fact
that his host himself sometimes wore a monocle.

Eszterhazy returned to the matter of canals: "Here is a
sketch of a proposed catchment basin—Yes, Lemkotch?"

"Lord Grumpkin!" said the Day Porter.

There followed a rather short man of full figure, with a
ruddy, shiny, cheerful face. There followed also a brief
clarification, by Lemkotch's employer, of the proper way to
refer to Professor Johanno Blumpkinn, the Imperial Geologist; there followed, also, an expression on the Porter's face,
indicative of his being at all times Doctor (of Medicine,
Law, Music, Philosophy, Science, and Letters) Eszterhazy's
loyal and obedient servant and all them words were not for
a ignorant fellow like him (the day porter) to make heads or
tails of; after which he bowed his usual brief, stiff bob and
withdrew. He left behind him a slight savor of rough rum,
rough tobacco, rough manhood, and rough soap . . . even
if not quite enough rough soap to erase the savor of the

others. The room also smelled of the unbleached beeswax with which they had been rubbing—polishing, if you like—the furniture's mahogany; of Prince Vlox, which some compared to that of a musty wolf (not perhaps to his face, though); of Eszterhazy himself (Pears soap and just a little bay rum) and of Professor Blumpkinn (Jenkinson's Gentleman's Cologne: more than just a little). Plus some Habana segars supplied by the old firm of Freibourg and Treyer in the Haymarket—London was a long way from Bella, capital of the Triple Monarchy of Scythia-Pannonia-Transbalkania (fourth largest empire in Europe) but so was Habana, for that matter. "Gentlemen, you have met, I believe," Eszterhazy said, anyway adding, "Prince Vlox, Professor Blumpkinn."

Further adding, "I am sorry that my servant did not get your name right, Han."

Blumpkinn waved his hand. "Calling me by the old-fashioned word for the smallest coin in his native province really helps me to remember a proper value of my own worth.—Ah. *Canal* plans. I hope that when the excavations are in progress you will be sure to keep me in mind if any interesting fossils turn up." It was not sure that Prince Vlox would be able to identify an interesting fossil if one hit him in the hough or bit him on the buttock, but Eszterhazy gave a serious nod. *He* knew how such things were to be done. Offer a small gift for reporting the discovery of "any of them funny elf-stone things as the old witch-women used to use"—they used to use them for anything from dropped stomach to teaching a damned good lesson to husbands with wandering eyes: but now all that had gone out of fashion—should certainly result in the reporting of enough interesting fossils, uninteresting fossils, and, indeed, non-fossils, to provide copingstones for the entire length of the Proposed Canal . . . if ever there was actually a canal. . . .

"And speaking of which," said Blumpkinn, and took two large sheets out between covers large enough to have contained the Elephant Folios; "I have brought you, Doctor

'Bert, as I had promised, the proof-sheets of the new photo-zinco impressions of the *Archaeopteryx,* showing far greater detail than was previously available . . . you see. . . ."

Doctor 'Bert did indeed now thrust in his monocle and scanned the sheets, said that he saw. Prince Vlox glanced, glanced away, rested a more interested glance at the funny French knick-knack picture . . . men, women, water, grass, children, women, women . . . all indeed composed of multitudes of tiny dots, speckles, . . . points, if you liked . . . a matter easily noticeable if you were up close, or had a hunter's eye.

"Yes, here are the independent fingers and claws, the separate and unfused metacarpals, the un-birdlike caudal appendage, all the ribs non-unciate and thin, neither birdlike nor very reptilian, the thin coracoid, the centra free as far as the sacrum, and the very long tail. . . ." His voice quite died away to a murmur, Professor Blumpkinn, perhaps thinking that it was not polite to lose the attention of the other guest, said, "This, you see, Prince Vlox, is the famous *Archaeopteryx,* hundreds of millions of years old, which the sensational press has rather inadequately described as the so-called 'no-longer-missing-link' between reptiles and birds . . . observe the sharp teeth and the feather . . . this other one unfortunately has no head . . . and this one—"

Here Prince Vlox, perhaps not an omnivorous student of paleontology, said, "Yes. Seen it."

"*Ah* . . . was that in London? or Berlin?"

"Never been in either place."

Blumpkinn gaped. Recovered himself. Looked, first amused, then sarcastic, then polite. Eszterhazy slowly looked up. "What do you mean, then, Roldry, 'seen it'? What—?"

Prince Vlox repeated, with a slight emphasis, that he had *seen* it. And he bulged his eyes and stared, as though to emphasize the full meaning of the verb, *to see.*

"What do you—Ah . . . 'Seen it,' seen it when, seen it where?"

"On our land. Forget just when. What do you mean, 'Am I sure?' I don't need a monocle to look at things. Why shouldn't I be sure? What about it?"

Blumpkinn and Eszterhazy for a moment spoke simultaneously. What about it? There were only two known *Archaeopteryx* specimens in the world! one in London, one in Berlin—think what a third would mean! Not only for science, but for Scythia-Pannonia-Transbalkania and its prestige.

Vlox, with something like a sigh, rose to his feet; clearly the subject no longer much engaged him . . . possibly because his own family and its prestige were incomparably older than the Triple Monarchy and *its* prestige. "Well, I'll have it looked for, then. Must be off. Things to do. My wine-merchant. My gunsmith. My carriage-maker. A turn of cards at The Hell-Hole. See if they've finished re-upholstering my railroad car. Tobacconist . . . new powder scales. . . . Can I execute any commissions for you, as they say? Haw haw! Tell you what, Engly, damned if I know what you want with this odd old bird, but tell you what: trade it for that funny French painting." And he donned his tattered seal-skin cap (so that he should not be struck by lightning) and his wisent-skin cape (also fairly tattered, but wisents weren't easy to get anymore), picked up his oak-stick, nodded his Roldry-nod, neither languid nor brisk, and went out into Little Turkling Street, where his carriage (as they say) awaited him. Some backwoods nobles kept a pied-à-terre in Bella in the form of a house or apartment. Prince Roldran preferred to keep a stable and to sleep in the loft. With taste and scent, no argument.

Silence for some seconds. Such was the prince's presence, that his immediate absence left a perceptible hole.

Blumpkinn: What do you say, Doctor 'Bert, is the prince *quite*, [a hesitation] . . . dependable?

Eszterhazy [removing his monocle]: In some things,

instantly. He would think nothing of striking a rabid wolf
with bare hands to save you. In others? well . . . let us say
that fossils are not quite in his line. We shall see. Any kind
of fossils from out that way should be interesting. If the old
witch-women have left any.

The Imperial Geologist blinked. "Yes . . . if they've left
any—Though I suppose . . . imagine, Doctor, they used
to grind up dinosaur bones and feed them with bread and oil
to pregnant women!!"

"That's what they did to my own dear Mother. Well, why
not? Calcium, you know."

The Imperial Geologist (the King-Emperor, Ignats Louis,
in authorizing the position, had hoped for gold and, no gold
being found, had shrugged and gone out to inspect the new
infantry boots)—the Imperial Geologist blinked some more.
"Yes," he said. "Well, why not. Calcium . . . I know."

Some years before there had appeared the book *From Ram's
Head to Sandy Cape on Camelback, by a New Chum*
(Glasscocke and Gromthorpe, No. 3, the Minories, 12/-),
and Eszterhazy had translated it into Modern Gothic, as he
had its successors, *Up the Fly River by Sail and Paddle*, and
*In Pursuit of Poundmaker, plus a General Survey of the
Northwest Territories* (available at Szentbelessel's Book
House near the New Model Road at two ducats *per* or all
three for five ducats, each with eleven half-tone illustrations
and a free patriotic bookmark; write for catalogue). From
these translations a friendship had developed. Newton
Charles Enderson was not really a "new chum," far from it;
he was a "currency lad"; and now he was on holiday from
the University of Eastern Australia and hoped to explore
some more, in the lands of the Triple Monarchy.

There were a number of not-very-well explored (not very
well explored by any scientific expeditions, that is; they had
all been very well explored by the River Tartars, the
Romanou, and by all the other non-record-keeping peoples
who had gone that way since the days of (and before the

days of: caches of amber had been found there, and Grecian pottery) the Getae, who may or may not have been close of kin to the ancient Scythian Goths) and rather languid waterways disemboguing into the Delta of the Ister. And New Chum Enderson had wanted Eszterhazy to go exploring with him, in a pirogue. And Eszterhazy had very much wanted to do so. There were several sorts of bee-eaters which had never been well engraved, let alone photographed; skins of course were in the museums, and several water-colors had been made by someone whose identity had been given simply as *An Englishwoman,* long ago; still semi-impenetrably wrapped in her modesty, she had withdrawn into her native northern mists, leaving only copies of the watercolors behind.

"But I am afraid that our schedules don't match. Really I do regret."

New Chum regretted, too. "But I must be back for the start of term."

"And I for the meeting of the Proposed Canal Committee. Well . . . I know that your movements are as precisely dated as those of Phileas Fogg, so just let me know when you'll be back, and I'll give you a good luncheon to make up for your privations. There's a person in the country who's promised me a fine fat pullet, and the truffles should be good, too, so—"

New Chum gave a bark, intended for a laugh, of a sort which had terrified Pommies and Aboes alike. "I'm not one of your European gourmets," he said. "Grew up on damper and 'roo. Advanced to mutton, pumpkin, and suet pud. More than once ate cockatoo—they'd told me it was chook—'chicken' to you—and I never knew the difference. Still, of course, I'll be glad to eat what you give me, with no complaint. . . . Ah, by the way. Don't depend on me much or at all to identify and bring back your bee-eaters. Know *nothing* of ornithology. Officially I'm Professor of Political Economy, but what I am, actually, is an explorer. Glad to give you a set of my notes, though." And on this they parted.

• • •

Two pieces of news. The country pullet would be on hand the next day. Also alas the sister-in-law's sister of Frow Widow Orgats, housekeeper and cook, had been Taken Bad with the Dropped Stomach—did she require medical advice?—an elf-stone?—no: she required the attentions of her sister's sister-in-law. The house, with the help of its lower staff, might keep itself for a little while. "And Malta, who I've hand-picked meself, will cook for you very well till I gets back, Sir Doctor." Malta, thought the Sir Doctor, had perhaps been handpicked so as to prevent the Sir Doctor from thinking of her as a suitable full-time replacement— she was not perhaps very bright—but merely he said, "Tomorrow they are bringing up a special pullet for the luncheon with the foreign guest and it may not look just exactly as the sort they sell here at the Hen Mark in town; so mind you do it justice."

Malta dropped several courtseys, but not, thank God, her stomach; said, "Holy Angels, my Lard, whatsoe'er I'm given to cook, I shall cook it fine, for Missus she's wrote out the words for me real big on a nice piece of pasteboard." Malta could read and she had the recipe? Well, well. Hope for the best. New Chum would perhaps not mind or even notice if the luncheon fell short of standard, but Eszterhazy, after all, would have to eat it, too.

However.

The roof of the Great Chamber did not indeed fall in on the meeting of the Proposed Canal Committee, but many other things happened, which he would hope had rather not. The chairman had forgotten the minutes of the last meeting and would not hear of the reading being skipped, *pro hac vice,* so all had to wait until they had been fetched in a slow hack, if not indeed a tumbril or an ox-cart. Then the Conservative delegation had wished to be given assurances the most profound that any land taken for the Canal would be paid for at full current market value; next, well before the Conservoes were made satisfied with such assurances, the

Workingchaps' delegation had taken it into its collective head that Asian coolie labor might be employed in Canal construction and demanded positive guarantees that it would not. Then the Commercial representation desired similar soothing in regard to brick and building-stone—not only that it would not be imported from Asia, but from anywhere else outside the Empire—"Even if it has to come from Pannonia!"—something which the Pannonian delegation somehow took much amiss. Cries of *Point of order!* and *Treason!* and *What has the Committee got to hide?* and *Move the Previous question!* were incessant. And Eszterhazy realized that he was absolutely certain to miss anyway most of his luncheon engagement with Enderson.

So he sent word that the meal was to proceed without him, and his apologies to his guest, and he (Eszterhazy) would join him as soon as possible.

"As soon as" was eventually reached, though he had feared it wouldn't be. As he was making his way out of the Great Chamber he encountered Professor Blumpkinn, almost in tears. "I have missed my luncheon!" said the Imperial Geologist (he did not look as though he had missed many) dolefully. "They have prepared none for me at home, and in a restaurant I cannot eat, because my stomach is delicate: if anything is in the least greasy or underdone or overdone, one feels rising, then, the bile: and one is dyspeptic for days!"

"Come home with me, then, Johanno," said Eszterhazy.

"Gladly!"

One might ask, How far can a pullet go? but the pullet was after all intended merely as a garnish to only one course of several; also a cook in Bella would sooner have suffered herself to be trampled by elephant cows rather than fail to provide a few Back-up Entrances, as they were called, in case of emergencies. A singularly greedy guest might become an Untoward Incident in a foreign *pension*: but not in a well-ordered house in Bella: What a compliment! God—who gives appetite—bless the man! and the order would be passed on, via an agreed-upon signal, to bring out one of the backups.

Going past the porte-cochère of the Great Hall, which was jammed with vehicles, Eszterhazy held up his hand and the red steam runabout darted forward from a nearby passage; almost before it had come to a stop, Schwebel, the engineer, had vaulted into the back to stoke the anthracite: Eszterhazy took the tiller. His guest, an appreciative sniff for the cedar wood-work (beeswax "compliments of Prince Vlox"), sat beside him.

"Who's *that?*" asked an Usher of a Doorkeeper, watching the deft work with the steering-gear.

"He'm Doctors Eszterhazy, th' Emperor's wizard," said Doorkeeper to Usher.

"So *that's* him!—odd old bird!" And then they both had to jump as the delegations poured out, demanding their coaches, carriages, curricles, hacks, and troikas. None, however, demanded steam runabouts.

"It will not offend you if we enter by way of the kitchen?" the doctor (although his doctorate was plural, he himself was singular . . . very singular) asked the professor.

Who answered that they might enter by way of the chimney. "Cannot you hear my stomach growling? Besides, it is always a pleasure to visit a well-ordered kitchen." Blumpkinn rang with pleasure the hand-bell given him to warn passers-by—the steamer was almost noiseless—and drivers of nervous horses.

"A moderate number of unannounced visits help keep a kitchen well-ordered." Besides, with a temporary cook and a guest with a very delicate stomach, an inspection, however brief, might be a good idea: and, in a few minutes, there they were!—but what was this in the alley? a heavy country wagon—and at the door, someone whose canvas coat was speckled with feathers—someone stamping his feet and looking baffled. "I tells you again that Poulterer Puckel-haube has told me to bring this country-fed bird, and to git

a skilling and a half for it! 'Tain't my fault as I'm late: the
roads about the Great Chamber was filled with kerritches."

But, like the King of Iceland's oldest son, Malta Cook
was having none. "You's heard I'm only temporal here," she
said, hands on hips, "and thinks to try your gammon on
me!—but you'll get no skilling and a half at this door! The
country chicking has already been delivered a couple hours
ago, with the other firm's compliments, and the foreign
guest is eating of it now. Away with ye, and—" She caught
sight of Eszterhazy, courtseyed, gestured towards the deliv-
eryman, her mouth open for explanation and argument.

She was allowed no time. Eszterhazy said, "Take the bird
and pay for it, we'll settle the matter later.—Give him a
glass of ale," he called over his shoulder. Instantly the man's
grievance vanished. The money would, after all, go to his
employer. But the beer was his . . . at least for a while.

At the table, napkin tucked into his open collar, sun-
burned and evidently quite content, sat Newton Charles
("New Chum") Enderson, calmly chewing. Equally calmly,
he returned the just-cleaned-off bone to its platter, on which
(or, if you prefer, whereon) he had neatly laid out the
skeleton. Perhaps he had always done the same, even with
the cockatoo and the kangaroo. Eszterhazy stared in intense
disbelief. Blumpkinn's mouth was opening and closing like
that of a barbel, or a carp. "Welcome aboard," said New
Chum, looking up. "Sorry you've missed it. The journey has
given me quite an appetite." At the end of the platter was a
single, and slightly odd, feather. Malta had perhaps heard, if
not more, of how to serve a pheasant.

"My God!" cried Blumpkinn. "Look! There is the centra
free as far as the sacrum, and the very long tail as well as the
thin coracoid, all the ribs nonunciate and thin, neither
birdlike nor very reptilian, the un-birdlike caudal appendage, the separate and unfused metacarpals, the independent
fingers and claws."

"Not bad at all," said Enderson, touching the napkin to
his lips. "As I've told you, I don't know one bird from

another, but this is not bad. Rather like bamboo chicken—
goanna, or iguana, you would call it. Though a bit far north
for that . . . but of course it must be imported! My
compliments to the chef! By the way. I understand that the
man who brought it said that there weren't any more . . .
whatever that means . . . You now how to treat a guest
well, I must say!"

Contentedly, he broke off a bit of bread and sopped at the
truffled gravy. Then he looked up again. "Oh, and speaking
of compliments," he said, "who's Prince Vlox?"

"I see the French picture is missing," said Eszterhazy.

Bernie

by
Ian McDowell

New writer Ian McDowell has made only a handful of science fiction sales to date, most of them to Asimov's Science Fiction, Amazing, *and* The Magazine of Fantasy and Science Fiction. *In the fantasy and horror fields he has been somewhat more prolific, with sales to* The Pendragon Chronicles, The Camelot Chronicles, Borderlands II, Book of the Dead III, Love in Vein: Tales of Gothic Vampirism, *and others. He has an MFA in creative writing from the University of North Carolina at Greensboro.*

Here's a slyly satirical, blackly funny, and suspensefully fast-paced story that takes on both children's television and the recent big upsurge in dino madness, as we get an inside look at TV's newest star . . .

*   *   *

Varla stared at the plastic carapace on Steve's desk. "Look, it's weird enough that our client is a six-foot-tall iguana, but do you really expect my team to work dressed up as Ninja Turtles? We're bodyguards, not kiddy show performers."

Steve grimaced and scratched his peeling nose. He'd just come back from the Bahamas, where she hoped he'd caught enough UV radiation to cause a melanoma. She hadn't had a paid vacation in two years, and she and her team were the ones who did all the real work.

He wasn't meeting her eyes. "First off, Bernie isn't an iguana, he's a genetically reconstructed deinonychus. . . ."

Varla popped her nicotine bubblegum, a vile habit she'd acquired in her umpteenth attempt at giving up smoking. "I know that, Steve, I was just being rhetorical. But why the goddam turtle costumes?"

He sighed and scratched his nose again. Clearly, the idea embarrassed him, too, and he wouldn't even have to wear one of the stupid outfits. "Disney wants us to keep a low profile on Bernie's tour, just like their own security people do at their parks. The masks and shells will disguise your helmets and body armor, and not alarm all the parents who've brought their brats out to the mall to see their favorite TV dinosaur in person. Just be glad Disney acquired the Turtles last year. You guys could be having to dress up like Mickey, Minnie, Donald, and Goofy."

Varla, who'd been pacing in outrage, settled her six-foot-two frame back into the vinyl chair and brushed black bangs out of her eyes. "Who are they so worried will be gunning for the big lizard, that they want us in full armor? I didn't know he was on any pro's hit list."

Steve fingered his remote and a holo freezeframe of Bernie began slowly revolving in the air above his desktop. At one-fifth scale, the image shouldn't have been particularly threatening, especially with the oversized purple Nikes and the balloon-like three-fingered gloves hiding his ripping talons, but his bipedal, stiff-tailed body radiated the same deadly power as a pit bull or a great white shark. Varla had serious trouble associating this brutally efficient-looking predator with the low-budget Bernie of her childhood, the sashaying actor in a baggy purple suit who sang nerdy songs about caring and sharing.

"They're not worried about terrorists," said Steve, his glasses reflecting the green and purple holo. "Just some crazed fundamentalist with a Saturday night special, who thinks reconstructed dinosaurs are a Satanic plot to undermine scripture. But suppose some loony does pop out of the crowd and take a shot at him? What does your team do, if the guy's not close enough to take out?"

Varla considered the matter. "Same as with a human client, I guess, get Bernie out of the line of fire."

Steve nodded through the holo. "Exactly. You'll have to dogpile him to get him down, and he won't like that, despite the tranquilizers. His teeth have been replaced with rubber implants, and the gloves and shoes will keep him from using his claws, but he could still do serious damage. The armor's as much to protect you from him as from flying bullets."

Varla put her motorcycle boots up on Steve's desk. "Great. If Godzilla here panics, he may try to kick our heads off. He looks strong enough to do it."

Steve nodded. "He is, no matter how much padding there is on the bottom of those giant shoes."

Varla dropped her gum in Steve's waste can. "When do we meet him?"

The combination ranch and studio was spread over a good sixty acres of Texas scrubbrush. They passed through three successive checkpoints, the last manned by two ruby-toothed, Baby-Eagle-toting *cholos* in Mickey Mouse base-ball caps, who directed Varla to park beside the purple barn, where Bernie's handler waited to meet the team.

A cluster of dirty white chickens scattered before the Range Rover, then regrouped, clucking in indignation, as Varla jumped down and stretched her cramped legs. The handler turned out to be a lanky woman in overalls and a EuroDisney T-shirt, with curly red hair and an infectious grin. "Jill Thompson," she said as she stuck out her hand, obviously bemused by having to look up. "God, I thought *I* was tall."

Varla smiled at that. "Varla Satana," she said as she shook Jill's hand. "And these are my guys, Tim, Dariush, and Tasha."

Tim and Dariush grinned and nodded, and Varla could tell they thought Jill was cute. So did Tasha, from the cold look in her big Walter Keene eyes. Tasha and Varla were intermittent lovers, and Tasha tended to pout in the presence of women she thought Varla might find attractive. Varla wished she'd get over herself. She was already pissed at Tasha for demanding they stop three times on the way to collect sun-bleached cow skulls.

Jill shook Tim's big hand and Dariush's small one, and didn't seem to notice that Tasha had not extended hers.

"Pleased to meet you all," she said as if she really meant it. "Let's get inside the barn where it's cool."

Inside were bales of hay, various tools, a Honda autotractor, an ancient refrigerator and four Emery Express crates containing armored Ninja Turtles costumes. Tim and Dariush scowled at the last items, but Tasha, for some perverse reason, smiled impishly. "It'll be like dressing up for Halloween," she said, idly kicking one of the crates with the toe of her scuffed red cowboy boot.

"Not today," said Jill. "I know the last thing you want to do is to climb into those costumes after a long drive. Besides, you won't start the real work with Bernie until tomorrow." She strode over to the fridge. "Today, all each of you need is a dead chicken."

Not sure she'd heard correctly, Varla walked over to see. Sure enough, the fridge was stuffed full of whole chickens, complete with feathers. "What are those for?"

Jill handed out rubber gloves, then chickens. "The way to Bernie's heart is through his stomach. Come with me out back and you'll see for yourself." Giving the last carcass to Varla, she strapped on a holstered dart pistol.

The back door of the barn opened into a large, electric-fenced enclosure. In the distance was a stand of post oaks and a small pond. Four men were waiting outside of the door. They were Mexican or Indian, in their mid-thirties to early fifties, all in jeans and work shirts. None of them was more than four and a half feet tall. They carried long metal and rubber poles with copper electrodes at the end, like extended cattle prods.

Tasha, never big on social graces, barely repressed a giggle, while Dariush and Tim exchanged a puzzled glance. Varla cocked an eyebrow at Jill.

Jill was clearly trying not to smile at their reaction. "Yeah, we hire a lot of little people to work with Bernie. Have you ever seen how a dog or cat that's grown up in a household without children reacts to kids when seeing them for the first time? Usually, it's with hostility or terror. They aren't used to people being that small. Child labor laws won't let us have kids working here, but having little people as ranch hands discourages him from thinking humans this size are potential prey."

"Where is the big lizard, anyway," said Varla. Standing there with a dead chicken in her hand, smiling at midgets, she wondered if this job could get any more surreal.

"He's not a lizard," said Jill with the tone of one who'd explained this many times. "He's a theropod dinosaur, as much like a bird as a reptile."

"Sorry," said Varla, used to a specialist's pedantry. "So where is the big rooster?"

Jill put two fingers in her mouth and whistled. Moments later, Bernie whistled back as he came trotting out of the trees.

Big, taciturn Tim let out what might have been a gasp, while Dariush gave his own low whistle. Tasha clapped her hands. "He's beautiful," she said.

Jill grinned. "Isn't he, though?"

Varla had to admit she was right. Bernie was surprisingly graceful as he loped toward them, his long muscular tail stuck out rigidly behind him, his narrow head held erect, his large amber eyes as coldly intelligent as an owl's. His coloration, a neon, almost fluorescent green, with broad maroon strips on his sides and narrower orange ones criss-crossing his belly, should have been garish, but somehow wasn't. Seen like this, without the white gloves and purple vest and shoes he wore on TV, everything was perfectly in balance, a work of nature's art that couldn't be improved on.

Varla estimated his overall length at just under four meters, which meant that his eye ridges came up to the level of her chin, and he looked like he weighed one-eighty, maybe two-hundred pounds. Certainly not big, as dinosaurs went, but plenty formidable for all that. His forelimbs were long, much more so than those of his distant cousin *Tyrannosaurus Rex,* and armed with three huge claws. His feet were also three-clawed, the middle being a six-inch bladelike talon that was raised off the ground. In his natural state, she had read, he would stand on one leg, balanced by the stiff tail, and grip his prey with his foreclaws while using his lifted hind foot to rip open its belly.

The midget ranch hands flanked them on either side, their poles ready, but Jill waved them back. "It's okay, Pablo," she said to one of them. "These people are professionals. They're paid to take the risk." She walked forward. "How's my pretty boy today?"

Bernie closed the space between himself and her with a fifteen foot leap. Dipping his head, he butted her gently in the thigh, and she scratched him behind the exposed membranes that were his ears. "Caring is sharing, " he said in a high, reedy voice.

"He really does talk," said Varla softly.

Jill nodded. "Not only is he about as smart as an African Grey parrot, but he has the same mimicking ability. I just wish the stuff I have to teach him to say wasn't so fucking inane."

"What about the singing?" asked Dariush. "My sisters' kids always sing along with him on TV. I never heard a bird sing that well."

Jill scratched under Bernie's chin. "Most of what you see on TV is computer simulation, but he sings during live appearances, too." Her expression grew pained. "That's done with a surgically implanted speaker. I hated that they did that to him, believe me. But what's a girl to do? If I protest too much, they'll fire me and hire someone else to babysit him. I try to give his corporate owners what they want while taking the best care of him I can."

Bernie looked up, fixing his glittering eye on Varla. "Friends are forever!" he said as he hopped forward.

"Better give him the chicken, Varla," said Jill. "Toss it, don't hand it."

Varla didn't need to be told. Bernie snapped it out of the air and began to chew on it. His rubber teeth might not have been much use, but his mouth was hard as a turtle's, and the chicken was pretty much pulped before it went down. Cocking his head to one side, he drooled bloody feathers and looked expectantly at Dariush, Tim, and Tasha.

Three chickens sailed through the air almost simultaneously. Bernie caught one and gulped it down without chewing while the other two bounced off him. He kicked one back into the air like a kid playing hackey-sack, swallowed it, then dipped his head to snap up the other.

Jill casually ran her hand along his muscular neck. "You can pet him now. His favorite spot is right behind the ears."

Gingerly, they gathered round. Bernie cocked his head from side to side, his large eyes blinking, the curve of his heavily muscled jaw giving him a crocodile's fixed smile. Varla was fascinated by the elegant geometry of his scales, their intricate patterns as regular as a digitized image. His skin felt like supple, carefully worked leather, and was warmer to the touch than any of the snakes and iguanas she'd owned as a child. The muscles under it could have been carved from marble, except when they flowed like water.

Bernie snuffled at Varla's leather jacket and Tasha's beaded purse. "Oh, shit," said Tasha, "he's *tasting* me," as a tongue the color and texture of a slab of calves' liver flicked out the end of his snout.

"Not really," said Jill. "What he's actually tasting are the scent particles in the air. His olfactory senses are better than the literature led me to expect."

"How many of these reconstructed dinosaurs are there now?" asked Dariush.

Jill frowned. "I'm not really sure. There's the deinonychus pack in Orlando that produced Bernie, and they're developing an apatasaurus herd in California. Disney's had less luck overseas; the Hokkaido park has yet to see any results from their seismosaurus project, and after the tyrannosaur debacle the French are sticking to Pleistocene mammals. Maybe a half-dozen zoos have adult specimens; I'd say there's about two hundred reconstructed dinosaurs worldwide. Less than there were last year, before that Macaw virus destroyed the Honduras preserve."

Tasha giggled as Bernie sniffed at her head, fascinated by the metallic sheen of the dye in her buzzcut hair. "How'd you get this job?" she asked, her initial hostility toward Jill evidently dissipated.

Jill grabbed hold of Bernie's dewlap and tugged him away from Tasha's reflective scalp. "Sorry, he's like a parrot, fascinated by shiny things." When she rubbed the wrinkled throat pouch between her palms, he tilted his head up and closed his eyes, looking for all the world like he was trying to purr. "I was Jacob Abrams's graduate assistant at UCLA, and I went with him when he took over the deinonychus project." Her face clouded over. "Jake died during the Manhattan quarantine. Bernie was little more than a hatchling. When it turned out he responded better to me than anyone else, Disney put me under contract as his permanent keeper. It's not a bad life, considering. We tape footage for the shows and videos and VR disks right out here, all the reference material for the computer guys who put Bernie's image through its paces. Two or three months a year we go on tour. At least I don't have to work at one of the damn parks. You guys are freelance, right? Outside security hired for the tour?"

Varla nodded.

"Be glad the Mouse is not your master. The perks are good, but the corporate culture sucks."

Tim stuck out a tentative hand and stroked the bony ridge on the back of Bernie's neck. "Disney seems to be buying up everything these days. At least, everything the Japanese and Koreans don't already own."

Jill shrugged. "Well, if they hadn't bought up the Bernie franchise, he might still be some guy in a baggy suit, and I'd never have gotten this job. Hey, watch it!"

Bernie had noticed Tim's earring. He nibbled at it, causing Tim to cover his ears with his hands and step quickly back. Jill rapped Bernie's plated snout. "Stop that, you oaf!"

Bernie cocked his head and blinked, his mouth frozen in that disconcerting smile. Pablo had come up with his stun pole, but Jill shook her head. "It's okay. If he's going to be a bad boy, he can play by himself for a while."

Bernie suddenly hissed like an air brake and swiveled his head around. Something had moved a hundred feet away, halfway between them and the stand of trees. Squinting in the harsh sunlight, Varla shaded her eyes and saw a rangy jackrabbit, sitting up on its haunches to look at them, its nose quivering in the air.

There was no obvious transition. One instant Bernie was still, his head doubled back, looking down his own spine at the rabbit; the next, he'd spun completely around and was bounding through the air like a kangaroo that had been shot out of a cannon, his charge kicking up a cloud of orange dust and showering Varla's team with a hailstorm of clods. He was almost halfway to the rabbit before it had even moved.

Jill stepped forward and took Varla's forearm. "Back inside," she said quietly. Looking over their shoulders as they were hustled back to the barn, they saw the chase was short, with Bernie catching the rabbit after two zig-zags. One taloned foot stamped it screaming into the dust, impaling it on the big raised claw. Standing on one leg like a stork, he picked it daintily off his foot and wolfed it down.

Pablo and the other hands followed them back inside. "Sorry," said Pablo to Jill, "those damn rabbits keep burrowing in."

"No big deal," said Jill. "We were done with him for the day." She turned back to Varla. "I'm sorry about that. Did you ever own a pet snake when you were a kid?"

Varla frowned at the apparent non-sequitur. "I look like the type, huh? Yeah, I had lots of snakes."

Jill walked toward the fridge. "Any of them ever eat anything other than live food?"

Varla remembered Stanley, six and a half shimmering feet of blue-black Florida Indigo snake. "One. I bought him turkey necks at Kroger's when I couldn't afford rats. He'd take them right out of my hand."

"But you didn't try giving him live rats by hand, did you?"

Varla shook her head vigorously. "God, no. I didn't dare stick my hand into his cage for at least thirty minutes after dropping in a rat."

Jill opened the fridge, tugged a twelve-pack of Kirin out from under the mass of dead chickens, and handed everyone a beer. "Bernie's the same way. It's like he's got two separate buttons in his head, an 'eat' button and a 'kill' button. Showing him a dead chicken, or any kind of nonliving food, that pushes the 'eat' button; he gets greedy, but basically he's fine. But if he sees potential prey scurrying about, that presses the 'kill' button. Believe me, you don't want to be around him then."

Varla remembered how Stanley, normally about as active and vicious as a scaly kielbasa, was transformed into a lightning-fast hunter at the sight of a quivering rodent. "No, I imagine not." She used her sleeve to wipe damp feathers off the beer can and pulled the tab.

A month later, Varla was on a loading dock outside Four Seasons Mall in Greensboro, North Carolina, finishing the chicken samosa and frozen lasie she'd bought at the McDonald's inside. Pulling off the sweaty T-shirt she wore over her green tights, she used it to wipe samosa crumbs from her face, then began strapping on her body armor. Beneath the outer kevlar and molded ceramic chest plate were bubble cells of liquid chloro-fluorocarbon. Having the cold, fluid-filled plastic near her skin felt like wearing a vest made from half-frozen Chillee Willies, not an unpleasant sensation in the sweltering July heat. Over the armor went the painted plastic shell, her holstered Astra A-85 accessible beneath its lower lip. Sitting on the steps to the dock, she pulled on the stupid two-toed boots. They'd drawn the line at gloves, so she rubbed green makeup over the backs of her hands. Last would be the helmet and wide-angle goggles and the stiff plastic mask that fit over them, but she was leaving all that off until it was time to go inside. God, but she wanted a cigarette.

Tim emerged from the van in full getup. Not for the first time, Varla thought that his long, biker-style beard and hair must be damned uncomfortable under all the stuff on his head, but with typical stubbornness, he'd refused to trim them. The domino "mask" painted around the eye-slits of his turtle headpiece was red, but she'd forgotten which one that meant he was. None of the kids expressed much interest in them, anyway. They knew that, unlike Bernie, the turtles were just people in costumes.

"All ready?"

He cocked a big green-smeared thumb toward the trailer. "I don't know what's up with Jill and Bernie, but Tasha says everything's cool inside the building." Filtered through the electronics in his mask, his normal baritone went up an octave.

Sighing, Varla finished her lasie and donned her own headgear for confirmation. "Lots of screaming kids and stressed-out parents waiting," buzzed Tasha's voice in her helmet, "but no sign-waving Christians." That was good. North Carolina was hardly the buckle of the Bible Belt, but a small contingent of fundamentalists had picketed them last week in Charlotte.

Everything seemed ready, so she tucked her seven-foot plastic and steel imitation of a Japanese bo stick under her arm and knocked on the side of the trailer, giving Jill the all-clear sign. There was no response. Tim shrugged. "I don't know why they're taking so long. Maybe there was some trouble with his dosage."

Opening the door on the back of the trailer, Varla stuck her head inside. The smell immediately explained the delay. Jill was kneeling behind Bernie, wiping beneath the base of his tail with a handful of paper towels. "Sorry," she said through clenched teeth, "But he just took a nasty dump and I have to clean off his cloaca. I hope he's okay; his plumbing is usually more regular than this." Fortunately, she hadn't gotten any green and white dinosaur shit on the nice black slacks and gold blouse she habitually wore for live appearances.

Ignoring Jill, Bernie turned his fixed grin on Varla. "I love you," he trilled, his big eyes more glassy than usual from the tranquilizers Jill had given him. Climbing inside the trailer, Varla stooped beside him and tied his left shoelace, which had come undone. She'd begun to hate seeing him laced into the big, clunky shoes and cartoonish gloves, although she understood the necessity of sheathing those damn talons. Bernie, for his part, didn't seem to mind. All in all, he was a remarkably well-tempered animal, even when not tranked to the gills.

Jill slipped his purple vest on him, and snapped the thin wire that served as Bernie's leash into its catch right behind his shoulder blades. It was actually more than a leash, for it was connected to a buttoned hand grip Jill could activate with her thumb. Should she do so, Bernie would receive a theoretically incapacitating electric shock. Varla wondered if Jill would have the heart to push that button if Bernie became unmanageable or took a snap at a kid. So far, the question had not been put to the test.

Varla held the door open as Jill urged Bernie out of the trailer. The foam heels of his shoes slapped clumsily against the concrete and corrugated steel of the loading dock, and when Tim punched in the security code, the service door opened with a grinding squeal. Fortunately, Bernie seemed used to such sounds by now. "Friends are better than ice cream," he said, as they entered the blessedly cool service corridor.

Varla and Tim flanked Bernie, their augmented bo sticks balanced on their shoulders, while Jill followed directly behind him, keeping a short rein on the leash. "Okay," said

Varla into her mike, "here we come." Up ahead she could
hear the murmur of the crowd above the slapping echo of
Bernie's giant Nikes.

The service corridor opened onto the mall's central hub,
a recessed commons that had once been an ice-skating rink.
The area just beyond the corridor had been cordoned off
with traffic barriers and uniformed mall security, creating an
empty circular space about fifty feet in diameter. It was
ringed by a crush of screaming, waving children and
grim-faced adults who struggled to restrain them. "Bernie,
Bernie, Bernie!" chanted the children, "we loooove you,
Bernie!"

Tasha and Dariush were already in position, waving
uncomfortably to the crowd in their bulky suits. As usual,
none of the children were paying them any attention. Varla
hoped Disney had acquired the Turtles cheap, for their glory
days were long past.

Varla and Tim joined Tasha and Dariush in fanning out,
so that the four of them faced the mob, each taking a quarter
of the circle. Last week's picketing in Charlotte had been the
only sign of trouble so far, but they were paid to never drop
their guard. Like Varla, the other three had sidearms
holstered under their shells, and the fighting sticks they all
carried were rigged to deliver an electric shock from one
end and an anesthetic injection from the other.

Behind Varla, Jill clapped her hands for Bernie to begin
his "dance," actually an exaggerated waddle, as she stood in
the center of the makeshift ring, extending his wired leash
and directing him around her like a show horse at the circus.
The crowd of children roared their approval as the speaker
implanted in Bernie's throat began his prerecorded theme
song.

> *When I'm with you,*
> *And you're with me,*
> *We're as happy as we can be!*
> *There's caring and sharing*

> *And hugs for free,*
> *When I'm with you and you're with me!*

Varla didn't turn her back on the crowd to watch Bernie, but she knew the routine. The song done, he would dip his head and bow to the audience, clapping gloved forelimbs together in apparent joy. Indeed, he seemed to like these live appearances well enough, and had yet to prove particularly intractable.

A glassy-eyed young woman in a Bernie T-shirt was lining up the dozen lucky winners in the local "Meet Bernie in Person" contest. This time it would be Varla and Tasha's turn to carry each child forward, so he or she could shake Bernie's gloved "hand." That was the part Varla really hated. Everybody's attention would be on making sure that Bernie didn't decide to bite his young fans, rather than scanning the crowd for potential assassins. Well, she hoped even fundamentalist loonies would hesitate to pop off a shot while kids were in the line of fire. If mall security was doing their job, no adults without children in tow were being allowed into the commons area, anyway.

The first winner was a fat, pop-eyed little boy with short seaweed-colored hair and the kind of acne that usually doesn't hit until adolescence. His mother, who couldn't have been more than twenty, and whose complexion was scarcely better, handed the child to Tasha, who hefted him with an audible grunt. Tasha wasn't very big, and the boy was certainly old enough to walk on his own, but it was better to carry the children rather than lead them by hand, as they were easier to restrain that way, and snatch away from Bernie if he got rambunctious. Behind her, Varla heard the little boy let out an excited piglet squeal as Tasha held him close to his idol, but Varla kept her eyes on the crowd.

Standing next in line was a thin, red-headed little girl with a Bernie nose ring and glittery eyeshadow. She was accompanied by an apple-cheeked, cherubic little man, apparently in his early fifties, with a high shiny forehead and a few

cottony wisps of disheveled white hair. His smooth pink
belly protruded out from under a faded, shrunken T-shirt of
comparatively ancient vintage, for it depicted Bernie in his
baggy purple incarnation, rather than as a real dinosaur. The
man had one restraining hand on the little girl's shoulder,
while in the other he held a heavy-looking Toys-R-Us bag,
no doubt laden with Bernie merchandise. "Hey, Uncle
Andy, that hurts," said the little girl, but he didn't ease his
grip on her shoulder. Despite his fixed smile, there was a
cold glint in his eyes.

"Tasha," Varla said softly into her mike, "watch the next
guy in line closely when I take his kid. I don't like the look
on his face." It might be an adult's normal reaction—both
Varla's mother and her mother's lover had despised Bernie
when Varla was a child—but you couldn't be too careful.

Tasha returned with the first contest winner. Varla slid her
stick into its socket on the back of her shell and bent to pick
up the little girl, who appeared to be about five or six years
old. Varla's goggles gave her an expanded field of vision,
and as she turned away from the cherubic man, the corner of
her left eye caught his right hand as it dipped into the
Toys-R-Us bag, to emerge clutching something with a
familiar black plastic sheen.

There was no time to pull a weapon, but she was close
enough to kick him, and she tossed the surprised little girl
away from her as she spun around, some distant part of her
thinking she'd just set the company up for a hellacious
lawsuit if the child was hurt. Then she was staring down the
barrel of a Glock 25 with a penlight laser undersight as the
cherubic man, his avuncular smile now a frozen grimace,
took a two-handed grip and sighted past Varla on Jill and
Bernie.

Varla's green Y-shaped boot connected with his chest and
he went over backward, firing into the air, her goggles
darkening against the muzzle flash, the huge pistol's thunderous retort ringing in her ears despite her helmet as the
skylight shattered far above their heads. She was much

bigger than him, it had been a strong roundhouse kick, and the tile floor was slick, so that the impact sent him skidding like a hockey puck into the crowd, which parted screaming to the left and right of him, effectively shielding his prone body from the mall's own security people. She'd surely knocked the wind out of him, maybe even broken a rib, but the little bastard was tougher than he looked, or at least inhumanly determined, for he hadn't dropped the damn gun. Yelling into her mike, Varla reached back for her fighting stick as she lunged forward.

Tasha was drawing her ACP from under her shell, and the little man made the mistake of sighting on her first, even though Varla was closer. The Glock roared again, the .50 caliber round splintering Tasha's carapace, and then Varla was jabbing the point of her stick into the gunman's exposed midriff. The little man *whuffed,* dropped the pistol and went into convulsions as 40cc of dinosaur-strength anesthetic hit his bloodstream. Varla reversed the stick, smashed it into his groin, and gave him a jolt from the electro-shock end for good measure, but he was already out cold, maybe even dead. She didn't particularly care, although the publicity would be ugly if she'd killed him. The little girl, thankfully unhurt, ran to his side. "Uncle Andy, you tried to shoot Bernie!" she squealed in outrage while aiming kicks at his limp form. Then a mall security officer scooped her up, while another called for paramedics on his portaphone.

Varla turned back to Tasha, whose shattered carapace hissed as it discharged chlorofluorocarbon vapor. Her ceramic chest plate had cracked, but the kevlar stopped the round, the impact triggering a phase change, so that the liquid in the bubble cells absorbed kinetic energy as it went gaseous, thus acting as a shock absorber, allowing a hundred-and-fifteen-pound woman to be hit at close range and stay on her feet. Thank God she'd taken it square in the chest, and that the Glock had been one of the older semi-autos, so she caught a single round and not a full burst. Tasha said something, but Varla couldn't make it out, despite the augmented hearing in her helmet. People were screaming all around her, as parents scooped up their children and bolted for the exits, slamming into and trampling over each other in their frenzy.

But what about Jill and Bernie? The broken glass had fallen behind Varla, back where they were. Cursing her own stupid negligence, Varla turned and saw that Jill was on her knees, looking dazed and bleeding slightly from the scalp, glass fragments glittering like snow in her frizzy red hair. Bernie was hopping from foot to foot, hissing, blood running from a dozen minor cuts on his neck and flanks. Jill had dropped the handle of his wired leash, and the plastic grip lay between her and him.

Shaking her head groggily, Jill dove for the leash, just as Tim and Dariush closed in on Bernie. That last was a mistake, for he leapt away from them as Jill grabbed the handle but before she could press the button, and when the wire brought him up short, the jack tore loose. Then he was bounding away into the mob, the clumsy shoes making him stumble each time he landed, but not appreciably slowing him down.

"Shit," roared Varla into her mike, "we've got to catch him!" Then she was charging full tilt into the crowd, cursing the awkwardness of her two-toed boots, but plowing through the panicked mass by virtue of her size and strength, hoping to God she didn't trample any kids. The others were behind her, but Tasha and Dariush had much shorter legs, and Tim was stocky where she was lean and rangy, so she rapidly outdistanced them. All around her, chainlink and plastic barriers were sliding in place, blocking off store entrances, while terrified customers crowded inside, their pale faces imitating Munch's "The Scream." The mob thinned out and she saw Bernie ahead of her, pausing to kick at his own reflection in one of the mirrored columns that lined the promenade. Despite the heavy padding on his shoes, the tough glass shattered, and then he was bounding away again, emitting a loud squawking cry like that of a crow amplified by stadium speakers.

The last store on the right was a pet shop, with a tiny corral in front containing a pair of miniature Zebu cattle. Bernie leapt over the plastic fence, grabbed the collie-sized bull by the head, and shook it fiercely. "Oh, shit," thought Varla, "his 'kill' button's been pushed." Still, she didn't draw her gun, for she could imagine the repercussions if she shot him. Maybe he'd stay busy with the bull long enough for her to get close and use her stick.

No such luck. Dropping the dead bull, and ignoring the terrified cow, Bernie bounded over the fake rail fence and began butting his head against the plexiglass that had slid down over the pet shop's entrance. Muffled by that barrier, dogs barked and parrots screamed inside, while some employees and customers pressed forward for a better look and others, more prudent, crowded back to the rear of the shop.

This wing of the mall ended in the entrance to a Sears Department Store, and there the steel grid had not descended all the way to the grooved floor, leaving about a foot of unobstructed space. Now a tiny little girl in a white dress, with huge eyes and blue and red ribbons in her curly blonde hair, wriggled out from underneath the grid. Bernie was between Varla and the child, and the girl was closer to him than Varla was. "Bernie!" she yelled with glee as she ran to him with outstretched arms. "I love you!"

Bernie cocked his head and watched her come, and Varla screamed in horror, expecting to see him kick the child like a soccer ball, but instead he reared back, opened wide, dipped down and *gulped,* then came back up with her entire upper body in his mouth, her plump legs kicking and her white dress bunched up around his bloodied snout, exposing her Bernie underoos, his jaws unhinging like those of a snake as he attempted to swallow her whole.

This last action had kept him in one place long enough for Varla to catch up, and she slammed into him, ramming the electro-shock end of her stick into his belly. Bernie vomited out the child as he went over backward, his Nikes kicking spasmodically, his cloaca letting go in an acrid spray of sludgy white and yellow fluid. Seemingly unhurt, the little girl rose shakily to her feet, all huge eyes and saliva-plastered hair. "Bad Bernie," she said in a high, tremulous voice, "bad!" Then she was stumbling away, bawling, stooping to scuttle safely back under the Sears barrier.

Before Varla could dose Bernie with the anesthetic end of her stick, he too was on his feet, shaking his head like a woozy boxer, his mouth open and his dewlap unfurled. "Caring means sharing," he squawked, his famous catch phrase sounding shriller than ever before. Then he leapt at her, one foot lashing out in a kick that would have done a champion *karateka* proud.

She jabbed as he jumped, and the injection went home as the padded size 32 sole of his left shoe smashed into her chest, knocking her onto her back and sending her sliding across the floor, much as Bernie's would-be assassin had gone sliding a few minutes earlier. Her plastic carapace was split neatly in two by the blow, and she felt constricting heat against her chest as the liquid in the bubble cells beneath her armor expanded into gas, but the phase change had done little to absorb the shock of such a widespread impact. She gasped for breath, unable to rise, and then he was kicking her hard, stomping on her chest, pieces of the turtle shell breaking off and sticking in the sole of his pounding Nike. *"Caring means sharing,"* he said in a voice like tearing sheet metal, *"caring means sharing!"* One more stomp and she'd pass out, but instead he straddled her, and all she could see was his calf's-liver-colored gullet as his mouth closed over her head.

The helmet would have protected her even if he'd had his original teeth, but his beaky "lips" could crush her throat if he shifted his grip, and one good shake would break her neck just like that of the little Zebu bull. She punched out blindly, first hitting nothing, then connecting with his ribcage. She pounded him harder than she'd ever pounded the heavy bag in her apartment, hard enough that her skin tore on his scales and a knuckle broke on his rocklike ribs, and kept on pounding, but her blows had no effect. Then the grip on her head loosened and his limp weight settled for a moment on her tortured chest before being rolled off her.

Three Ninja Turtle faces bent over her, their painted smiles mocking her pain, polarized lenses peering out impassively from their eye slits, and she heard Tasha's voice in her ringing ears.

"Honey, are you all right?"

She tried to sit up, but the effort cost too much. They eased her back. "The paramedics are coming, boss, just lie still," buzzed Tim's disembodied voice. Looking at them like this, all stooped over her, her own vision dim, she had no idea who was who. For the first time she was scared, scared that she'd been hurt worse than she thought, and might die without seeing their faces.

"Bernie?" she gasped. "What about Bernie?"

Then Jill was bending over her, too, and she was glad for the sight of an unadorned human face, even if the blood trickling down Jill's forehead made it look like her red hair was melting. "He's out," she said, gently squeezing Varla's arm, "your injection did the trick. Thanks for not shooting him." Jill disappeared, presumably to check on her charge.

Varla held someone's green hand and shut her eyes. There were sirens in the distance.

Later, in the hospital, they all brought her flowers, even Jill, and the floral shop delivered a dozen roses from Steve, although she suspected Disney was giving him hell about how everything turned out. It was all over the news, of course, with lawsuits flying everywhere, and she couldn't imagine what it meant for Bernie's future.

"No kids were badly hurt, so the judge ruled he doesn't have to be destroyed," said Jill, idly fingering the stitches in her scalp. "Instead, Disney's selling him. To my Alma Mater.

UCLA wants to test his problem-solving and language-learning abilities, and they're hiring me to work with him. Thank God. I've had enough of show business to last a lifetime."

Varla agreed with that. She leaned back in the hospital bed, wishing she could smoke. She was getting out tomorrow, but it would be a while before her ribs and collar bone were fully mended, even with calcium acceleration. "Did you hear the latest shit? The guy who tried to shoot Bernie is suing us, claiming I used excessive force, that the combination of dino tranquilizer and electric shock stopped his heart, and he nearly died."

"I wish he had," said Jill. "What was his deal, anyway? God knows, I've been trying to avoid the news."

Tim twirled his chestnut beard, which for once looked freshly washed. "His name's Andrew Whaley. Used to wear the purple suit, back before Disney owned Bernie. When they got themselves a real dinosaur, he was out a job. Harbored a grudge ever since. He borrowed his sister's kid, bribed somebody involved with the promotion to make sure his niece got one of the 'Meet Bernie' tickets, and used her to get close to him. Pretty cold, for such a harmless-looking little guy."

"He'll get his," said Dariush. "Let's hope he's sentenced before his lawsuit comes to trial. A lot of cons are big Bernie fans. I don't think he'll do very well in prison."

"At the very least, he'll learn a lot about caring and sharing in the pen," said Varla.

Small Deer
by
Clifford D. Simak

The late Clifford D. Simak sold his first story in 1931, and was a towering ancestral figure in SF for more than fifty years. His famous novel City *won him the International Fantasy Award; he has also won two Hugo Awards, one in 1958 for his short story "The Big Front Yard," and one in 1964 for his novel* Way Station. *His other books include the novels* Time and Again, Ring around the Sun, Time Is the Simplest Thing, They Walked Like Men, The Goblin Reservation, *and* A Choice of Gods, *and the collections* All the Traps of Earth, The Worlds of Clifford Simak, Skirmish, *and* The Best of Clifford Simak.

Here he comes up with one of the most peculiar, and yet strangely logical, explanations for the extinction of the dinosaurs that anyone has yet devised . . .

*　　*　　*

Willow Bend, Wisconsin
June 23, 1966
Dr. Wyman Jackson,
Wyalusing College,
Muscoda, Wisconsin

My dear Dr. Jackson:

I am writing to you because I don't know who else to write to and there is something I have to tell someone who can understand. I know your name because I read your book, "Cretaceous Dinosaurs," not once, but many times. I tried to get Dennis to read it, too, but I guess he never did. All Dennis ever was interested in were the mathematics of his time concept—not the time machine itself. Besides, Dennis doesn't read too well. It is a chore for him.

Maybe I should tell you, to start with, that my name is Alton James. I live with my widowed mother and I run a fix-it shop. I fix bicycles and lawn mowers and radios and television sets—I fix anything that is brought in to me. I'm not much good at anything else, but I do seem to have the knack of seeing how things go together and understanding how they work and seeing what is wrong with them when they aren't working. I never had no training of any sort, but I just seem to have a natural bent for getting along with mechanical contraptions.

Dennis is my friend and I'll admit right off that he is a strange one. He doesn't know from nothing about anything, but he's nuts on mathematics. People in town make fun of him because he is so strange and Ma gives me hell at times for having anything to do with him. She says he's the next best thing to a village idiot. I guess a lot of people think the way that Ma does, but it's not entirely true, for he does know his math.

I don't know how he knows it. He didn't learn it at school and that's for sure. When he got to be 17 and hadn't got no farther than eighth grade, the school just sort of dropped him. He didn't really get to eighth grade honest; the teachers after a while got tired of seeing him on one grade and passed him to the next. There was talk, off and on, of sending him to some special school, but it never got nowhere.

And don't ask me what kind of mathematics he knew. I tried to read up on math once because I had the feeling, after seeing some of the funny marks that Dennis put on paper, that maybe he knew more about it than anyone else in the world. And I still think that he does—or that maybe he's invented an entirely new kind of math. For in the books I looked through I never did find any of the symbols that Dennis put on paper. Maybe Dennis used symbols he made up, inventing them as he went along, because no one had ever told him what the regular mathematicians used. But I don't think that's it—I'm inclined to lean to the idea Dennis came up with a new brand of math, entirely.

There were times I tried to talk with Dennis about this math of his and each time he was surprised that I didn't know it, too. I guess he thought most people knew about it. He said that it was simple, that it was plain as day. It was the way things worked, he said.

I suppose you'll want to ask how come I understood his equations well enough to make the time machine. The answer is I didn't. I suppose that Dennis and I are alike in a lot of ways, but in different ways. I know how to make contraptions work (without knowing any of the theory) and Dennis sees the entire universe as something operating mathematically (and him scarcely able to read a page of simple type).

And another thing. My family and Dennis's family live in the same end of town and from the time we were toddlers, Dennis and I played together. Later on, we just kept on together. We didn't have a choice. For some reason or other, none of the kids would play with us. Unless we wanted to play alone, we had to play together. I guess we got so, through the years, that we understood each other.

I don't suppose there'd been any time machine if I hadn't been so interested in paleontology. Not that I knew anything about it; I was just interested. From the time I was a kid I read everything I could lay my hands on about dinosaurs and saber-tooths and such. Later on I went fossil hunting in the hills, but I never found nothing really big. Mostly I found brachiopods. There are great beds of them in the Platteville limestone. And lots of times I'd stand in the street and look up at the river bluffs above the town and try to imagine what it had been like a million years ago, or a hundred million. When I first read in a story about a time machine, I remember thinking how I'd like to have one. I guess that at one time I thought a little about making one, but then realized I couldn't.

• • •

Dennis had a habit of coming to my shop and talking, but most of the time talking to himself rather than to me. I don't remember exactly how it started, but after a while I realized that he had stopped talking about anything but time. One day he told me he had been able to figure out everything but time, and now it seemed he was getting that down in black and white, like all the rest of it.

Mostly I didn't pay too much attention to what he said, for a lot of it didn't make much sense. But after he'd talked, incessantly, for a week or two, on time, I began to pay attention. But don't expect me to tell you what he said or make any sense of it, for there's no way that I can. To understand what Dennis said and meant, you'd have to live with him, like I did, for twenty years or more. It's not so much understanding what Dennis says as understanding Dennis.

I don't think we actually made any real decision to build a time machine. It just sort of grew on us. All at once we found that we were making one.

We took our time. We had to take our time, for we went back a lot and did things over, almost from the start. It took weeks to get some of the proper effects—at least, that's what Dennis called them. Me, I didn't know anything about effects. All that I knew was that Dennis wanted to make something work a certain way and I tried to make it work that way. Sometimes, even when it worked the way he wanted it, it turned out to be wrong. So we'd start all over.

But finally we had a working model of it and took it out on a big bald bluff, several miles up the river, where no one ever went. I rigged up a timer to a switch that would turn it on, then after two minutes would reverse the field and send it home again.

We mounted a movie camera inside the frame that carried the machine, and we set the camera going, then threw the timer switch.

I had my doubts that it would work, but it did. It went away and stayed for two minutes, then came back again.

When we developed the camera film, we knew without any question the camera had traveled back in time. At first there were pictures of ourselves, standing there and waiting. Then there was a little blur, no more than a flicker, across a half a dozen frames, and the next frames showed a mastodon walking straight into the camera. A fraction of a second later his trunk jerked up and his ears flared out as he wheeled around with clumsy haste and galloped down the ridge.

Every now and then he'd swing his head around to take a look behind him. I imagine that our time machine, blossoming suddenly out of the ground in front of him, scared him out of seven years of growth.

We were lucky, that was all. We could have sent that camera back another thousand times, perhaps, and never caught a mastodon—probably never caught a thing. Although we would have known it had moved in time, for the landscape had been different, although not a great deal different. But from the landscape we could not have told if it had gone back in time a hundred or a thousand years. When we saw the mastodon, however, we knew we'd sent the camera back 10,000 years at least.

I won't bore you with how we worked out a lot of problems on our second model, or how Dennis managed to work out a time-meter that we could calibrate to send the machine a specific distance into time. Because all this is not important. What is important is what I found when I went into time.

I've already told you I'd read your book about Cretaceous dinosaurs and I liked the entire book, but that final chapter about the extinction of the dinosaurs is the one that really got me. Many a time I'd lie awake at night thinking about all the theories you wrote about and trying to figure out in my own mind how it really was.

So when it was time to get into that machine and go, I knew where I would be headed.

Dennis gave me no argument. He didn't even want to go. He didn't care no more. He never was really interested in the time machine. All he wanted was to prove out his math. Once the machine did that, he was through with it.

I worried a lot, going as far as I meant to go, about the rising or subsidence of the crust. I knew that the land around Willow Bend had been stable for millions of years. Sometime during the Cretaceous a sea had crept into the interior of the continent, but had stopped short of Wisconsin and, so far as geologists could determine, there had been no disturbances in the state. But I still felt uneasy about it. I didn't want to come out into the Late Cretaceous with the machine buried under a dozen feet of rock or, maybe, hanging a dozen feet up in the air.

So I got some heavy steel pipes and sunk them six feet into the rock on the bald bluff top we had used that first time, with about ten feet of their length extending in the air. I mounted the time frame on top of them and rigged up a ladder to get in and out of it and tied the pipes into the time field.

One morning I packed a lunch and filled a canteen with water. I dug the old binoculars that had been my father's out of the attic and debated whether I should take along a gun. All I had was a shotgun and I decided not to take it. If I'd had a rifle, there'd been no question of my taking it, but I didn't have one. I could have borrowed one, but I didn't want to. I'd kept pretty quiet about what I was doing and I didn't want to start any gossip in the village.

I went up to the bluff top and climbed up to the frame and set the time-meter for 63½ million years into the past and then I turned her on. I didn't make any ceremony out of it. I just turned her on and went.

I told you about the little blur in the movie film and that's the best way, I suppose, to tell you how it was. There was this little blur, like a flickering twilight. Then it was sunlight once again and I was on the bluff top, looking out across the valley.

Except it wasn't a bluff top any longer, but only a high hill. And the valley was not the rugged, tree-choked, deeply cut valley I had always known, but a great green plain, a wide and shallow valley with a wide and sluggish river flowing at the far side of it. Far to the west I could see a shimmer in the sunlight, a large lake or sea. But a sea, I thought, shouldn't be this far east. But there it was, either a great lake or a sea—I never did determine which.

And there was something else as well. I looked down to the ground and it was only three feet under me. Was I ever glad I had used those pipes!

Looking out across the valley, I could see some moving things, but they were so far away that I could not make them out. So I picked up the binoculars and jumped down to the ground and walked across the hilltop until the ground began to slope away.

I sat down and put the binoculars to my eyes and worked across the valley with them.

There were dinosaurs out there, a whole lot more of them than I had expected. They were in herds and they were traveling. You'd expect that out of any dozen herds of them, some of them would be feeding, but none of them was. All of them were moving and it seemed to me there was a nervousness in the way they moved. Although, I told myself, that might be the way it was with dinosaurs.

They all were a long way off, even with the glasses, but I could make out some of them. There were several groups of duckbills, waddling along and making funny jerky movements with their heads. I spotted a couple of small herds of thescelosaurs, pacing along, with their bodies tilted forward. Here and there were small groups of triceratops. But strangest of all was a large herd of brontosaurs, ambling nervously and gingerly along, as if their feet might hurt. And it struck me strange, for they were a long ways from water and from what I'd read in your book, and in other books, it didn't seem too likely they ever wandered too far away from water.

And there were a lot of other things that didn't look too much like the pictures I had seen in books.

The whole business had a funny feel about it. Could it be, I wondered, that I had stumbled on some great migration, with all the dinosaurs heading out for some place else?

I got so interested in watching that I was downright careless and it was foolish of me. I was in another world and there could have been all sorts of dangers and I should have been watching out for them, but I was just sitting there, flat upon my backside, as if I were at home.

Suddenly there was a pounding, as if someone had turned loose a piledriver, coming up behind me and coming very fast. I dropped the glasses and twisted around and as I did something big and tall rushed past me, no more than three feet away, so close it almost brushed me. I got just a brief impression of it as it went past—huge and gray and scaly.

Then, as it went tearing down the hill, I saw what it was and I had a cold and sinking feeling clear down in my gizzard. For I had been almost run down by the big boy of them all—Tyrannosaurus rex.

His two great legs worked like driving pistons and the light of the sun glinted off the wicked, recurved claws as his feet pumped up and down. His tail rode low and awkward, but there was no awkwardness in the way he moved. His monstrous head swung from side to side, with the great rows of teeth showing in the gaping mouth, and he left behind him a faint foul smell—I suppose from the carrion he ate. But the big surprise was that the wattles hanging underneath his throat were a brilliant iridescence—red and green and gold and purple, the color of them shifting as he swung his head.

I watched him for just a second and then I jumped up and headed for the time machine. I was more scared than I like to think about. I had, I want to testify right here, seen enough of dinosaurs for a lifetime.

But I never reached the time machine.

Up over the brow of the hill came something else. I say something else because I have no idea what it really was. Not as big as rex, but ten times worse than him.

It was long and sinuous and it had a lot of legs and it stood six feet high or so and was a sort of sickish pink. Take a caterpillar and magnify it until it's six feet tall, then give it longer legs so that it can run instead of crawl and hang a death mask dragon's head upon it and you get a faint idea. Just a faint idea.

It saw me and swung its head toward me and made an eager whimpering sound and it slid along toward me with a side-wheeling gait, like a dog when it's running out of balance and lop-sided.

I took one look at it and dug in my heels and made so sharp a turn that I lost my hat. The next thing that I knew, I was pelting down the hill behind old Tyrannosaurus.

And now I saw that myself and rex were not the only things that were running down the hill. Scattered here and there along the hillside were other running creatures, most of them in small groups and herds, although there were some singles. Most of them were dinosaurs, but there were other things as well.

I'm sorry I can't tell you what they were, but at that particular moment I wasn't what you might call an astute observer. I was running for my life, as if the flames of hell were lapping at my heels.

I looked around a couple of times and that sinuous creature was still behind me. He wasn't gaining on me any, although I had the feeling that he could if he put his mind to it. Matter of fact, he didn't seem to be following me alone. He was doing a lot of weaving back and forth. He reminded me of nothing quite so much as a faithful farm dog bringing in the cattle. But even thinking this, it took me a little time to realize that was exactly what he was—an old farm dog bringing in a bunch of assorted dinosaurs and one misplaced human being.

At the bottom of the hill I looked back again and now that I could see the whole slope of the hill, I saw that this was a bigger cattle drive than I had imagined. The entire hill was alive with running beasts and behind them were a half dozen of the pinkish dogs.

And I knew when I saw this that the moving herds I'd seen out on the valley floor were not migratory herds, but they were moving because they were being driven—that this was a big roundup of some sort, with all the reptiles and the dinosaurs and myself being driven to a common center.

I knew that my life depended on getting lost somehow, and being left behind. I had to find a place to hide and I had to dive into this hiding place without being seen. Only trouble was there seemed no place to hide. The valley floor was naked and nothing bigger than a mouse could have hidden there.

Ahead of me a good-size swale rose up from the level floor and I went pelting up it. I was running out of wind. My breath was getting short and I had pains throbbing in my chest and I knew I couldn't run much farther.

I reached the top of the swale and started down the reverse slope. And there, right in front of me, was a bush of some sort, three feet high or so, bristling with thorns. I was too close to it and going too fast to even try to dodge it, so I did the only thing I could—I jumped over it.

But on the other side there was no solid ground. There was, instead, a hole. I caught just a glimpse of it and tried to jerk my body to one side, and then I was falling in the hole.

It wasn't much bigger than I was. It bumped me as I fell and I picked up some bruises, then landed with a jolt. The fall knocked the breath out of me and I was doubled over, with my arms wrapped about my belly.

My breath came slowly back and the pain subsided and I was able to take a look at where I was.

The hole was some three feet in diameter and perhaps as much as seven deep. It slanted slightly toward the forefront of the slope and its sides were worn smooth. A thin trickle of dirt ran down from the edge of it, soil that I had loosened and dislodged when I had hit the hole. And about halfway up was a cluster of small rocks, the largest of them about the size of a human head, projecting more than half their width out of the wall. I thought, idly, as I looked at them, that some day they'd come loose and drop into the hole. And at the thought I squirmed around a little to one side, so that if they took a notion to fall I'd not be in the line of fire.

Looking down, I saw that I'd not fallen to the bottom of the hole, for the hole went on, deeper in the ground. I had come to rest at a point where the hole curved sharply, to angle back beneath the swale top.

I hadn't noticed it at first, I suppose because I had been too shook up, but now I became aware of a musky smell. Not an overpowering odor, but a sort of scent—faintly animal, although not quite animal.

A smooth-sided hole and a musky smell—there could be no other answer: I had fallen not into just an ordinary hole, but into a burrow of some sort. And it must be the burrow of quite an animal, I thought, to be the size it was. It would have taken something with hefty claws, indeed, to have dug this sort of burrow.

And even as I thought it, I heard the rattling and the scrabbling of something coming up the burrow, no doubt coming up to find out what was going on.

I did some scrabbling myself. I didn't waste no time. But about three feet up I slipped. I grabbed for the top of the hole, but my fingers slid through the sandy soil and I couldn't get a grip. I shot out my feet and stopped my slide short of the bottom of the hole. And there I was, with my back against one side of the hole and my feet braced against the other, hanging there, halfway up the burrow.

While all the time below me the scrabbling and the clicking sounds continued. The thing, whatever it might be, was getting closer, and it was coming fast.   ·

Right in front of me was the nest of rocks sticking from the wall. I reached out and grabbed the biggest one and jerked and it came loose. It was heavier than I had figured it would be and I almost dropped it, but managed to hang on.

A snout came out of the curve in the burrow and thrust itself quickly upward in a grabbing motion. The jaws opened up and they almost filled the burrow and they were filled with sharp and wicked teeth.

I didn't think. I didn't plan. What I did was instinct. I dropped the rock between my spread-out legs straight down into that gaping maw. It was a heavy rock and it dropped four feet or so and went straight between the teeth, down into the blackness of the throat. When it hit it splashed and the paws snapped shut and the creature backed away.

How I did it, I don't know, but I got out of the hole. I clawed and kicked against the wall and heaved my body up and rolled out of the hole onto the naked hillside.

Naked, that is, except for the bush with the inch-long thorns, the one that I'd jumped over before I fell into the burrow. It was the only cover that there was and I made for the upper side of it, for by now, I figured, the big cattle drive had gone past me and if I could get the bush between myself and the valley side of the swale, I might have a chance. Otherwise, sure as hell, one of those dogs would see me and would come out to bring me in.

For while there was no question that they were dinosaur herders, they probably couldn't tell the difference between me and a dinosaur. I was alive and could run and that would qualify me.

There was always the chance, of course, that the owner of the burrow would come swarming out, and if he did I couldn't stay behind the bush. But I rather doubted he'd be coming out, not right away, at least. It would take him a while to get that stone out of his throat.

I crouched behind the bush and the sun was hot upon my back and, peering through the branches, I could see, far out on the valley floor, the great herd of milling beasts. All of them had been driven together and there they were, running in a knotted circle, while outside the circle prowled the pinkish dogs and something else as well—what appeared to be men driving tiny cars. The cars and men were all of the same color, a sort of greenish gray, and the two of them, the cars and men, seemed to be a single organism. The men didn't seem to be sitting in the cars; they looked as if they grew out of the cars, as if they and the cars were one. And while the cars went zipping along, they appeared to have no wheels. It was hard to tell, but they seemed to travel with the bottom of them flat upon the ground, like a snail would travel, and as they travelled, they rippled, as if the body of the car were some sort of flowing muscle.

I crouched there watching and now, for the first time, I had a chance to think about it, to try to figure out what was going on. I had come here, across more than sixty million years, to see some dinosaurs, and I sure was seeing them, but under what you might say were peculiar circumstances. The dinosaurs fit, all right. They looked mostly like the way they looked in books, but the dogs and car-men were something else again. They were distinctly out of place.

The dogs were pacing back and forth, sliding along in their sinuous fashion, and the car-men were zipping back and forth, and every once in a while one of the beasts would break out of the circle and the minute that it did, a half dozen dogs and a couple of car-men would race to intercept it and drive it back again.

The circle of beasts must have had, roughly, a diameter of a mile or more—a mile of milling, frightened creatures. A lot of paleontologists have wondered whether dinosaurs had any voice and I can tell you that they did. They were squealing and roaring and quacking and there were some of them that hooted—I think it was the duckbills hooting, but I can't be sure.

Then, all at once, there was another sound, a sort of fluttering roar that seemed to be coming from the sky. I looked up quickly and I saw them coming down—a dozen or so spaceships, they couldn't have been anything but spaceships. They came down rather fast and they didn't seem too big and there were tails of thin, blue flame flickering at their bases. Not the billowing clouds of flame and smoke that our rockets have, but just a thin blue flicker.

For a minute it looked like one of them would land on top of me, but then I saw that it was too far out. It missed me, matter of fact, a good two miles or so. It and the others sat down in a ring around the milling herd out in the valley.

I should have known what would happen out there. It was the simplest explanation one could think of and it was logical. I think, maybe, way deep down, I did know, but my surface mind had pushed it away because it was too matter-of-fact and too ordinary.

Thin snouts spouted from the ships and purple fire curled mistily at the muzzle of those snouts and the dinosaurs went down in a fighting, frightened, squealing mass. Thin trickles of vapor drifted upward from the snouts and out in the center of the circle lay that heap of dead and dying dinosaurs, all those thousands of dinosaurs piled in death.

It is a simple thing to tell, of course, but it was a terrible thing to see. I crouched there behind the bush, sickened at the sight, startled by the silence when all the screaming and the squealing and the hooting ceased. And shaken, too—not by what shakes me now as I write this letter, but shaken by the knowledge that something from outside could do this to the earth.

For they were from outside. It wasn't just the spaceships, but those pinkish dogs and gray-green car-men which were

not cars and men, but a single organism, were not things of
earth, could not be things of earth.

I crept back from the bush, keeping low in hope that the
bush would screen me from the things down in the valley
until I reached the swale top. One of the dogs swung around
and looked my way and I froze, and after a time he looked
away.

Then I was over the top of the swale and heading back
toward the time machine. But half way down the slope, I
turned around and came back again, crawling on my belly,
squirming to the hilltop to have another look.

It was a look I'll not forget.

The dogs and car-men had swarmed in upon the heap of
dead dinosaurs, and some of the cars already were crawling
back toward the grounded spaceships, which had let down
ramps. The cars were moving slowly, for they were heavily
loaded and the loads they carried were neatly butchered
hams and racks of ribs.

And in the sky there was a muttering and I looked up to
see yet other spaceships coming down—the little transport
ships that would carry this cargo of fresh meat up to another
larger ship that waited overhead.

It was then I turned and ran.

I reached the top of the hill and piled into the time
machine and set it at zero and came home. I didn't even stop
to hunt for the binoculars I'd dropped.

And now that I am home, I'm not going back again. I'm not
going anywhere in that time machine. I'm afraid of what I
might find any place I go. If Wyalusing College has any
need of it, I'll give them the time machine.

But that's not why I wrote.

There is no doubt in my mind what happened to the
dinosaurs, why they became extinct. They were killed off
and butchered and hauled away, to some other planet,
perhaps many light years distant, by a race which looked

upon the earth as a cattle range—a planet that could supply a vast amount of cheap protein.

But that, you say, happened more than sixty million years ago. This race did once exist. But in sixty million years it would almost certainly have changed its ways or drifted off in its hunting to some other sector of the galaxy, or, perhaps, have become extinct, like the dinosaurs.

But I don't think so. I don't think any of those things happened. I think they're still around. I think earth may be only one of the many planets which supply their food.

And I'll tell you why I think so. They were back on earth again, I'm sure, some 10,000 or 11,000 years ago, when they killed off the mammoth and the mastodon, the giant bison, the great cave bear and the sabretooth and a lot of other things. Oh, yes, I know they missed Africa. They never touched the big game there. Maybe, after wiping out the dinosaurs, they learned their lesson and left Africa for breeding stock.

And now I come to the point of this letter, the thing that has me worried.

Today there are just a few less than three billion of us humans in the world. By the year 2000 there may be as many as six billion of us.

We're pretty small, of course, and these things went in for tonnage, for dinosaurs and mastodon and such. But there are so many of us! Small as we are, we may be getting to the point where we'll be worth their while.

Dinosaur Pliés
by
R. V. Branham

With only a handful of elegant and intricate stories like the one that follows, R. V. Branham has established a reputation for himself in the last couple of years as a writer to watch, and as one of the most distinctive and original new voices in SF. Branham's fiction has appeared in Asimov's Science Fiction, Midnight Graffiti, Full Spectrum, Writers of the Future, *and others, and at last report he was at work on a novel. Born in Calexico, California, he put in stints as an assistant X-ray technician, a rape crisis counselor, and an engineering research consultant on his way to becoming a writer.*

Here he gives us a wry, tongue-in-cheek, and not *very likely look at what dinosaur culture might have been like . . .*

* * *

An Introduction

Welcome to audition and placement examinations for the Academy of Mesozoic Dance, First Year Forms. Applications are open to any dinosaur between two and six years of age, and must be stamped by a *parent*. (Biological parent only. No Guardians, except for Orphans *or* Parricides. If one has questions, one should wait until *after* the examination results are announced.)

As with years past, we shall use *Le Sacre du Printemps* for ambience.

And may the better dinosaur rip the flesh of the lesser, figuratively speaking of course.

Adolescent Dances

Will the Hadrosaurs—yes, *all duckbills*, please come to the bars as one's name is announced: Parasaurolophus, Lambeosaurus, Saurolophus, Corythosaur.

Please, Madame Maiasaurus! One must either watch impartially or be asked to leave! We do not want to have to resort to calling in Officer Rex, now do we?

Excuse me, girls.

When I call out a position, it will be executed punctually and without inquiry. Are we understood? Failure to follow instructions accurately may result in immediate disqualification.

Okay! Now—music, please! Girls: Demiplié, all positions, *except* the third. *Very* good. Watch your heads, use the second position of the head until told otherwise. *Mademoiselle Lambeosaurus, must one be reminded that one is not holding a violin?* Watch those positions *ouvertes*, Mademoiselle Corythosaur . . . do not separate the feet so wide. This is the *Dance*, not the ablution. Five poses *derrières*, followed by ten poses *devants*. Please give it more than your all, better than your very best.

And what is the meaning of this?!

Dress Rehearsal Abduction

Who's responsible for this?!

Who let those Heterodontosauruses in, the randy buggers!?

Girls, come back! Where is Officer Rex when one needs him?

We might as well continue . . .

Rounds of Spring

Please come to the bars, yes, to the bars, when your name is announced. Now: Mr. Brontosaurus—you changed your

name to *what*? To *Apato*saurus? That all may be fine and
well for your egocentric parents, but it *wiillll* not do for the
Academy, it will not do at all. Mr. *Bronto*saurus, Mesde-
moiselles Stegosaurus and Plateosaurus, Mr. Megalosaurus—
please, members of the audience, one must refrain from fat
jokes, *one must shut up.*

Yes. Music.

Please, young ladies and young gentlemen. Keep a very
wide distance between one's face and one's neighbor's tail.
Speaking of tails, one must be *very very* careful to control
the motions of one's tail during the Dance. It is the essence
of the Dance.

Now! Five grand pliés! Fair—not bad, not good, but not
bad. At all times both head *and* tails in first position. Very
good, it shows pride. Positions *soulevées,* all of them—in
no particular order. Improvise. Think *cloud.*

Better than one would expect. *Interes*ting.

Games of the Rival Neighborhoods

Everyone, being *all applicants*, to the bars! Stretching
exercises! One may play, but no duels, no combat.

We, being your examiner and head of this Academy, will
take a brief break for evaluation considerations.

Again, *behave.* There will be monitors in *our* absence.

The Sagacious Elder's Public Appearance

At this point in our auditions it is customary to wait for the
public appearance of the Sagacious Elder, who founded this,
the Academy of the Mesozoic Dance. But . . . the Elder
never appears. Never has, in anybody's memory. But we are
not barbarians. We wait.

Sixty seconds of quiet meditation, please.

The Earth Adored

And what time is it? Is it time for our lunch break? Is it time yet?

Earth Dance

It is, I believe, time for our lunch break.
    Let us reconvene these auditions in one hour or so.
    Let us now, then, fall upon the earth and feed our faces.

Another Introduction

Welcome back.
    I am sure you have heard some rumors—it being a smallish community—about my departure. Some of them have regarded the theft of some eggs from the hatchery.
    It is not true. And the parties responsible—*we all know who they are*—shall be hearing from my solicitor.
    It is *true*, however, that we are retiring. But not *departing* from this dear circle of friends.
    I can tell, from your restraint, from your lack of response, that you are deeply moved. *We* are deeply moved. One must, we suppose, show dignity.
    This will be our last audition together. Let us strive, together, to make it the best in living memory.

Mysterious Arcs and Secants of the Adolescents

Oh, so our duckbills return, as supplicants, if these garlands indicate anything. We must suppose that one cannot be held to blame when one is being pursued by platoons of paramours.
    But what, we must ask, are these arcs and secants upon the floor of the Dance? Is there a significance oracular, occult? Are they drawings of divinity or of delinquents?

Glorification of the Chosen Candidate

But, girls? You lay these garlands, these offerings, at my feet? It moves me to tears, to be so honored, and by those who will not even be my students (though I do indeed have a decision in their fates, as students of the Dance).

Conjuring the Ancients

It is now time, as tradition dictates, that we introduce our new Mistress. However, during lunch, she suggested a break with custom which would allow me a few more moments of glory.

I have gone over the examination results with our new Mistress, and selections have been made.

These selections will be announced later, at the banquet, to which all and sundry are invited.

So let us, instead, have another sixty seconds of quiet meditation. If not the Elder, then perhaps one of the Ancients may return.

The Ancients Ritual

No Ancients. No rituals.

Perhaps next year there should be a discussion among the Board regarding changing the format of these ceremonies.

Sacred Dance, the Chosen Candidate

Again, to the bars. I have decided to give you your first lesson. Why, some of you may ask, does one need the Dance? After all, it is instinctive with us dinosaurs. Yes and no, because yes you are born with basic techniques and the vocabulary of the Dance, and *no* because you are primi*tive* and *un*refined, with no sense of nuance or subtlety.

Also, there is no place in the Dance for humor, for japes,

for puns. We *heard* that silly joke about us not being *at* the banquet, but *being* the banquet. Jokes about our weight are in *bad* form, and form is the essence of the Dance.

So, let us see some demipliés—I feel like a ringmaster, standing in these rings.

Demipliés, first *and* second positions—*what's this*?

Back to the bars, everyone!

And would our audience be so kind as to return to their seats?

Now. Heads and tails erect, proud! Do not bare your teeth! It is rude to bare your teeth on the dance floor. It is a sort of sacrilege and a definite act of aggression! Do not wag your tails—we only do that when we are hungry. And have we not already had our lunch? Don't wag your tails! Back, we say, back!

For Igor S., Pro Forma

Day of the Hunters
by
Isaac Asimov

*A good case could be made for the proposition that the late Isaac Asimov was the most famous SF writer of the last half of the twentieth century. He was the author of more than three hundred books, including some of the best-known novels in the genre (*The Caves of Steel, I, Robot, *and the* Foundation *trilogy, for example); his last several novels kept him solidly on the nationwide bestseller lists throughout the 1980s; he won two Nebulas and two Hugos, plus the prestigious Grandmaster Nebula; he wrote an enormous number of nonfiction books on a bewilderingly large range of topics, everything from the Bible to Shakespeare, and his many books on scientific matters made him perhaps the best-known scientific popularizer of our time; his nonfiction articles appeared everywhere from* Omni *to* TV Guide; *he was one of the few SF writers whose face was recognizable to the general public, due to his frequent appearances on late-night and daytime talk shows (he even did television commercials)—and he is* also *the only SF writer famous enough to ever have had an SF magazine named after him,* Isaac Asimov's Science Fiction Magazine. *A mere sampling of Asimov's other books, even restricting ourselves to fiction alone (we should probably say, to SF alone, since he was almost as well-known in the mystery field), would include* The Naked Sun, The Stars Like Dust, The Currents of Space, The Gods Themselves, Foundation's Edge, The Robots of Dawn, Robots and Empire, *and* Foundation's Earth. *His most recent fiction titles include two expansions of famous Asimov short stories into novel form,* The Ugly Little Boy *and* Nightfall, *written in collaboration with Robert Silverberg, and his last solo novel,* Forward the Foundation.

Here, with typical inventiveness, Asimov comes up with a

totally different *explanation for the death of the dinosaurs
than the one Simak gave us earlier . . . but one equally
ingenious and, sadly, considering its ominous implications,
perhaps considerably more plausible . . .*

*   *   *

It began the same night it ended. It wasn't much. It just
bothered me; it still bothers me.

You see, Joe Bloch, Ray Manning, and I were squatting
around our favorite table in the corner bar with an evening
on our hands and a mess of chatter to throw it away with.
That's the beginning.

Joe Bloch started it by talking about the atomic bomb,
and what he thought ought to be done with it, and how who
would have thought it five years ago. And I said lots of guys
thought it five years ago and wrote stories about it and it
was going to be tough on them trying to keep ahead of the
newspapers now. Which led to a general palaver on how lots
of screwy things might come true and a lot of for-instances
were thrown about.

Ray said he heard from somebody that some big-shot
scientist had sent a block of lead back in time for about two
seconds or two minutes or two thousandths of a second—he
didn't know which. He said the scientist wasn't saying
anything to anybody because he didn't think anyone would
believe him.

So I asked, pretty sarcastic, how *he* came to know about
it. —Ray may have lots of friends but I have the same lot
and none of them know any big-shot scientists. But he said
never mind how he heard, take it or leave it.

And then there wasn't anything to do but talk about time
machines, and how supposing you went back and killed
your own grandfather or why didn't somebody from the
future come back and tell us who was going to win the next
war, or if there was going to be a next war, or if there'd be
anywhere on Earth you could live after it, regardless of who
wins.

Ray thought just knowing the winner in the seventh race while the sixth was being run would be something.

But Joe decided different. He said, "The trouble with you guys is you got wars and races on the mind. Me, I got curiosity. Know what I'd do if I had a time machine?"

So right away we wanted to know, all ready to give him the old snicker whatever it was.

He said, "If I had one, I'd go back in time about a couple or five or fifty million years and find out what happened to the dinosaurs."

Which was too bad for Joe, because Ray and I both thought there was just about no sense to that at all. Ray said who cared about a lot of dinosaurs and I said the only thing they were good for was to make a mess of skeletons for guys who were dopy enough to wear out the floors in museums; and it was a good thing they did get out of the way to make room for human beings. Of course Joe said that with *some* human beings he knew, and he gives us a hard look, we should've stuck to dinosaurs, but we pay no attention to that.

"You dumb squirts can laugh and make like you know something, but that's because you don't ever have any imagination," he says. "Those dinosaurs were big stuff. Millions of all kinds—big as houses, and dumb as houses, too—all over the place. And then, all of a sudden, like that," and he snaps his fingers, "there aren't any anymore."

How come, we wanted to know.

But he was just finishing a beer and waving at Charlie for another with a coin to prove he wanted to pay for it and he just shrugged his shoulders. "I don't know. That's what I'd find out, though."

That's all. That would have finished it. I would've said something and Ray would've made a crack, and we all would've had another beer and maybe swapped some talk about the weather and the Brooklyn Dodgers and then said so long, and never think of dinosaurs again.

Only we didn't, and now I never have anything on my mind but dinosaurs, and I feel sick.

Because the rummy at the next table looks up and hollers, "Hey!"

We hadn't seen him. As a general rule, we don't go around looking at rummies we don't know in bars. I got plenty to do keeping track of the rummies I do know. This fellow had a bottle before him that was half empty, and a glass in his hand that was half full.

He said, "Hey," and we all looked at him, and Ray said, "Ask him what he wants, Joe."

Joe was nearest. He tipped his chair backward and said, "What do you want?"

The rummy said, "Did I hear you gentlemen mention dinosaurs?"

He was just a little weavy, and his eyes looked like they were bleeding, and you could only tell his shirt was once white by guessing, but it must've been the way he talked. It didn't *sound* rummy, if you know what I mean.

Anyway, Joe sort of eased up and said, "Sure. Something you want to know?"

He sort of smiled at us. It was a funny smile; it started at the mouth and ended just before it touched the eyes. He said, "Did you want to build a time machine and go back to find out what happened to the dinosaurs?"

I could see Joe was figuring that some kind of confidence game was coming up. I was figuring the same thing. Joe said, "Why? You aiming to offer to build one for me?"

The rummy showed a mess of teeth and said. "No, sir. I could but I won't. You know why? Because I built a time machine for myself a couple of years ago and went back to the Mesozoic Era and found out what happened to the dinosaurs."

Later on, I looked up how to spell "Mesozoic," which is why I got it right, in case you're wondering, and I found out that the Mesozoic Era is when all the dinosaurs were doing whatever dinosaurs do. But of course at the time this is just so much double-talk to me, and mostly I was thinking we had a lunatic talking to us. Joe claimed afterward that he knew about this Mesozoic thing, but he'll have to talk lots longer and louder before Ray and I believe him.

But that did it just the same. We said to the rummy to come over to our table. I guess I figured we could listen to him for a while and maybe get some of the bottle, and the others must have figured the same. But he held his bottle tight in his right hand when he sat down and that's where he kept it.

Ray said, "Where'd you build a time machine?"

"At Midwestern University. My daughter and I worked on it together."

He sounded like a college guy at that.

I said, "Where is it now? In your pocket?"

He didn't blink; he never jumped at us no matter how wise we cracked. Just kept talking to himself out loud, as if the whiskey had limbered up his tongue and he didn't care if we stayed or not.

He said, "I broke it up. Didn't want it. Had enough of it."

We didn't believe him. We didn't believe him worth a darn. You better get that straight. It stands to reason, because if a guy invented a time machine, he could clean up millions—he could clean up all the money in the world, just knowing what would happen to the stock market and the races and elections. He wouldn't throw all that away, I don't care what reasons he had. —Besides, none of us were going to believe in time travel anyway, because what if you *did* kill your own grandfather.

Well, never mind.

Joe said, "Yeah, you broke it up. Sure you did. What's your name?"

But he didn't answer that one, ever. We asked him a few more times, and then we ended up calling him "Professor."

He finished off his glass and filled it again very slow. He didn't offer us any, and we all sucked at our beers.

So I said, "Well, go ahead. What happened to the dinosaurs?"

But he didn't tell us right away. He stared right at the middle of the table and talked to it.

"I don't know how many times Carol sent me back—just a few minutes or hours—before I made the big jump. I didn't care about the dinosaurs; I just wanted to see how far the machine would take me on the supply of power I had available. I suppose it was dangerous, but is life so wonderful? The war was on then—One more life?"

He sort of coddled his glass as if he was thinking about things in general, then he seemed to skip a part in his mind and keep right on going.

"It was sunny," he said, "sunny and bright; dry and hard. There were no swamps, no ferns. None of the accoutrements of the Cretaceous we associate with dinosaurs,"—anyway, I think that's what he said. I didn't always catch the big words, so later on I'll just stick in what I can remember. I checked all the spellings, and I must say that for all the liquor he put away, he pronounced them without stutters.

That's maybe what bothered us. He sounded so familiar with everything, and it all just rolled off his tongue like nothing.

He went on, "It was a late age, certainly the Cretaceous. The dinosaurs were already on the way out—all except those little ones, with their metal belts and their guns."

I guess Joe practically dropped his nose into the beer altogether. He skidded halfway around the glass, when the professor let loose that statement sort of sadlike.

Joe sounded mad. "*What* little ones, with whose metal belts and which guns?"

The professor looked at him for just a second and then let his eyes slide back to nowhere. "They were little reptiles, standing four feet high. They stood on their hind legs with a thick tail behind, and they had little forearms with fingers. Around their waists were strapped wide metal belts, and from these hung guns. —And they weren't guns that shot pellets either; they were energy projectors."

"They were what?" I asked. "Say, when was this? Millions of years ago?"

"That's right," he said. "They were reptiles. They had scales and no eyelids and they probably laid eggs. But they used energy guns. There were five of them. They were on me as soon as I got out of the machine. There must have been millions of them all over Earth—millions. Scattered all over. They must have been the Lords of Creation then."

I guess it was then that Ray thought he had him, because he developed that wise look in his eyes that makes you feel like conking him with an empty beer mug, because a full one would waste beer. He said, "Look P'fessor, millions of them, huh? Aren't there guys who don't do anything but find old bones and mess around with them till they figure out what some dinosaur looked like. The museums are full of these here skeletons, aren't they? Well, where's there one with a metal belt on him? If there were millions, what's become of them? Where are the bones?"

The professor sighed. It was a real, sad sigh. Maybe he realized for the first time he was just speaking to three guys in overalls in a barroom. Or maybe he didn't care.

He said, "You don't find many fossils. Think how many animals lived on Earth altogether. Think how many billions and trillions. And then think how few fossils we find. —And these lizards were intelligent. Remember that. They're not going to get caught in snow drifts or mud, or fall into lava, except by big accident. Think how few fossil men there are—even of these subintelligent apemen of a million years ago."

He looked at his half-full glass and turned it round and round.

He said, "What would fossils show anyway? Metal belts

rust away and leave nothing. Those little lizards were warm-blooded. I *know* that, but you couldn't prove it from petrified bones. What the devil? A million years from now could you tell what New York looks like from a human skeleton? Could you tell a human from a gorilla by the bones and figure out which one built an atomic bomb and which one ate bananas in a zoo?"

"Hey," said Joe, plenty objecting, "any simple bum can tell a gorilla skeleton from a man's. A man's got a larger brain. Any fool can tell which one was intelligent."

"Really?" The professor laughed to himself, as if all this was so simple and obvious, it was just a crying shame to waste time on it. "You judge everything from the type of brain human beings have managed to develop. Evolution has different ways of doing things. Birds fly one way; bats fly another way. Life has plenty of tricks for everything. —How much of your brain do you think you use? About a fifth. That's what the psychologists say. As far as they know, as far as anybody knows, eighty per cent of your brain has no use at all. Everybody just works on way-low gear, except maybe a few in history. Leonardo da Vinci, for instance. Archimedes, Aristotle, Gauss, Galois, Einstein—"

I never heard of any of them except Einstein, but I didn't let on. He mentioned a few more, but I've put in all I can remember. Then he said, "Those little reptiles had tiny brains, maybe quarter-size, maybe even less, but they used it all—every bit of it. Their bones might not show it, but they were intelligent; intelligent as humans. And they were boss of all Earth."

And then Joe came up with something that was really good. For a while I was sure that he had the professor and I was awfully glad he came out with it. He said, "Look, P'fessor, if those lizards were so damned hot, why didn't they leave something behind? Where are their cities and their buildings and all the sort of stuff we keep finding of the cavemen, stone knives and things. Hell, if human beings got the heck off of Earth, think of the stuff *we'd* leave behind us. You couldn't walk a mile without falling over a city. And roads and things."

But the professor just couldn't be stopped. He wasn't even shaken up. He just came right back with, "You're still judging other forms of life by human standards. We build cities and roads and airports and the rest that goes with us—but they didn't. They were built on a different plan. Their whole way of life was different from the ground up. They didn't live in cities. They didn't have our kind of art. I'm not sure what they did have because it was so alien I couldn't grasp it—except for their guns. Those *would* be the same. Funny, isn't it. —For all I know, maybe we stumble over their relics every day and don't even know that's what they are."

I was pretty sick of it by that time. You just *couldn't* get him. The cuter you'd be, the cuter he'd be.

I said, "Look here. How do you know so much about those things? What did you do; live with them? Or did they speak English? Or maybe you speak lizard talk. Give us a few words of lizard talk."

I guess I was getting mad, too. You know how it is. A guy tells you something you don't believe because it's all cockeyed, and you can't get him to admit he's lying.

But the professor wasn't mad. He was just filling the glass again, very slowly. "No," he said, "I didn't talk and they didn't talk. They just looked at me with their cold, hard, staring eyes—snake's eyes—and I knew what they were thinking, and I could see that they knew what I was thinking. Don't ask me how it happened. It just did. Everything. I knew that they were out on a hunting expedition and I knew they weren't going to let me go."

And we stopped asking questions. We just looked at him, then Ray said, "What happened? How did you get away?"

"That was easy. An animal scurried past on the hilltop. It was long—maybe ten feet—and narrow and ran close to the ground. The lizards got excited. I could feel the excitement in waves. It was as if they forgot about me in a single hot flash of blood lust—and off they went. I got back in the machine, returned, and broke it up."

It was the flattest sort of ending you ever heard. Joe made a noise in his throat. "Well, what happened to the dinosaurs?"

"Oh, you don't see? I thought it was plain enough. —It was those little intelligent lizards that did it. They were hunters—by instinct and by choice. It was their hobby in life. It wasn't for food; it was for fun."

"And they just wiped out all the dinosaurs on the Earth?"

"All that lived at the time, anyway; all the contemporary species. Don't you think it's possible? How long did it take us to wipe out bison herds by the hundred million? What happened to the dodo in a few years? Supposing we really put our minds to it, how long would the lions and the tigers and the giraffes last? Why, by the time I saw those lizards there wasn't any big game left—no reptile more than fifteen feet maybe. All gone. Those little demons were chasing the little, scurrying ones, and probably crying their hearts out for the good old days."

And we all kept quiet and looked at our empty beer bottles and thought about it. All those dinosaurs—big as houses—killed by little lizards with guns. Killed for fun.

Then Joe leaned over and put his hand on the professor's shoulder, easylike, and shook it. He said, "Hey, P'fessor, but if that's so, what happened to the little lizards with the guns? Huh? —Did you ever go back to find out?"

The professor looked up with the kind of look in his eyes that he'd have if he were lost.

"You still don't see! It was already beginning to happen to them. I saw it in their eyes. They were running out of big game—the fun was going out of it. So what did you expect them to do? They turned to other game—the biggest and most dangerous of all—and really had fun. They hunted that game to the end."

"What game?" asked Ray. He didn't get it, but Joe and I did.

"Themselves," said the professor in a loud voice. "They finished off all the others and began on themselves—till not one was left."

And again we stopped and thought about those dinosaurs—big as houses—all finished off by little lizards with guns. Then we thought about the little lizards and how they had to keep the guns going even when there was nothing to use them on but themselves.

Joe said, "Poor dumb lizards."

"Yeah," said Ray, "poor crackpot lizards."

And then what happened really scared us. Because the professor jumped up with eyes that looked as if they were trying to climb right out of their sockets and leap at us. He shouted, "You damned fools. Why do you sit there slobbering over reptiles dead a hundred million years. That was the first intelligence on Earth and that's how it ended. That's *done*. But we're the second intelligence—and how the devil do you think *we're* going to end?"

He pushed the chair over and headed for the door. But then he stood there just before leaving altogether and said: *"Poor dumb humanity! Go ahead and cry about that."*

Herding with the Hadrosaurs

by
Michael Bishop

Michael Bishop is one of the most acclaimed and respected members of that highly talented generation of writers who entered SF in the 1970s. His renowned short fiction has appeared in almost all the major magazines and anthologies, and has been gathered in three collections: Blooded on Arachne, One Winter in Eden, *and* Close Encounters with the Deity. *In 1981 he won the Nebula Award for his novelette "The Quickening," and in 1983 he won another Nebula Award for his novel* No Enemy but Time. *His other novels include* Transfigurations, Stolen Faces, Ancient Days, Catacomb Years, Eyes of Fire, The Secret Ascension, Unicorn Mountain, *and* Count Geiger's Blues. *His most recent novel is the baseball fantasy* Brittle Innings, *which has been optioned for a major motion picture. Bishop and his family live in Pine Mountain, Georgia.*

Here he takes us, in company with a determined scientist, back millions of years for a visit with a group of hadrosaurs—a voyage of discovery that turns out to be full of surprises for both *sets of creatures . . .*

* * *

In '08, my parents—Pierce and Eulogy Gregson of Gipsy, Missouri—received permission to cross the geologic time-slip west of St. Joseph. They left in a wood-paneled New Studebaker wagon, taking provisions for one month, a used 'Zard-Off scent-generator, and, of course, their sons, sixteen-year-old Chad (me) and five-year-old Cleigh, known to all as "Button." Our parents rejected the security of a caravan because Daddy had only contempt for "herders," detested taking orders from external authority, and was sure that when we homesteaded our new Eden beyond the temporal divide, reptile men, claim jumpers, and other scalawags would show up to murder and dispossess us. It struck him as politic to travel alone, even if the evident dangers of the Late Cretaceous led most pioneers to set forth in groups.

That was Pierce Gregson's first, biggest, and, I suppose, last mistake. I was almost a man (just two years away from the vote and only an inch shy of my adult height), and I remember everything. Sometimes, I wish I didn't. The memory of what happened to our folks only two days out from St. Jo, on the cycad-clotted prairie of the old Dakotas, pierces me yet. In fact, this account is a eulogy for our folks and a *cri de coeur* I've been holding back for almost thirty years.

(Sweet Seismicity, let it shake my pain.)

The first things you notice crossing over, when agents of the World Time-Slip Force pass you through the discontinuity locks, are the sharp changes in temperature and humidity. The Late Cretaceous was—in many places, at least—hot and moist. So TSF officials caution against winter, spring, or fall crossings. It's best to set out, they say, in late June, July, or August, when atmospheric conditions in northwestern Missouri are not unlike those that hold, just beyond the Nebraska drop-off, in the Upper Mesozoic.

Ignoring this advice, we left in February. Still, our New Stu wagon (a sort of a cross between a Conestoga wagon and a high-tech *Ankylosaurus*) plunged us into a strength-sapping steam bath. All our first day, we sweated. Even the sight of clown-frilled *Triceratops* browsing among the magnolia shrubs and the palmlike cycads of the flood plains did nothing to cool our bodies or lift our spirits. It was worse than going to a foreign country knowing nothing of its language or mores—it was like crawling the outback of a bizarre alien planet.

Button lived it. Daddy pretended that the heat, the air, the grotesque fauna—all of which he'd tried to get us ready for— didn't unsettle him. Like turret-gunners, Mama and I kept our eyes open. We missed no chance to gripe about the heat or our wagon's tendency to lurch, steamroller seedling evergreens, and vibrate our kidneys. Daddy, irked, kept his jaw set and his fist on the rubber knob, as if giving his whole attention to steering would allow him to overcome every obstacle, physical or otherwise.

It didn't. On Day Two, twenty or thirty miles from the eastern shore of the Great Inland Sea, we were bumping along at forty-five or fifty mph when two tyrannosaurs— with thalidomide forelegs dangling like ill-made prosthetic hooks—came shuffle-waddling straight at us out of the north.

Sitting next to Daddy, Button hooted in delight. Behind him, I leaned into my seat belt, gaping at the creatures in awe.

The tyrannosaurs were stop-motion Hollywood mockups— except that, gleaming bronze and cordovan in the ancient sunlight, they weren't. They were alive, and, as we all soon realized, they found our wagon profoundly interesting.

"Isn't that 'Zard-Off thing working?" Mama cried.

Daddy was depressing levers, jiggling toggles. "It's on, it's on!" he said. "They shouldn't be coming!"

The scent generator in our wagon was supposed to aspirate an acrid mist into the air, an odor repugnant to saurians, carnivores and plant-eaters alike.

But these curious T-kings were approaching anyway— proof, Mama and I decided, that our scent-generator, a secondhand model installed only a few hours before our departure, was a dud. And it was just like Daddy, the biggest of scrimps, to have paid bottom dollar for it, his perfectionism in matters not money-grounded now disastrously useless.

"Daddy, turn!" I shouted. "We can outrun them!"

To give him credit, Daddy had already ruddered us to the right and was squeezing F-pulses to the power block with his thumb. The plain was broad and open, but dotted with palmate shrubs, many of which looked like fluted pillars crowned by tattered green umbrella segments; we ran right over one of the larger cycads in our path before we'd gone thirty yards. Our wagon tilted on two side wheels, tried to right itself, and, failing that, crashed down on its passenger box with a drawn-out *KRRRRR-ack!*

Mama screamed, Daddy cursed, Button yowled like a vivisected cat. I was deafened, dangling in an eerie hush from my seat belt. And then Button, upside-down, peered quizzically into my face while mouthing, urgently, a battery of inaudible riddles.

Somehow, we wriggled out. So far as that goes, so did Daddy and Mama, although it would have been better for them—for all of us—if we had just played turtle.

In fact, our folks undoubtedly struggled free of the capsized wagon to *look for* Button and me. What Button and I saw, huddled behind an umbrella shrub fifty yards away, was that awkward but disjointedly agile pair of T-kings. They darted at Mama and Daddy and seized them like rag dolls in their stinking jaws, one stunned parent to each tyrannosaur.

Then the T-kings—lofty, land-going piranhas—shook our folks unconscious, dropped them to the ground, crouched on their mutilated bodies with crippled-looking foreclaws, and vigorously tore into them with six-inch fangs.

At intervals, they'd lift their huge skulls and work their lizardly nostrils as if trying to catch wind of something tastier. Button and I, clutching each other, would glance away. Through it all, I cupped my hand over Button's mouth to keep him from crying out. By the time the T-kings had finished their meal and tottered off, my palm was lacerated from the helpless gnashing of Button's teeth.

And there we were, two scared human orphans in the problematic Late Cretaceous.

Every year since recrossing the time-slip, I see a report that I was a feral child, the only human being in history to have been raised by a nonmammalian species. In legend and literature, apes, wolves, and lions sometimes get credit for nurturing lost children, but no one is idiot enough to believe that an alligator or a Komodo dragon would put up with a human child any longer than it takes to catch, chew, and ingest it. No one should.

On the other hand, although I, Chad Gregson, was too old to be a feral child, having absorbed sixteen years of human values at the time of our accident, my little brother Cleigh, or Button, wasn't. And, indeed, it would probably not be wrong to say that, in quite a compelling sense, he was raised by hadrosaurs.

I did all I could to pick up where our folks had left off, but the extended tribe of duckbills—*Corythosaurus*—with whom we eventually joined also involved themselves in Button's parenting, and I remain grateful to them. But I jump ahead of myself. What happened in the immediate aftermath of our accident?

Button and I lay low. A herd of *Triceratops* came snuffling through the underbrush, grunting and browsing. Overhead, throwing weird shadows on the plains, six or seven pterosaurs—probably vulturelike *Quetzalcoatli*—circled our wagon's wreck on thermal updrafts, weighing the advisability of dropping down to pick clean the bones of Pierce and Eulogy Gregson. They stayed aloft, for the departed T-kings may have still been fairly near, so Button and I likewise stayed aloof.

Until evening, that is. Then we crept to the wagon—I held on to Button to keep him from trying to view the scattered, collopy bones of our folks—and unloaded as much gear as we could carry: T-rations, two wooden harmonicas, some extra all-cotton clothing, a sack of seed, etc. TSF officials allowed no synthetic items (even 'Zard-Off was an organic repellent, made from a Venezuelan herb) to cross a time-slip, for after an early period of supply-dependency, every pioneer was expected to "live off the land."

A wind blew down from the north. Suddenly, surprisingly, the air was no longer hot and moist; instead, it was warm and arid. We were on a Dead Sea margin rather than in a slash-and-burn Amazonian clearing. Our sweat dried. Hickories, oaks, and conifers grew among the horsetails along the meander of a river by the Great Inland Sea. Button and I crept through the glowing pastels of an archaic sunset, looking for fresh water (other than that sloshing in our leather botas) and shelter.

Which is how, not that night but the following dawn, we bumped into the hadrosaurs that became our new family: a lambeosaurine tribe, each creature bearing on its ducklike head a hollow crest, like the brush on a Roman centurion's helmet.

Becoming family took a while, though, and that night, our first beyond the divide without our parents, Button snuggled into my lap in a stand of cone-bearing evergreens, whimpering in his dreams and sometimes crying out. Small furry creatures moved about in the dark, trotting or waddling as their unfamiliar bodies made them—but, bent on finding food appropriate to their size, leaving us blessedly alone. Some of these nocturnal varmints, I understood, would bring forth descendants that would evolve into hominids that would evolve into men. As creepy as they were, I was glad to have them around—they clearly knew when it was safe for mammals to forage. Q.E.D.: Button and I had to be semisafe, too. "Where are we?" Button asked when he awoke.

"When are we?" or *"Why are we here?"* would have been better questions, but I told Button that we were hiding from the giant piranha lizards that had killed Daddy and Mama. Now, though, we had to get on with our lives.

About then, we looked up and spotted a huge camouflage-striped *Corythosaurus*—green, brown, burnt yellow—standing on its hind legs, embracing a nearby fir with its almost graceful arms. With its goosy beak, it was shredding needles, grinding them into meal between the back teeth of both jaws. Behind and beyond it foraged more *Corytho-*

sauri, the adults nearly thirty feet tall, the kids anywhere from my height to that of small-town lampposts. Some in the hadrosaur herd locomoted like bent-over kangaroos; others had taken the posture of the upright colossus before us.

Button began screaming. When I tried to cover his mouth, he bit me. *"They wanna eat us!"* he shrieked even louder. *"Chad—please, Chad!—don't let them eat me!"*

I stuffed the hem of a cotton tunic into Button's mouth and pinned him down with an elbow the way the T-kings, yesterday, had grounded our folks' corpses with their claws. I, too, thought we were going to be eaten, even though the creature terrifying Button had to be a vegetarian. It and its cohorts stopped feeding. In chaotic unison, they jogged off through the grove on their back legs, their fat, sturdy, conical tails counter-balancing the weight of their crested skulls.

"They're gone," I told Button. "I promise you, they're gone. Here—eat this."

I snapped a box of instant rice open under his nose, poured some water into it, and heated the whole shebang with a boil pellet. Sniffling, Button ate. So did I. Thinking, "safety in numbers," and setting aside the fact that T-kings probably ate duckbills when they couldn't find people, I pulled Button up and made him trot along behind me after the *Corythosauri*.

In a way, it was a relief to be free of the twenty-second century. (And, God forgive me, it was something of a relief to be free of our parents. I *hurt* for them. I *missed* them. But the possibilities inherent in the Late Cretaceous, not to mention its dangers, pitfalls, and terrors, seemed crisper and brighter in our folks' sudden absence.)

The asteroid that hit the Indian Ocean in '04, gullywashing the Asian subcontinent, Madagascar, and much of East Africa, triggered the tidal waves that drowned so many coastal cities worldwide. It also caused the apocalyptic series of earthquakes that sundered North America along a jagged north-south axis stretching all the way from eastern Louisiana to central Manitoba.

These catastrophic seismic disturbances apparently produced the geologic divide, the Mississippi Valley Time-Slip, fracturing our continent into the ruined Here-and-Now of the eastern seaboard and the anachronistic There-and-Then of western North America. Never mind that the West beyond this discontinuity only existed in fact over sixty-five million years ago. Or that you can no longer visit modern California because California—along with twenty-one other western states and all or most of six western Canadian provinces—has vanished.

It's crazy, the loss of half a modern continent and of every person living there before the asteroid impact and the earthquakes, but you can't take a step beyond the divide without employing a discontinuity lock. And when you do cross, what you see is fossils sprung to life, the offspring of a different geologic period. In Europe, Asia, Africa, South America, Australia, Antarctica, it's much the same—except that the time-slips in those places debouch on other geologic time divisions: the Pleistocene, the Paleocene, the Jurassic, the Silurian, etc.

We're beginning to find that many parts of the world we used to live in are, temporally speaking, vast subterranean galleries in which our ancestors, or our descendants, stride like kings and we are unwelcome strangers. I survived my time in one such roofless cavern, but even if it meant losing Button to the Late Cretaceous forever, I'd be delighted to see all our world's cataclysm-spawned discontinuities melt back into normalcy tomorrow. . . .

The *Corythosauri* were herding. The tribe we'd just met flowed into several other tribes, all moving at a stately clip up through Saskatchewan, Alberta, and the northeastern corner of old British Columbia. Button and I stayed with them because, in our first days beyond the divide, we saw no other human pioneers and believed it would be more fun to travel with some easy-going nonhuman natives than to lay claim to the first plot of likely-looking ground we stumbled across.

Besides, I didn't want to begin farming yet, and the pace set by the duckbills was by no stretch burdensome—fifteen to twenty miles a day, depending on the vegetation available and the foraging styles of the lead males.

It was several weeks before we realized that the *Corythosauri*, along with six or seven other species of duckbill and a few distant groups of horned dinosaurs, were migrating. We supposed—well, *I* supposed, Button being little more than a dumbstruck set of eyes, ears, and boyish tropisms—only that they were eating their way through the evergreens, magnolias, and cycad shrubs along routes well-worn by earlier foragers.

Where, I wondered, were our human predecessors? The time-slip locks at St. Joseph and other sites along the divide had been open two full years, ever since Tharpleton and Sykora's development of cost-effective discontinuity gates. To date, over 100,000 people had reputedly used them. So where was everyone? A few, like our parents, had met untimely deaths. Others had made the crossing elsewhere. Still others had headed straight for the Great Inland Sea—to trap pelicanlike pterosaurs, train them on leads, and send them out over the waters as captive fishers. It beat farming, said some returning pioneers, and the westerly salt breezes were always lovely. In any event, Button and I trailed our duckbills a month before happening upon another human being.

How did we become members of the *Corythosaurus* family? Well, we stayed on the lumbering creatures' trail every day and bedded down near them every night. At first, sighting us, the largest males—like four-legged, thirty-foot-tall woodwinds—would blow panicky bassoon notes through the tubes winding from their nostrils through the mazelike hollows in their mohawk crests. These musical alarms echoed back and forth among the tribe, alerting not only our family but every other nearby clan of hadrosaurs to a possible danger. At first, this was flattering, but, later, simply frustrating.

Button got tired of dogging the *Corythosauri*. They stank, he said, "like the snake house in the St. Louis Zoo." He griped about all the mushy green hadrosaur patties along our route. He said that the insects bumbling in clouds around the duckbills—gnats, flies, a few waspish pollinators—were better at "poking our hides than theirs." He whined that we couldn't "become duckbills because we don't eat what they eat!" And he was right. We were living on T-rations, tiny rodentlike mammals that I caught when they were most sluggish, and the pulpy berries of strange shrubs. We often had tight stomachs, loose bowels, borderline dehydration.

But I kept Button going by ignoring his gripes, by seeing to it that he ate, and by carrying him on my shoulders. Weirdly, it was after hoisting him onto my shoulders that the duckbills stopped running from us at first sight. By that trick, we ceased being two bipedal strangers and became a single honorary hadrosaur.

When he sat on my shoulders, Button's dilapidated St. Louis Cardinals baseball cap gave us both the crest and the bill we needed to pass as one of their youngsters. Then, in fact, the *Corythosauri* let us travel at the heart of their group, with all the other juveniles. There, we were relatively secure from the flesh-eaters—*T. rex, Daspletosaurus*, and *Albertosaurus*—that would track us through the Dakota flood plains or try to intercept us in the lush Canadian woods.

The *Corythosauri* did a lot of noisy bassooning. They did it to warn of predators, to let the members of other duckbill clans—*Parasaurolophus, Hypacrosaurus, Maiasaura*, etc.— know of their nearness (probably to keep them from trespassing on their foraging grounds), and to chase off rival duckbills or timid carnivores.

Button and I took part in some of these performances

with our wooden harmonicas. I'd sound a few notes, echoing the call of an upright male in a register too high to make the imitation precisely accurate, and Button would blow an impromptu score of discordant notes that, totally silencing our duckbill kin, would drift across the landscape like the piping of a drunken demigod.

Anyway, by the time we had hiked almost five hundred miles, we were adopted members of the family. Or, rather, one adopted member when Button rode my shoulders, but tolerated hangers-on when he didn't. Trapping small mammals, picking berries, and digging up tubers that we could clean and eat (our T-rations ran out on the twenty-seventh day), we scurried about under the duckbills' feet, but made ourselves such fixtures in their lives that none of the creatures had any apparent wish to run us off.

Thus, we came to recognize individuals, and Button—when I asked him to name the creatures—gave most of them the names of his favorite anserine or ducky characters: Daffy, Mother Goose, Howard, Donald, Daisy, Huey, Dewey, Louie, Scrooge McDuckbill. Adult females, because of their bulk, got monikers like Bertha, Mama Mountain, Beverly Big, Hulga, and Quaker Queen. (I helped with some of these.) We spent the better parts of three days baptizing our *Corythosauri*. Button had such a good time that he wanted me to help him come up with last names, too. I protested that we'd never be able to remember them all. When Button began to sulk, I told him to do the stupid naming himself.

Anyway, we wound up with three McDuckbills, some O'Mallards, a Gooseley, and a covy of Smiths: Daffy Smith, Mama Mountain Smith, Hulga Smith, etc. If, that is, I remember the baptisms correctly. On the other hand, how could I forget any aspect of the most vivid period of my life?

About a month into our trek, we ran into Duckbill Jay McInturff and Bonehead Brett Easley, self-proclaimed "dinosaur men," hunters who traded "lizard beef" and "gator skins"—welcome supplements to a marine-based economy—to the people in the fishing villages along the northern coastal arc of the Great Inland Sea.

We ran into them because they leapt from the forest through which we were hiking and filled Dewey O'Mallard, a lissome juvenile, with handmade arrows. They shot their arrows, fletched with *Hesperornis* feathers, from polished bows fashioned from *Centrosaurus* ribs and strung with rodent gut. The other duckbills yodeled in dismay, reared, thrashed their tails, and trotted off bipedally in twelve different directions at once. I'd been walking four or five animals behind Dewey, with Button on my shoulders, and when Dewey trumpeted and fell, causing general panic, I simply froze.

The dinosaur men emerged from their natural blinds to butcher Dewey. When they saw Button and me, they started. Then they began asking questions. I took Button, now crying hysterically, from my shoulders. He spat at the men and ran off into the woods. I would have chased him, but the shorter of the two men caught my arm and squeezed it threateningly.

I spent that night with the two dinosaur men. They made camp near Dewey's corpse, tying me to a cycad with a rope of hand-woven horsetail fibers. Why were they tying me? Why weren't they helping me find Button? As they field-dressed Dewey, I shouted, *"Button, come back!"* realizing, even as I yelled, that it would be stupid for him to return to the uncertain situation he had instinctively fled. I shut up.

McInturff and Easley, who had politely introduced themselves, built a fire and roasted over it a white-skinned portion of their kill. They tried to get me to eat with them, but I refused, not because I wasn't hungry or despised dinosaur flesh, but because Button and I had *named* Dewey. How could I turn cannibal?

Despite their Wild West nicknames, Duckbill Jay and Bonehead Brett weren't uneducated yahoos. (To receive permission to use a discontinuity lock, you couldn't be.) But they had separated themselves from other pioneers, dressed up in spiked *Nodosaurus*-hide vests, duckbill-skin leggings, and opossum-belly moccasins, and begun a two-man trading company inspired by North America's rugged trappers of the early 1800's. Playing these parts, they had come to believe that a selfish lawlessness was their birthright.

Unable to coax me to eat, McInturff, a slender, sandy-haired man with a splotchy beard, and Easley, a simian gnome with a high, domed forehead, tried to talk me into joining them. They could use another set of hands, and I'd learn to make arrows, shoot a bow, skin *Parkosauri*, butcher duckbills, and sew "fine lizardly duds"—if I let them teach me. They'd also help me find Button so that he, too, could benefit from their woodsy self-improvement program.

I talked to the hunters, without agreeing to this proposal. So they began to ignore me. Easley left the clearing and returned a little later with a half-grown panoplosaur to which was rigged a travois. On this sled, they piled the hide, bones, and butchered flesh of Dewey, after conscientiously treating the meat with sea salt. Then they ambled over to the cycad to which I was bound.

"Any idea where those flute-crests of yours happen to be going, Master Gregson?" McInturff said.

"No, sir."

"Four months from now, the middle of June, they'll hit the Arctic rim, the shore of what Holocene-huggers used to call the Beaufort Sea."

"Holocene-huggers?"

"Stay-at-homes," Easley said. "Baseline-Lubbers."

"You want to traipse eighteen hundred more miles, kid? That's what's in store for you."

"Why?" I said. "Why do they go there?"

"It's a duckbill rookery," McInturff said. "A breeding site. Quite a ways to go to watch a bunch of lizards screw."

"Or," Easley said, "you could link up with some bone-heads in the Yukon and tail them across the land bridge into Old Mongolia."

"Where are we now?" I asked.

"Montana," McInturff said. "If Montana existed."

"Its relative vicinity," Easley said. "Given tectonic drift, beaucoups of climatic changes, and the passage of several million years."

I had no idea what to reply. The dinosaur men put out their fire, lay down under the chaotically arrayed stars, drifted off to sleep. Or so I thought. For, shortly after lying down, McInturff and Easley arose again, walked over, unbound my hands, and, in the alien woods, far from any human settlement, took turns poking my backside. I repeatedly cried out, but my tormentors only laughed. When dawn came, they debated whether to kill me or leave me tied up for a passing carnivore. They decided that the second option would free them of guilt and give a human-size predator—a dromaeosaur or a stenonychosaur—several hours of amusing exercise.

"Wish you'd change our mind," Bonehead Brett Easley said. He prodded the sleepy panoplosaur out of its doze.

"Yeah, Master Gregson," Duckbill Jay McInturff said. "We could make good use of you."

Guffawing, they left. The woods moved with a hundred balmy winds. A half hour after the dinosaur men had vanished, Button came running into the clearing to untie me.

It took us most of the day, but using the telltale spoors of shredded vegetation and sour-smelling *Corythosaurus* patties, we tracked our family—Scrooge McDuckbill, Mama Mountain Smith, etc.—to a clearing in the Montana forest. There we tried to rejoin them. But our arrival spooked them, and it was two more days, Button on my shoulders like a tiny maharajah, before we could catch up again, reconvince the duckbills of our harmlessness, and resume our communal trek northwestward.

Long-distance dinosaurs, I reflected. We're going to walk all the way to the Arctic rim with them. Why?

Because the Gregsons had always been loners, because I

had good reason not to trust any of the human beings over here, and because we had already forged a workable bond with our "flute crests." Besides, I didn't want to homestead, and there was no one around—close to hand, anyway—to tell us we couldn't attempt anything we damned well pleased.

So Button and I traveled on foot all the way to a beautiful peninsula on the Beaufort Sea, where we heard the duckbills bassoon their melancholy lovesongs and watched hundreds of giant lizards of several different species languidly screw. The males' upright bodies struggled athwart the females' crouching forms, while the tribes' befuddled juveniles looked on almost as gaped-beaked as Button and I. The skies were bluer than blue, the breezes were softer than mammal fur, and the orgasmic bleats of some of the lovesick duckbills were like thunder claps.

Button was dumbstruck, fascinated.

"Sex education," I told him. "Pay attention. Better this way than a few others I can think of."

The males in the mild Arctic forest blew rousing solos and showed off their crests. Those with the deepest voices and the most elaborate skull ornaments were the busiest, reproductively speaking, but there were so many dinosaurs in the rim woods, foraging and colliding, that in less than a month Button and I could see through the shredded gaps as if a defoliant had been applied. We saw boneheads—macho pachycephalosaurs half the size of our duckbills banging their helmeted-looking skulls in forest sections already wholly stripped of undergrowth. The clangor was spooky, as were the combatants' strategic bellows.

Button and I stayed out of the way, fishing off the coast, gathering berries, trapping muskratlike creatures on the banks of muddy inlets, and keeping a lookout for the human hunters that prowled the edges of the herbivore breeding grounds. We did well staying clear of godzillas like *T. rex* and the *Daspletosaurs*, but, more than once, we narrowly avoided being kicked to tatters by an eleven-foot-tall midnight skulker called—I've since learned—*Dromiceiomimus*. Resembling a cross between an ostrich and a chameleon, this beast could run like the anchor on a relay team. And so Button and I began weaving tree platforms and shinnying upstairs to sleep out of harm's way.

Sexed out and hungry for fresh vegetation, our *Corythosaurus* clan stayed in its breeding haunts only until late July, at which time Scrooge McDuckbill, Daffy Smith, and Donald Gooseley led the group southeastward. Button and I, more comfortable with these lummoxy herbivores than apart from them, tagged along again.

In October, catching the placental odor of the Great Inland Sea, the gravid females (including Quaker Queen, Beverly Big, Mama Mountain, Hulga, Bertha, and several demure ladies from clans that had joined us after our run-in with McInturff and Easley) split off from the unperturbed males and led their youngsters into a coastal region of northern Montana. We went with the females rather than with the males because the females, seeing Button and me as one more gawky kid, matter-of-factly mother-henned us on this journey. Their bodies gave us protection, while their clarinet squeaks and oboe moans offered frankly unambiguous advice.

Then, at an ancestral hatching ground, they dug out mud-banked nests that had fallen in, or fashioned new nests near the old ones. Working hard, the ladies built these nests at least a body-length apart; each nest was about eight feet in diameter and four feet deep at the center of its bowl. When the nests were complete, the female duckbills squatted above the bowls and carefully deposited their eggs (as few as twelve, as many as twenty-four) in concentric rings inside the drying pits. Then they left, cropped ferns and other plant materials, waddled back, and conscientiously covered their tough-skinned eggs.

Although I tried to discourage him, warning that he could get trampled or sat upon, Button got involved. He carried dripping loads of vegetation back to the hatching grounds to help Beverly Big and Quaker Queen incubate their lizard-lings. And when their eggs broke open and baby hadrosaurs poked their beaked noggins out, Button not only helped the mama duckbills feed them, but sometimes crawled into the muck-filled nests and hunkered among the squeaking youngsters. No mother seemed to resent his presence, but what *almost* cured Button of this behavior was having Quaker Queen drop a bolus of well-chewed fruit on him. Even that accident didn't keep him from stalking the mud bridges between nests, though, watching and waiting as our dinosaur siblings rapidly grew.

Button and I stayed with our *Corythosauri* for more than three years (if "years" beyond a discontinuity divide have any meaning). We migrated seasonally with our duckbill family, going from south to north in the "winter" and from north to south toward the end of "summer." We saw the hadrosaurs mate in their breeding grounds, and, after the females had laid their eggs, we stayed in the muddy hatching grounds like bumbling midwives-in-training.

On each seasonal trek, we saw animals for whom we had developed great affection—Daffy, Bertha, a host of name-less youngsters—run down and murdered by the T-kings and the *Albertosauri* that opportunistically dogged our marches. During our third year with the duckbills, in fact, I figured out that only sixty-four of over eight hundred hatchlings made it out of the nest and less than half the survivors reached the Arctic breeding grounds with their adult relatives. Agility, stealth, and even simple puniness often saved Button and me, but the hadrosaurs weren't so lucky. Many of those that didn't fall to predators succumbed to parasites, accidents, or mysterious diseases. The forests and uplands of the Late Cretaceous could be beautiful, but life there wasn't always pretty. (Maybe our folks, escaping it so soon, had known true mercy.)

As for human pioneers from the blasted twenty-second century, A.D., Button and I had no desire to consort with them. At times, we saw smoke from their villages; and, on each of our migrations, bands of human nomads, archers in lizard-skin clothing, helped the T-kings cull the weakest members of the herds, whether duckbills, boneheads, fleet-footed hypsilophodonts, or horned dinosaurs. In large bands, though, the archers sometimes risked everything and went after a *Tyrannosaurus*. Once, from a mountainside in eastern Alberta, Button and I watched a dozen Lilliputian archers surround and kill an enraged Gulliver of a T-king. Neither of us was sorry, but it isn't always true that the killer of your greatest enemy is automatically your friend.

McInturff and Easley came into our lives again the year that Button—who had long ago given up talking in favor of playing duckbill calls on his harmonica—turned eight. Along with nine or ten other raiders, they targeted the duckbills' Montana hatching grounds, shooed off as many of the mothers as possible, and killed all those inclined to defend their nests. The men were egg gathering, for reasons I never fully understood—restocking the fishing villages' larders, providing a caulking substance for boats—and Button and I escaped only because the men came into the nesting grounds shouting, banging bones together, and blowing *Triceratops* trumpets. There was no need for stealth; they *wanted* the females to flee. So Button and I hurried out of there along with the more timid hadrosaur mothers.

The next day, I crept back to the area to see what was going on. On a wooded hillside above the main nesting floor, I found an egg that had long ago petrified, hefted it as if it were an ancient cannonball, and duck-walked with it to an overlook where the activity of the nest raiders was all too visible. Easley, his bald pate gleaming like a bleached pachycephalosaur skull, was urging his men to gather eggs more quickly, wrap them in ferns, and stack them gently in their shark-skin sacks.

The sight of Easley's head was an insupportable annoyance. I raised myself to a crouch, took aim, and catapulted my petrified egg straight at his head. The egg dropped like a stone, smashing his skull and knocking him into one of the hollowed-out nests. He died instantly. All his underlings began to shout and scan the hillside. I made no effort to elude discovery. Three or four of them scrambled up the overlook's slope, wrestled me down, secured my hands with horsetail fibers, and frog-marched me back down to the hatching site to meet Duckbill Jay McInturff.

"I remember you," McInturff said. "Brett and I had a chance to kill you once. I'll bet Brett's sorry we didn't do it."

It seemed likely that McInturff would order me killed on the spot, but maybe the presence of so many other men, not all of them as indifferent to judicial process as he, kept him from it. After finishing their egg collecting, they tied my hands at the small of my back, guyed my head erect with a lizard-skin cord knotted to my bindings, and made me walk, dragging behind an ankylosaur travois loaded with egg sacks and another hammocking Easley's corpse.

At a village on the Great Inland Sea, I was locked for at least a week in a tool shed with a dirt floor. Through the holes in its roof, I could sometimes see gulls and pteranodons wheeling.

I had lost my parents, I had lost Button, I had lost our family of hadrosaurs. It seemed clear that McInturff and his egg-hunting cohorts would either hang me from a willow tree or paddle me out to sea and toss me overboard to the archaic fishes or ichthyosaurs that yet remained. I was almost resigned to dying, but I missed Button and feared that, only eight years old, he wouldn't last too long among the harried duckbills.

The last night I spent in the tool shed, I heard a harmonica playing at some distance inland and knew that Button was trying to tell me hello, or good-bye, or possibly "It's all right, brother, I'm still alive." The music ceased quickly, making me doubt I'd really heard it, then played again a little nearer, reconvincing me of Button's well-being, and stopped forever a moment or so later. Button himself made no appearance, but I was glad of that because the villagers would have captured him and sent him back through a discontinuity lock to the Here-and-Now.

That, you see, is what they did to me. The sheriff of Glasgow, the fishing settlement where I was confined, knew a disaffected family who had applied for repatriation. He shipped me with them, trussed like a slave, when they made their journey back toward the Mississippi Valley Time-Slip, just across from St. Jo, Missouri, and the unappealing year known as 2111 A.D. Actually, because of a fast-forward screw-up of some esoteric sort, we recrossed in 2114. Once back, I was tried for Easley's murder in Springfield, found guilty of it on the basis of affidavits from McInturff and several upright egg raiders, and sentenced to twenty-five years in prison. I have just finished serving that sentence.

From the new accounts that sometimes slip back through, Button grew up with the *Corythosauri*. Over there, he's still with them, living off the land and avoiding human contact. It's rumored that, at nineteen, he managed to kill Duckbill Jay McInturff and to catch in deadfalls some of McInturff's idiot henchmen. (God forgive me, I hope he did.)

Because of my murder conviction, I'm ineligible to recross, but more and more people in our desolate century use the locks every year, whether a gate to the Late Cretaceous or a portal on another continent to a wholly different geologic or historical time. This tropism to presumably greener stomping grounds reminds me of the herding and migrating instincts of the dinosaurs with whom Button and I lived so many "years" ago. And with whom Button, of course, is probably living yet.

One gate, I'm told, a discontinuity lock in Siberia, debouches on an epoch in which humanity has been extinct for several million years. I'd like to use that lock and see the curious species that have either outlived us or evolved in our absence. Maybe I will. A document given me on leaving prison notes that this Siberian lock is the only one I am now eligible to use. Tomorrow, then, I intend to put in an application.

Ontogeny Recapitulates Phylogeny

by

R. Garcia y Robertson

Here's another fast-paced and compelling story by R. Garcia y Robertson, whose "The Virgin and the Dinosaur" appeared earlier in this anthology. In this one he keeps us safely in the present—or is it safe? And is the dead past really all that safely dead . . . ?

* * *

Like the marks of a great three-toed bird the dinosaur tracks ran right down the old dead river bed; deep prints of a hunting carnosaur, cut crisply into the hardened mud. Casting caution aside, the scientist crouched down, running her excited fingers over the tracks. Fused metatarsals gave the huge beast that bird-like strut. Carol felt the print and pictured an animal that she had known only from books. The stiff print from the fused foot made identification easy—order *Saurischia,* suborder *Theropoda,* family *Ceratosauridae,* and genus *Ceratosaurus*—a strong, tall killing machine.

Morning light streamed through high canopy and lower foliage, picking out the next print. Estimating stride length, Carol decided she was on the trail of an adult, well over twenty-five feet from stiff tail to shearing teeth. In her mind Carol captured the entire creature; long tail, powerful hind limbs, and a thick neck supporting a massive head, blade-like horn and heavy brow ridges.

Kneeling on the exposed riverbed, Carol felt a vibration in the air, a chill underneath the morning heat. The yellow dust around her was disturbed and broken. Here was a killer that hunted in packs, so why was it stalking alone? Was it old or ill? Where was the great beast headed? Carol tried to

tell from the tracks. Feeling the nearest print she found the
outer edge deeper and broken down. Here the monster
turned a bit, craning its neck to one side. Carol had never
seen a dinosaur duck like that, but she had seen birds in the
wild leave the same mark when they made a ducking and
turning motion. She inspected the next print. Now the toes
dug into the stone. Spotting something, the carnosaur
shifted its weight forward, leaning on its toes, getting ready
to run.

There Carol stopped. She could follow the dinosaur no
further; not until workmen broke up the remaining rocks
covering the old stream bed. The fossil footprints vanished
under a short shelf of more recent marine sediment. She
straightened up slowly, and early morning nausea crept over
her. She would rest, maybe even sleep, and come back when
the work gang had exposed more of the footprints. Perhaps
then Carol would know where the *Ceratosaurus* had gone.

Dividing the vegetation with its flat horn, the carnosaur
poked its head through the tangle at the river's edge, finding
an especially broad clearing beside the shrinking stream. A
centuries old sequoia had come crashing down along the
bank, its shallow roots undermined by ground water. The
fall of that forest titan had taken the smaller trees with it.
Since that time the stream had sunk further, uncovering
wide mud flats, while fast growing things had filled the
clearing. A low green carpet of ferns and horsetails was
broken by an occasional barrel-shaped cycadophyte with
bright flowers and a rich crown of long tough leaves.

Humming insects droned in the hot still air. Wherever
there was a break in the canopy insects came down to feed
on the decay. Little animals would lurk in the thin boundary
between undergrowth and mud flats, drawn by the insects
and the need to drink. Right now the carnosaur's prey might
be there, panting in the heat.

Nothing stirred. Except for the drumming of its huge
heart and rumblings in its belly the carnosaur kept com-

pletely still. Only its head poked into the clearing. Too old
to hunt with the pack, the crafty beast lived on carrion and
small prey. There was not a whiff of carrion in the morning
air and the old carnosaur had not eaten. The smallest bit of
flesh and blood would be welcomed by its starved belly.

A faint shiver ran through the leaves of a cycadophyte.
Something small hid at the edge of the mud flats. The
ceratosaur decided to cut a diagonal across the clearing, an
indirect approach, tempting its prey into false and fatal
movement. Breaking cover, the huge carnivore strutted
upstream on three-toed feet, cutting its victim off from the
tree line. Turning in the mud, the carnosaur dug in its toes.

In the same part of the forest, a hundred and twenty million
years away, Carol bent over a low patch of herbs. Bird song
filtered through jungle canopy, so different from the Upper
Jurassic foliage. The sequoias had all fallen, leaving not a
forest of titans, but a lush barrens supporting few creatures
bigger than a songbird.

The land had both fallen and risen during the last hundred
thousand millennia. The sinking Jurassic plain had become
a shallow sea bottom, and then been thrust back up by
volcanism. Green folds of highland forest hugged a spine of
smoking mountains, peaks standing in solid blue waves
where the sea had been. Only the ferns remained the same,
unchanged by the ages but hidden by a riot of newer
broad-leafed undergrowth. For a blink of time this jungle
had been plantation land. When the bottom fell out of the
coffee market the wilds began reclaiming their own. Vines
and weeds fought for air and light, crowding the coffee
bushes and climbing the tall shade trees. In places this
undergrowth had been cut back to make room for banana
trees and maize fields, but each tiny open space was
enclosed in a great green wall.

While the work gang uncovered more *Ceratosaurus*
tracks Carol was finding wild raspberry. She had spent
almost all her life far from a pharmacy, in jungles stocked

with fever and primitive sanitation. Herbal remedies had been her first medicines, and forty years later she fell back on them. Flows of mud had submerged the dirt road and landing strip. There would be no hospital, no flying doctor here. The nearest village had nothing to offer but chronic dysentery and an aged midwife. The midwife had given Carol the unicorn root in her pocket. Carol half-trusted the herb to be pure, but the root had brought on strange dreams.

She was glad to find wild raspberry, *rubus strigosus;* long used by local Indians to combat nausea, and as a uterine tonic. This double purpose was significant, since Carol knew that her particular morning sickness was early pregnancy. Carol even knew precisely how pregnant she was. The baby could only be the result of a single bout of unsafe sex the night she left New York. Could she call it a baby? Carol was a scientist, and knew life came in stages. What was in her would hardly look human under a dissecting scope.

Had she not been leaving New York the baby would never have happened. Carol wished she had the charm or beauty to keep men. The prospect of flying off always gave her courage. Leaving town, the States, and phone service, said "No complications" loud and clear. So now she was alone, far from civilization, with the ultimate complication. A biologist will tell you that the chances of two humans conceiving in a single night are low, but a paleontologist lives by much more minute odds. A fossil is far rarer than conception. Multitudes live and die, never leaving their mark on a rock. Finding a sharp set of *Ceratosaurus* prints so far south was a major discovery, a missing link between Mesoamerican shale and the Morrison Formation of the northern plains.

Standing among the green growing things, with new life growing inside her, Carol still felt very alone. In the summer the forest teemed with Ivy League students, young graduate anthropologists imitating the Indians and despising the Spanish-speaking middle class. By now they had flown back to their upper class homes and fall semesters. The autumn rains had come, drowning the roads in mud, swamping the dirt airfield, stranding Carol among the Indians. Even when the students were there Carol had felt cut off. She was a generation ahead of them and a working scientist, a bottom of the heap paleontologist, turning over rocks in the wilds and trading her findings for modest grants. Each year it became harder, competing with younger fossil hunters equipped with echo amplifiers and electronic strata maps.

Carol had only wits and experience, and that bit of clairvoyance that lets a good bone hunter see through the rocks into ages past. Trained intuition told her she was close to a big bone bed. She had seen only tracks, but marks in the mud convinced her that there had been surface pools and plenty of ground water. Downstream she guessed there had been quicksand. There she expected to find the soft spots where bones collected from carcasses washed down by floods, or thirsty creatures caught in the mud. Carol had seen such bone reefs, but never found one all her own. Now she needed such a find desperately, to justify this trip into the jungle, to pay for the baby.

Training, wit, and intuition had not prepared Carol for a baby. A forty-year-old only child, she never had children, sisters, brothers, nor nieces and nephews. Her own childhood had been among strangers. Carol's parents had been anthropologists, studying and living with little known peoples on three continents. Carol had worn loincloth diapers and run barefoot with village children. Her baby talk had been a mix of forgotten tongues. The languages kept changing, but she was always the different one, the one with white skin. Even when she was old enough for boarding school in the States, she was still the stranger, the one who did not know the pop stars and could only swear in Swahili. Carol never had her parents' way with people, so she turned her attention to old bones and life long ago turned to stone.

Now she was no longer the barefoot little white girl

running through the jungle. Walking made her weary. After a life on her feet it seemed unfair that her steps should now come harder. With unicorn root in her pocket and raspberry leaves for her tea she headed back to her tent, skirting around the dig. Noon was not far off, and the Indians clearing marine sediment from the Mesozoic riverbed would be working slower. Carol would spare them the worry of having their *gringa* boss watching over them. In solitude she brewed her herbs, then tried to make up the sleep that she had lost to strange dreams and morning sickness.

The dream started in amniotic darkness. Carol felt herself shrinking into her abdomen, lying curled within herself listening to the sea surge of her own bloodstream. After many ages a spark of light shone in the distance. The spark grew, fueled by the heat of a young sun. Air came thick and went into her lungs and daylight blazed over a primeval forest bounded by a shrinking river with a wide muddy bed. Tall palms shaded the far bank, and a row of young sequoias towered nearer at hand. Heavy air buzzed with insects, but there were no birds in this forest to scold the hunter and warn the hunted. A web of tiny trails disappeared between the trees. Thirsty heat tugged Carol towards the stream, but fear fought with the urge.

Then she saw it. Hanging as still as the air, half hidden by the pines, a boney head protruded into the clearing. From behind that hideous mask a sharp eye fixed on her. Frozen in her dream she watched the head and horned snout come forward out of the forest. A powerful neck and thick shoulders followed; heavy thighs pushed the plants aside, trodding down horsetails and snapping young trees. This walking tower reached the mud bank, then turned toward her, faster than she thought something so large could move.

Frightened, Carol became aware of her small body. Her oversized eyes seemed at proper height because she was crouching atop a four-foot cycadophyte. Clawed fingers held her there, and a thin tail steadied her. The stiff hairs on her back bristled in terror. The carnivore came one stride closer and Carol was fleeing, leaping off her perch and running blindly along the riverbank.

Dust motes danced in shafts of sunlight above the dank dirt floor. The closeness inside the midwife's shed was stifling. An iron roof trapped the tropic heat even in late September, while chinks in the packing crate walls let in light but not a breath of air. The old midwife sat cross-legged in one dark corner looking lean and withered, her shrunken eyes fierce and hollow. She listened while Carol recounted her dream.

"I discovered that I was a tiny furry animal, hunted by this huge beast. I ran, or tried to run. My legs moved, but the soft mud sucked at my feet. I awoke in a cold sweat despite the noontime sun." Carol stopped and stared at the packed earth, not wanting to look at the haggard woman, tasting the sickly sweetness of waking all over again.

The crone in the corner stirred her tea with a stick. "Women with child have strong dreams. There is more to this or you would not have come back to me."

Tracing a slow line in the oily dirt, Carol continued, "Yes, there is more. I returned to the dig and ordered them to clear away the rock in the direction that the monster was turning. Right where I had been in the dream, between the hunter and the river, we found the tracks of a small mammal. Stamped on top of them were more of the carnosaur's tracks." She shook herself. "How could I have known just what the thing was chasing?"

"How could you have known?" The midwife returned the question to the scientist, bright little eyes peering out from wrinkled flesh.

Carol drew a second line in the dirt, exactly across the first. "The dream began with the baby inside me. I was seeing things through the baby's eyes. Was there something in the unicorn root you gave me, something that would cause dreams?" Her hands went into her pockets, searching for the unicorn root.

The crone made a flat motion that meant "no." She followed the motion with more words. "The unicorn root is pure, but I said a prayer over it. You are old to be having a first child. You came to me afraid. I prayed that you would come closer to the child within you, and know whether the baby is well."

Hands still in her jeans, the scientist looked up from her pattern in the dust, staring back at the tiny bright eyes. "But I dreamed about a little animal long ago."

"The baby inside you is a little animal, a creature still growing. After giving goldenseal I have seen babies that never became human. They came out as worms, or sala-manders, or little animals with big eyes and a tail."

Carol let go of the unicorn root, brought her hand from her pocket and brushed out the pattern in the dirt. "Non-sense, this is an animal of long ago, ages ago. It has been gone so long that the mud has turned to stone."

The crone shook her head. "We all come from ages past, and a little bit is passed on with each generation."

Carol cursed the rains and mud that sealed her off from civilized contact, and civilized medicine. "Oh yes, micro-scopic bits of material are passed on, but not memories."

Laughter rippled through the hut, sharp but soft, like a rippling shroud. "What do you know of memory? You have writing and recording machines to remember for you. You have forgotten memory. I carry the memories of generations in my head. I remember my mother's mother, and her mother's mother. I can tell you the tales of the Temple Builders, and of the time when the Black Robes first came out of the forest. Even in you memory is not dead. Your baby knows neither machines nor paper, and remembers for you. How else could you know that the little animal's tracks would be by the stream?"

The crone stabbed a bony finger at Carol's womb. "Right now your baby is that animal, whether it will ever become human is not mine to say. You want this baby very much, and now it is at risk, even as that little animal is."

"At risk from what?" The scientist stood up, hands hidden again in her pockets, shivering in the heat.

"Perhaps it is your age, perhaps the fever. I cannot say for you. You must sleep to dream again."

"I never want a dream like that again."

Carol left the midwife's hut feeling weak for even listening to that woman. The old woman had no training, no degrees; nothing to recommend her but the awe and respect of *los Indios,* nothing but batches of healthy babies delivered in a dirt-poor village. Still that did not make her a doctor. Carol heard the indignant voice of her own mentor, her *Herr Doctor,* castigating old fables in scornful accents. "Embryology is not evolutionary history. In the last century one could say 'Ontogeny recapitulates phylogeny'—but not so today." Equating growth in the womb with growth of the species was a notion that science had left behind.

She wandered through the afternoon, trying to feel the changes in her body, telling herself that she had a touch of fever, that her hormones were adjusting. Each explanation seemed as silly and puny as the midwife's. The tracks in the rock were hard evidence that she had seen further into the past than she should; no longer making educated guesses, but knowing things that she had no way of knowing. Rationality battled with despair. She wanted the baby with selfish desperation. Her life had been long and lonely. Inside her was someone who would share it; no more one night loves, no more flying away the next day.

Standing by the dig increased her frustration. The two parts of the dig were clearly converging. The original ceratosaur tracks turned straight toward the area where they mixed with the mammal's footprints. Frozen in the stone was the record of a few seconds of time, and it was taking hours to unearth it. The upper layers of marine shale were soft, but the workers had to dig slowly so their tools did not smash the older rock beneath. Carol was almost certain that they would find nothing. A simple movement of the shrinking river, or a flaw in the deposit, would hide what had happened eons ago. They should be searching downstream for the bone bed instead.

Night falls fast in the tropics. When it was too dark to dig by natural light, Carol stood over the work with a lantern. She would not let the workers leave until the two sets of tracks had been joined into a single pattern, and the chase was as clear in the rock as it had been in her dream. Science seemed merely to confirm superstition. She told them to quit work, and ordered that *mañana* they should dig farther downstream and try to find that big bone pile that she so badly needed.

Workers went home to their families, leaving nothing for Carol to do but sit up and wait for dawn. After midnight the village noises died, the last dogs slept silent. Carol sat watching the insects smash and sizzle against her lantern. Still she did not dare sleep for fear of dreaming. Now and again she would look up at the shadows cast on the tent fabric, trying to puzzle out their pattern.

Reaching deep into her pocket she pulled out the unicorn root. Using her bush knife she pared off bits to put in her tea. Science had not helped her. It had only confirmed her fears. Maybe just this once ontogeny was phylogeny, or maybe it was all in her head. None of that mattered. Carol had to get control of what was happening inside her, even if it was only fever, even if it meant giving in to her dreaming.

Carol sipped the unicorn root tea and lay back against her pillow, closing her eyes, too scared to snuff out the hurricane lantern.

The race went on under the heavy Jurassic sky. Thick clouds clung to the treetops, hiding a cruel hot sun. Hunter and hunted dripped with moisture as they ran along the sunken river. Carol scampered across the slimy mud and the stream seemed to rise up, blocking her path. Instinctive fear of water brought her little feet to a halt. Though the current was neither swift nor deep, it could sweep her away. She would thrash about with water clinging to her fur until the hunter's jaws plucked her up and crushed her.

Carol turned. Baring sharp tiny teeth she arched her back, each hair straining to make her look larger. She had let the frightened feet carry her this far. Now she had to take command. Wit and training told her where safety lay. Half waking, half asleep, she forced her dream feet to run downstream, straight at the dinosaur.

Rearing up, the startled carnosaur was framed against the dense white sky, forearms raking the steaming air. Carol saw the horned jaws open, and the rows of knife-sized teeth. She dashed past a huge taloned foot. The head came down, ducking after her, jaws snapping; a huge featherless chicken pecking at an ant. Holding its tail high the carnosaur spun around. Carol's charge had been a surprise, but now it was back to the flat-out chase that only the carnosaur could win.

Carol ran downstream searching for the soft bog. Half her life had been spent looking for bone traps, and she needed one now like never before. The stream widened. The ground quaked as the carnosaur's heavy steps caught up with her. She felt the shudder of a great clawed foot skidding into the mud.

Carol turned again. The carnosaur teetered on the edge of the bog, one leg sinking, three bird-like toes clawing at solid ground, sliding toward the muck. Carol forced her little feet back toward the monster, dancing on thin slime, daring the carnosaur to take another snap at her.

Ancient hatred gleaming in its eyes, the horned head lunged at her. Overbalancing, the huge beast fell fully onto the bog, splattering mud in all directions. Carol stepped back. The struggling wreck tipped slowly over, sinking feet first, tail following. Watching the carnosaur twist and founder, Carol started to lick at her fur coat. The big surging ripples stilled. Buried up to its shoulders in the muck, the horned mask glared back at her. Carol finished cleaning her fur and skipped off across the swampy surface, so happy to be little and alive.

• • •

She awoke to find the hurricane lantern burning uselessly in daylight. Insect bodies lay in a circle of death around the lamp. Her head felt stuffed and she could still taste the terror of her dream. With clothes wrinkled and hair wild Carol stumbled out of the tent. It was already noon, and a mob of happy workers were waiting outside, cheering her emergence, plucking at her sleeves. With broad gestures and broken Spanish they led their disheveled *gringa* down the packed earth trail, past the women patting tortillas, past the rows of decayed coffee plants, into the forest.

The workers would not say what they had found. Confused by their good humor, her questions produced only wide smiles and secreted laughter. Stopping at the edge of the dig, she looked into the rock and saw why they were so happy. There was the bone pile she had hoped to find, a reef of dinosaur bodies mixed together in the fossil mud.

From atop the pile a hideous horned mask glared up at her out of the newly opened shale. Trapped in a distorted dance of death lay the stone skull and twisted neck bones of a huge *Ceratosaurus*. The beast had surely lost its footing and sank into the river mud, sliding down under its own great weight. Kneeling at the edge of the newly opened sepulcher, Carol's body felt at peace; her stomach hungry instead of hollow. After all, there was a baby growing inside her. Young men slapped her back, cracking ribald jokes about spending the money that would come pouring down from *el norte*. Triumphant little omnivores are always so ready to crow over a tall carnivore smothered in dust.

Trembling Earth
by
Allen Steele

Allen Steele made his first sale to Asimov's *in 1988. It didn't take him long to follow it up with a string of sales to the magazine that quickly established him with the readership as one of its most popular new writers. In 1990 he published his critically acclaimed first novel,* Orbital Decay, *which subsequently won the Locus Poll as Best First Novel of the year, and soon Steele was being compared to golden-age Heinlein by no less an authority than Gregory Benford. His other books include the novels* Clarke County, Space; Lunar Descent; *and* Labyrinth of Night. *His most recent books are a novel,* The Jericho Iteration, *and a collection,* Rude Astronauts. *He lives in St. Louis, Missouri.*

Here he gives us a taut and edge-of-your-seat suspenseful story of a close encounter with a savage pack of killer dinosaurs, not in the distant past, but in present-day Florida . . .

* * *

"OKEFENOKEE SWAMP, also spelled Okefinokee, primitive swamp and wildlife refuge in southeastern Georgia and northern Florida . . . The swamp's name probably is derived from the Seminole Indian word for 'trembling earth,' so called because of the floating islands of the swamp."

—Encyclopedia Britannica

1. The Mesozoic Express

A high-pitched chop of helicopter rotors from somewhere high above the treetops, the faint invisible perception of drifting on still waters, hot sunlight on his face and cold water on his back. An amalgam of sensations awakened Steinberg, gradually pulling him from a black well. Awake, but not quite aware; he lay in the muddy bottom of the fiberglass canoe and squinted up at the sunlight passing through the moss-shrouded tree branches. His clothes were soaked through to the skin and even in the midday sun he was chilled, but somehow that didn't register. All that came through his numbed mind was the vague notion that the canoe was drifting downstream, bobbing like a dead log in the current of the . . .

Where was he? What was the name of this place? "Suwannee Canal," a voice from the fogged depths of his mind informed him. Yeah. Right. The Suwannee Canal. How could he have forgotten? "Up Shit Creek and no paddle," another voice said aloud. It took him a moment to realize that the voice was his own.

The helicopter seemed to be getting closer, but he couldn't see it yet. Well, if I'm drifting, maybe I need to find a paddle. Steinberg sat up on his elbows and his eyes roamed down the length of the canoe. Muddied backpacks, soaked and trampled sleeping bags, a rolled-up tent, a propane lantern with a broken shield, a black leather attache case which for some reason looked entirely appropriate for being here . . . but no paddle. Must have fallen out somewhere back there. Yes, Denny, you're definitely up Shit Creek . . .

"That's a joke, kid." The new voice in his head belonged to Joe Gerhardt. "Laugh when the man tells you a joke . . ."

No. Don't think about Joe. Don't think about Pete. He shook his head and instantly regretted it; it felt as if someone had pounded a railroad spike through his brain. He winced, gasping a little at the pain. Aspirin. Tiffany has the aspirin bottle . . .

Where's Tiffany? The thought came through in a rare instant of clarity. Where's Tiffany? She was right behind me when we were running, she was right behind when . . .

Something bumped the bottom of the canoe, behind his head. He slowly looked around, his gaze travelling across sun-dappled water the color of tea, and saw the long, leathery head of an alligator just below the gunnel of the canoe, slit-pupilled green eyes staring up at him. Startled, Denny jerked upward a little and the gator disappeared beneath the water without so much as a ripple. If his hand had been dangling in the water the gator could have chomped it off, yet somehow Denny wasn't frightened. Just Old Man Gator, coming by to visit his canoe without a paddle here on Shit Creek . . .

Where's Tiffany?

Now the sound of rotors was much louder. The exertion and the headache had drained him; feeling as if all life had been sucked from his bones, Steinberg sank back into the bottom of the canoe, the back of his throbbing head finding a cool puddle of water. Mosquitos purred around his ears and before his eyes, but he couldn't find the strength to swat them away. He stared back up at the blue sky and listlessly watched as the twin-prop Osprey hove into view above the treetops. I know that thing, he thought. I was in it just yesterday. Me . . . and Joe Gerhardt . . . and Pete Chambliss . . .

And now he really didn't want to think about them. Especially not about what happened to them, because if he did he might remember the sound of jaws tearing into flesh, of screams that go on and on and on . . . and if that happened he might just jump right out of the canoe and take his chances with Mister Old Man Alligator, because even if he didn't know what happened to Tiffany, he knew what happened to Gerhardt and the senator. And that's not a joke, kid. That's not funny at all . . .

He watched as the Osprey grew closer and found to his relief that there was a little mercy to be found in Shit Creek, because his eyes closed and he rediscovered the bliss of oblivion.

Transcript of the Kaplan Commission Hearings on the Assassination of Senator Petrie R. Chambliss; Washington, DC, July, 2004. George Kaplan, former United States

Attorney General, presiding. From the testimony of Daniel
Steinberg, former legislative aide to Sen. Chambliss.

KAPLAN: Thank you for being here with us today, Mr.
Steinberg. The Commission realizes that you're involved in
serious litigation in regards to this incident, so we're
especially appreciative of the effort you've taken to speak to
us.

STEINBERG: Yes, sir. Thank you, sir.

KAPLAN: Many of the facts of this case are already
known to us, Mr. Steinberg, both from public accounts and
from the testimony of witnesses before you. However, there
has been a great deal of confusion and . . . might I add for
the benefit of the press pool reporters in the hearing
room . . . obfuscation on the part of the media. There has
also been some lack of corroboration among the testimonies
of prior witnesses. It's important for this Commission to get
the facts straight, so some questions we might ask you may
seem redundant. So I hope you don't mind if . . . well,
please bear with us if we seem to be beating the same
ground that's been beaten before.

STEINBERG: Not at all, sir . . . I mean, yes, sir. I
understand completely.

KAPLAN: Good. To start with, Mr. Steinberg, can you
tell us why you and the late Senator Chambliss went to the
Okefenokee National Wildlife Reserve last April?

STEINBERG: Well, the senator felt as if he needed to
take a vacation, sir. We . . . that's his staff and the senator,
sir . . . I mean, his Washington staff, not the campaign
committee.

KAPLAN: We understand that. Please, just relax and take
your time.

STEINBERG: Uhh . . . yes sir. Anyway, Pete . . . that is, the senator . . . had just come back from Moscow, after his discussions with the new government regarding the unilateral nuclear disarmament treaty. Everyone had been burning the candle at both ends, both with the Moscow arms talks and the presidential campaign. The campaign for the Super Tuesday primaries was coming up and the Senate had gone into recess, so Pete . . . I'm sorry if I'm so informal, Mr. Kaplan . . .

KAPLAN: That's quite all right. We understand that you were on a first-name basis with the senator. Carry on.

STEINBERG: Anyway, Pete wanted to take some time off, do something just for fun. Well, he is . . . I'm sorry, he was . . . an avid outdoorsman, and he had taken an interest in the paleontological research being done at the Okefenokee Wildlife Refuge because of his position on the Senate Science Committee, so he decided that he wanted to take a canoe trip through the refuge and . . .

KAPLAN: Excuse me, Mr. Steinberg. The chair recognizes Dr. Williams.

FREDERICK WILLIAMS, Ph.D; Chancellor, Yale University: Mr. Steinberg, you say the senator wanted to visit the Okefenokee Swamp. I can understand that he might have wanted to take a break by taking a canoe trip, since I'm an aficionado of the sport myself, but I'm still not sure of his intent. Was it because he wanted to paddle where he had not paddled before, or was it because he wanted to see the dinosaurs?

STEINBERG: Well, it was both, sir. I mean, he could have taken a raft trip down the Colorado River, but he had done that a couple of times before already. And he did want to see the dinosaur project and it was going to be in a Super

Tuesday state besides, so the exposure couldn't hurt . . . well, he just came to me and said, "Denny, what do you say to a little canoe trip down South?"

DR. WILLIAMS: And what did you say?

STEINBERG: I said, "Sounds great, Pete. Let's go."

DR. WILLIAMS: And you didn't consider this to be an unsafe venture?

STEINBERG: No, sir. Not at the time, at least. Why should I?

DR. WILLIAMS: I would think that you would want to ask yourself that question, seeing as how you're facing a charge of second-degree murder . . .

The Bell/Boeing V-22 Osprey which had carried them the last leg of the trip, from Moody Air Force Base in Valdosta to the Okefenokee National Wildlife Refuge, had barely settled on the landing pad when Pete Chambliss unsnapped his seat harness and stood up in the VTOL's passenger compartment. "Okay, boys, let's go!" he yelled over the throb of the rotors.

Before anyone could stop him, the senator had twisted up the starboard passenger door's locking lever and was shoving open the hatch. Denny Steinberg looked across the aisle at Joe Gerhardt. The Secret Service escort only shrugged as he unsnapped his own harness, then stepped to the rear cargo deck to pick up Chambliss's backpack. Gerhardt had barely lifted it from the deck when it was grabbed from his hands by Chambliss. Hefting it over his shoulder, Chambliss turned around and pounded Denny's shoulder with his huge right hand.

"C'mon, Denny!" he boomed. "Let's go get that river!" Then Chambliss jumped out of the Osprey and was trotting out from beneath the swirling blades of the starboard nacelle. Two officials from the Deinonychus Observation Project, a man and a woman who had come out to the pad to greet their honored guest, seemed unprepared for the sight of Senator Petrie R. Chambliss—dressed in jeans, red flannel shirt, and hiking boots—suddenly appearing in their midst, grabbing their hands and pumping them so hard it seemed as if he were about to dislocate their elbows. Their expressions, to Steinberg's eye, matched that of the Soviet Foreign Minister's, the first time Kamenin had met Pete Chambliss in Moscow last week. The senator from Vermont was an awful lot to take in one dose.

The Osprey's pilot, who had watched everything through the door from his right-hand seat in the forward compartment, looked at Steinberg. "Is he always this enthusiastic?" he asked loudly, grinning at the young aide from beneath his mirrored aviator shades.

Steinberg nodded and the pilot shook his head and looked away. Just then the rear cargo hatch raised open and a ground crewman pulled down the loading ramp. A handful of men and women tromped up the ramp and walked to the front of the aircraft. They pulled down the folding seats, barely taking notice of Gerhardt and Steinberg. One of them, a redneck with shoulder-length hair, glanced out through a porthole, then looked at Denny. "That the guy who's running for president?" he yelled. Denny nodded and the redneck nodded back. "Sheeit, I shoulda gotten an autograph. Hey, Jake, gimme a cigarette!"

The guy he called Jake, who had a greasy mustache and wore a John Deere cap, fumbled in his shirt pocket for a pack of Marlboros. "Buy some yourself sometime, Al. Hey, Greg! Take us outta here, willya? This place gives me the creeps!"

"Lemme get rid of the VIPs first, okay?" The co-pilot leaned around to look at Denny and jerk his thumb at the open passenger hatch. "Get going!" he yelled. "We gotta go up again! Time to take the part-timers home and come back for feeding time!"

Before Denny could ask what the co-pilot meant, Gerhardt had grabbed both of their packs and clambered out of the VTOL, holding his straw cowboy hat down on his head against the prop-wash. Steinberg picked up the attache case containing the senator's communications system and clumsily lowered himself from the hatch, then dashed out from under the rotors. As soon as he was clear, the engines roared to a higher pitch and the Osprey—Air Force surplus, dark gray with a scowling, cigar-chomping Albert Alligator from the Pogo comic strip stencil-painted on its fuselage above the words *"The Mesozoic Express"*—lofted into the air once again. Denny watched as the hybrid aircraft cleared the treetops, then the two engine nacelles swiveled forward on their stub wings to their horizontal cruise configuration and the Osprey roared away, heading east.

Steinberg turned around and scanned the compound in which he had just been deposited. Once, when the refuge had been open to the general public, this had been a big tourist attraction of southeastern Georgia: campgrounds, a picnic area, a visitor's center and museum, a concession stand and a boat ramp. Now it looked like the last outpost of civilization on the edge of the Early Cretaceous period. The visitor's center had been converted into a main lodge for the University of Colorado science team which presently used the place; the concession stand and picnic tables were gone, replaced by Quonset hut dorms, laboratories, generator shack and the chopper pad. Fresh stumps showed where trees had been felled throughout the compound, which was enclosed by a high fence topped with concertina barbed wire. Beyond the fence was the vast morass of the Okefenokee Swamp—and it didn't look like the sort of place where Pogo Possum and Albert Alligator were likely to be found.

Eying the phlegm-like strands of Spanish moss dangling from the cypress trees on the other side of the fence,

swatting away a bat-sized mosquito from his face, Denny
Steinberg—legislative aide to Senator Petrie Chambliss,
alumnus of George Washington University, owner of a
two-bedroom condo in Georgetown and an antique apple-
red '68 Corvette Stingray which he'd rather be polishing
right now—had to ask himself: How the hell did I get talked
into this trip?

Because he had mentioned to Pete that he was once a
canoe instructor at a Boy Scout camp in Tennessee, that's
how. And because the senator didn't forget anything. And
because if the man goes to the White House next year,
Denny Steinberg wanted a new office just down the hall and
that meant buttering up the presidential frontrunner when-
ever possible. Even if that entailed going along on a canoe
trip in a godforsaken hellhole like this.

Chambliss was still talking to the project officials, his arms
folded across his broad chest; he wore a faintly bemused
smile on his face as he listened to them, probably because—if
prior experience were any indicator—someone was over-
explaining things to Chambliss. There was a natural as-
sumption people made that, because Pete Chambliss looked
like a barroom armbreaker, he also had the mind of one. At
six-foot-four, with the muscle-bound build of a former
Notre Dame linebacker, Chambliss did have the appearance
of a former bouncer. When he had first taken office, his
political foes on the Hill had tried to smear him with the
label "Conan the Senator" until it quickly became apparent
that Petrie Chambliss was no Green Mountains hillbilly.
Thuggish looks notwithstanding, the Democratic chairman
of the Senate Foreign Relations Committee was now re-
garded as one of the most intelligent legislators in Congress.
It was only when Chambliss ventured beyond the Beltway
that he ran into people who equated physical size with lack
of intelligence. That was a handicap in this race; in his
sound bites, the big lug came off as King Kong trying to
sound like Thomas Jefferson. The staff was still working on

him, for instance, to be careful to use "isn't" instead of his habitual "ain't." But so far, the polls hadn't shown this to be a major liability. Considering that the Republican incumbent sounded like a squeamish English teacher from a prep school for girls, perhaps the voters were ready for—as one *Washington Post* columnist put it—"the reincarnation of Teddy Roosevelt."

Joe Gerhardt was standing about a dozen feet away with their backpacks, casually gazing around the compound. As Steinberg watched, the Secret Service man reached into the pocket of his denim jacket, pulled out a pack of Camels, shook one loose and stuck it in his mouth. Steinberg sauntered over, and Gerhardt held out the pack to offer him a smoke.

"No, thanks." Denny cocked his head towards Chambliss. "Shouldn't you be with your man?"

The two of them had met only this morning when they had boarded the senator's chartered jet at Washington National. Instead of the normal business suit favored by the agency's dress-code, Gerhardt was wearing jeans, a T-shirt and denim jacket. Otherwise, he had the bland, unnoticeable features of a Secret Service bodyguard. He didn't look at Denny as he lit his cigarette with a butane lighter. "Nope," he replied drily. "Not unless he changes his mind."

"What's that supposed to mean?"

"Remember when we took a pee-break at the airport? Well, the senator told me that, considering that this is his vacation and that Secret Service protection was something that had been forced on him, he would prefer it if I didn't shadow him."

Gerhardt exhaled pale blue smoke. " 'It's okay if you're nearby,' he said. 'But if you're close enough to be able to tell the color of my piss, then you're too close.' " He grinned and shrugged. "We aims to please."

"Maybe you should be a little less considerate." Steinberg lowered his voice. "In case nobody briefed you earlier,

Pete's been in the thick of some crucial events lately. There's a lot of people who don't appreciate his role in the strategic arms talks and a few would like to see him dead before he becomes president. We've got the death threats to prove that somebody out there means business . . ."

"The New American Minutemen Enclave. Uh-huh." Gerhardt ashed his cigarette and cast a wary eye at the compound. "Yessir, this looks just like a NAME stronghold to me, all right."

"Cute. It would be appreciated if you were a little more observant, okay? Like, do your job? Pay a little attention?"

Gerhardt nonchalantly blew smoke through his nostrils and looked down at the muddy ground. "Looky here, son . . ."

With his left hand, he opened his jacket a couple of inches. The butt of a submachine pistol stuck out from the holster suspended under his left armpit. "That's an Ingram MAC-10," he softly drawled, "and I don't think I need to give you a lecture on its specs to show you I mean business, too. But if you don't believe me, there's a buzzard on the top of that big cypress behind me, on the other side of the fence." Gerhardt didn't look around. "If you want, I'll pick it off for you."

Denny peered in the direction Gerhardt had indicated. The tree was about a hundred yards away and the turkey vulture in it was nearly invisible against the sleet gray sky; Steinberg saw it only once as it lazily stretched one taloned foot up to scratch its long head.

"That's okay," Steinberg said. "I'll believe you."

"Good. Then stay off my case. I know what I'm doing." Gerhardt took another drag from his cigarette, dropped it on the ground and stomped on it with his boot before walking off. "The senator wants to start his vacation. I think I'll join him."

Chambliss was walking away with one of the officials. The other one, the woman, was walking towards them.

Gerhardt politely touched the brim of his cowboy hat as she passed, then looked back over his shoulder at Steinberg. "Get the packs, won't you, son?" he called out. "The man needs his bodyguard."

Steinberg looked down at the three forty-pound nylon backpacks and the attache case piled on the landing pad. Gerhardt was through with playing porter; now it was his turn.

"Son of a bitch," Denny hissed. He managed to pick up two of the heavy North Face packs and was struggling to grab the top loop of the third pack between his forefingers when the young woman, whose blond hair was braided down her back and who had the longest legs this side of a Ford Agency model, recovered the third pack from his fingertips.

"Let me get that." Before he could object, she grabbed the third pack and effortlessly hoisted it over her shoulder. "Looks like your pal left you in the lurch."

"Umm . . . yeah. Something like that." Feeling vaguely emasculated, but nonetheless relieved to be free of the extra burden, Steinberg grasped the handle of the attache case. "I take it you're with the science team?"

"Uh-huh," she replied, starting off in the direction of the lodge. "I'm Tiffany Nixon, refuge naturalist. Team Colorado's out at the Chessier Island observation tower. Bernie Cooper's taking the senator and your friend out there now. We'll catch up with them after we dump this stuff at the lodge."

A few dozen yards away, Bernie Cooper—a thin, balding man in his early forties—was climbing into the driver's seat of an open-top Army surplus Hummer, with Pete Chambliss taking the shotgun seat and Joe Gerhardt climbing into the rear. Gerhardt glanced in their direction and gave him a sardonic wave, then the Hummer started off down the narrow paved roadway leading to the side gate. Denny suddenly didn't mind; he was trading one ride with an SS asshole for another with one of the most beautiful women he had met in a long time. Things were beginning to look up . . .

"Secret Service?" she asked.

"Hmm? Excuse me?"

"Your friend." She nodded towards the departing vehicle. "Is he the Secret Service escort or are you?"

"Him. I'm the senator's aide. He's the one packing a gun."

She frowned as they reached the lodge's front porch. A second Hummer was parked out front. "If he shoots at one of my gators," she said as she dropped the backpacks next to the pine railing, "I'm going to smack him upside the head with a paddle. C'mon inside and I'll give you a gronker. Bernie had the ones for the senator and the other guy in his jeep, but I was supposed to take care of you."

Tiffany opened the screen door and led him into the cathedral-ceilinged lodge. Ah, so, he thought as he walked down a short hallway past a couple of offices to a supply closet. This was the guide they were going to have for their canoe trip. "From what I hear, alligators aren't the worst things we have to worry about out there," Steinberg said nonchalantly, watching as she unlocked the door with a key. "If he shoots at any lizards, it's going to be one of the big ones."

To his surprise, Nixon gave a bitter laugh. "Okay by me. I didn't ask for those monsters to be put here." The naturalist turned on the light, picked a couple of yellow plastic cartridges the size of cigarette packs off a shelf, and handed one to him. "Clip this on your belt and switch it on when I tell you. You know what it's for?"

Steinberg nodded. He had already been told about the reflex inhibitors. When the dinosaurs were still in their infant state, pain-inducers guided by Intel microchips had been surgically implanted in the pain centers of their brains. The tiny nanocomputers were powered by hemodynamic microgenerators which kept the batteries perpetually charged by the blood flow to the brain. The inhibitors—for some reason called "gronkers"—also held Intel nanochip boards, wired to short-range radio transmitters fixed to the same frequency as the receivers in the pain-inducers and, once switched on, were continuously transmitting a signal on that bandwidth.

If one of the dinosaurs came within a hundred yards of a person wearing an inhibitor, the aversion program hard-wired into the microchip nestled deep within the dinosaur's cranium automatically sent a painful electric charge into the beast's nervous system . . . and if the big bastard didn't get the hint and kept coming, the charge continued at quickly increasing intensity until, at approximately one hundred feet, voltage sufficient to knock it cold was delivered into its brain.

The idea was to allow the researchers to get near enough to the deinonychi to observe them at close range without imperilling themselves. Steinberg knew the technology was proven and sound, but it still made him uneasy to trust his life to a plastic box. Idly turning it over in his hand, he noticed a strip of white masking tape on the side; written on it was the name NIXON. "Hey, I think I got your . . . uh, gronker. Why do you call 'em that anyway?"

"Um? Oh, it doesn't matter." Tiffany was already clipping the other unit, marked STEINBERG, onto her belt. Once Denny had fastened his own inhibitor to his belt, she gave it a quick tug to make sure it was secure. "They all work the same," she added. "Don't worry about it. If the ni-cad battery dies, it'll beep three times before it goes down. If that happens, tell one of us and we'll get you out of there. Just don't lose it, okay?"

"Why do you . . . ?" he repeated.

"Because when they get zapped, they go 'gronk' just before they fall down." She switched off the light, relocked the door and walked past him towards the front door. "Well, you guys came here to see some dinosaurs. So let's go meet Freddie and his playmates."

DANGER!

NO UNAUTHORIZED PERSONNEL
BEYOND THIS POINT!

Enter this area with EXTREME CAUTION! Stay on the roadways or the boardwalk at all times. Make no unnecessary noises. Do not smoke. Food is absolutely forbidden. Menstruating women and persons with untreated cuts or scratches should avoid this area.

Wear your inhibitor at ALL TIMES! In case of failure, proceed to this gate AT ONCE and LEAVE THE AREA IMMEDIATELY!

Log in when you enter the area and log out when you leave.

Failure to comply with any of these regulations may subject you to criminal prosecution under federal law, punishable by fines (up to $1,000) and/or jail sentence (up to 1 year).

On the bottom margin, someone had hand-written in pen: "Please do not feed or harass the dinosaurs." And someone else had scrawled below that: "Dinosaurs! Please do not eat or harass the humans!"

"You've got some funny people working here," Steinberg muttered.

"If you say so." Nixon signaled them into the logbook within the box. "You can turn on your gronker now." Steinberg reached down, pushed a switch on the little unit, and watched as a green status light came on and the gronker beeped once. Nixon did the same, then she pulled a two-way headset radio out of the box and fitted it over her ears. She touched the lobe where the bone convection mike rested against her upper jaw, softly said something that Steinberg didn't catch, then locked the box and walked around in front of the cart to unlock the gate and swung it open. Steinberg obligingly drove the Hummer through the gate and Nixon shut the gate behind them and relocked it.

The roadway was getting more narrow now, invaded by dense vegetation which had not been trimmed back in some time. They passed picnic sites which had been usurped by tall grass and weeds; a wooden sign with an arrow pointing to the Peckerwood Trail was almost completely over-whelmed by vines. Through the trees and underbrush he could see aluminum fencing and rows of coiled razorwire. The park which time forgot. "So tell me," Steinberg asked. "How did a nice girl like you . . . ?"

"Get in a swamp like this?" Nixon cast him an amused glance. "I haven't heard a line like that since I quit going to health clubs." She swerved the Hummer around a pothole in the road. "Gotta fix that sometime," she observed. "I hope this isn't a pick-up scene, because it's too weird if it is."

"What? Me?" he protested. Yet that was his intent, whether he cared to admit it or not. Studying her out of the corners of his eyes, Denny couldn't help but to fantasize about a neat little sexual encounter over the next couple of days. A one-night stand in a tent, perhaps; the great outdoors already did things to his libido. Pete wouldn't mind—since his divorce two years ago the senator had made time with some of the more desirable women on the Hill, discreetly out of view of the press—and the trip shouldn't be a total loss. But he was careful not to let on how close to the mark Tiffany had come. "This is probably much the same thing as a gym," he murmured, waving a hand at the jungle around them. "The reptiles here are only bigger, that's all."

"How true." She paused thoughtfully. "I was a lawyer before this. Contracts attorney with Meyers, Larousse & Sloane in Atlanta. I was your typical sixty-hour-a-week legal droid, working my butt off to become a full partner and unhappy as hell . . . all I really wanted to do was paddle a canoe around the Okefenokee on the weekends. I spent each week shuffling paperwork and waiting for Friday when I could load up my canoe and head down here." She shrugged. "So one day I decided to pull the plug. Turn life into one long weekend."

"And become a naturalist in a wildlife refuge? That's a switch."

"I know. The partners still haven't figured it out. Ask me if I care what they think. Anyway, I had been working here for about two years when the Interior Department decided to turn the refuge into a research center for the project. They canned most of the staff when they closed the place to the public, but as luck would have it they still needed a naturalist who knew the swamps, so they kept me around."

Denny nodded his head, but remembered something she had said earlier. "But I take it you're not happy about the dinosaurs."

"Take it any way you want," Tiffany said noncommittally. She slapped the steering wheel with her hands. "So here I am . . . and here we are."

The other Hummer was parked next to a trailhead; she steered their own vehicle off the road, switched off the engine, and climbed out. As Steinberg got out and joined her on the edge of the raised wooden boardwalk leading into the bushes, he heard the clatter of distant rotors. "C'mon," Tiffany said, heading down the boardwalk to a gate in the fence. "It's almost time for the main event."

"Hmm?" Denny shaded his eyes with his hand and peered up at the sky. Was that the Osprey coming back? The swamp seemed more dense now, as if the green maze were moving in around them like the fronds of a pitcher plant curling in around its prey. "What's that?"

"Feeding time," Tiffany said. "You'll love it." She opened the unlocked gate and looked over her shoulder at him. "Just like a budget hearing back in DC."

It was the second time that day he had heard about feeding time, but she was already striding down the boardwalk before he could ask what she meant. He hurried to catch up with her.

From the testimony of Dr. Bernard Cooper:

KAPLAN: We realize that you're upset with Rep. Mc-Caffrey's characterization of the project as reckless, in regards to the species of dinosaur which your team revived . . .

DR. COOPER: "Upset" isn't the word for how I feel, Mr. Kaplan . . .

KAPLAN: . . . yet you have to realize that the burden of proof is upon you to convince this Commission that the project was not reckless, that you had taken adequate safeguards to protect visitors to the refuge. . . .

DR. COOPER: Mr. Kaplan, the primary goal of The Deinonychus Observation Project was not to establish a dinosaur petting zoo. When the Department of the Interior leased the Okefenokee refuge to the project, we did our best to make sure that the specimens would be isolated from the outside world and that the scientists conducting the observations would be thoroughly protected from the dinosaurs. Besides the fact that the Okefenokee Swamp was the most available site which approximately matched the natural environment of the Early Cretaceous era, it was also selected because of its isolation. Safety was a top priority and a considerable part of our NSF budget was spent on just that priority. The refuge was hemmed in with high fences with limited access to the swamp. Waterways such as Suwannee Canal were equipped with underwater fences to keep the dinosaurs from swimming out, even though this species isn't amphibious by nature. Roads were blocked to prevent vehicles from entering so that entrance to the refuge could only be made by aircraft. The specimens themselves were surgically implanted with the electronic inhibitors I described earlier. Every precaution imaginable was taken to prevent injury or death to anyone entering the refuge . . .

KAPLAN: And yet . . .

DR. COOPER: Please allow me to finish, sir. We anticipated that we might have some privileged visitors to the project, such as members of Congress who oversee the National Science Foundation, and we were thoroughly prepared to make certain that they were safe. However, I must point out to the Commission that we did not expect that a presidential candidate might decide to spend his vacation with us, let alone one who might be a target for assassination by a right-wing extremist group. We did not invite Senator Chambliss and his party to the refuge. To be quite blunt, Mr. Kaplan, if it had been within my power to do so, I would have refused to let him in.

KAPLAN: Then why did you allow the late senator to visit you?

DR. COOPER: Because the project is at the mercy of congressional funding, and we need all the friends on Capitol Hill we can get. You know the old saw about where an 800-pound gorilla wants to sit? Mr. Kaplan, with all due respect to the deceased, he was an 800-pound gorilla. He sat wherever he damned well pleased.

Under the rattle of an approaching aircraft, Steinberg heard the voices of the science team as he and Nixon arrived at the end of the boardwalk.

"Pack acquired at three-ten degrees northwest, down-range two-point-two miles . . ."

"Onboard telemetry good. We've got a clear fix. They're still in the trees . . ."

"Okay, bring in the Osprey for the drop . . ."

The observation platform looked like a giant pinewood

treehouse, perched fifty feet above the ground on the big toe of the foot-shaped Chessier Island. A high steel fence and more razorwire surrounded the platform; Denny was suddenly made uncomfortably aware how exposed they had been while on the boardwalk. One of the men on the platform noticed Steinberg and Nixon and buzzed them through the boardwalk gate. Nixon led the way up the spiral stairway to the top of the platform.

The swamp opened up before him as a vast, primordial prairie. The plain of floating peat moss had been here for seemingly countless years, its mass having gradually bubbled up from the bottom of the swamp to form an almost-solid surface. The edges of the clearing were fringed with pine and cypress trees draped with Spanish moss; the prairie was covered with high, yellow grass which rippled like ocean waves as a warm breeze wafted across it. The rippling grew more intense as the Osprey came in over the treetops and hovered above the plain. A covey of white sandhill cranes, startled by the VTOL's arrival, lifted off from the ground and flapped across the prairie straight towards the tower, irritably honking their distress, until they veered away from the tower and disappeared beyond the trees.

Under the canvas awning stretched above the platform, a couple of researchers were standing ready around their instruments: tripod-mounted Sony camcorders, Nikon cameras with humongous telephoto lenses, shotgun mikes, a dish antenna all pointed at the prairie. At a bench behind, a young man with a goatee beard and a ponytail was watching the screens of two Grid laptop computers on a bench, hardwired into a couple of CD-ROM datanets. The reels of an old-fashioned tape deck slowly turned, while a couple of monochrome TV monitors showed closeups of the swamp.

Chambliss and Gerhardt were standing with Cooper behind the scientists, watching all that was happening before them. Like almost everyone else on the platform, they had high-power binoculars draped on straps around their necks. Stepping over the tangled cables on the floor of the deck,

Steinberg walked over to them, hearing Cooper speak in a low voice: ". . . dropping them in just about . . ."

"Sorry I'm late, Pete," Denny interrupted. "I had to . . ."

Chambliss impatiently shushed him. Cooper irritably glanced at him, then continued. "The pack won't emerge until the Osprey's gone," he said quietly. "They're pretty shy about the chopper and they tend to hide from it, but once they come out they'll make pretty quick work of the bait. It's not much of a challenge for them. That's why the team has to record everything. Everything happens too fast to make many on-the-spot calls."

Denny watched as the Osprey settled down to within a few feet of the peat moss surface. Although its landing gear was lowered, the aircraft never actually landed on the swamp, undoubtedly because the floating surface of the swamp would never sustain its weight. The rear cargo hatch cranked open and he could dimly make out one of the crew members climbing out to pull down the tail ramp. Steinberg ducked beneath Chambliss's line of sight and scuttled over to Gerhardt. "What's going on?" he whispered.

"Feeding time at the OK Corral," the Secret Service agent murmured, still watching the swamp.

"I keep hearing that. What are they feeding 'em?"

Gerhardt looked at him and said, "Mooooo . . ."

Steinberg glanced down at one of the close-up monitors in time to see the bait being led down the Osprey's ramp by the crewmember: a full-grown cow, its bovine head twisting back and forth as it was dragged out of the hatch by a rope around its neck. "I don't fucking believe this," he murmured.

"There's a ranch in Folkston where they're kept," Tiffany supplied. He hadn't noticed that she had slid up beside him. She handed a spare pair of binoculars to him. "Did you know there's an overabundance of cattle in the country?" she asked softly. "This is how they get rid of the surplus. Feedstock for the dinosaurs." She smiled grimly. "They're not vegetarians and Purina doesn't make Dinosaur Chow, even if they would eat it. And they won't touch dead meat. They like their food fresh, if you know what I mean."

"Don't they get enough to eat out there?" Gerhardt asked.

"Are you kidding? They'd knock off every bear and deer in the refuge in a week if we let them forage, and the ambient ecosystem would be shot to hell. Even the gators are too scared to take 'em on." She grimaced. "Not that the fuckers don't try," she added.

"Hmm? The gators?"

"The dinosaurs. They're eating the swamp alive. That cow's just subsistence rations for them." There was an expression in her face which was hard to interpret; there was something in her eyes which was hidden as she raised her binoculars to study the prairie.

Once the cow was on the ground, about two hundred yards from the platform, the crewman hastily pushed the tail ramp back into the Osprey and pulled himself into the hatch. He looked like he was in a hurry and Denny couldn't blame him one bit. The Osprey ascended, twin rotors counter-rotating like scimitars, and peeled away toward the distant compound. Abandoned in the middle of the prairie, the cow watched the aircraft depart. It lowed once, a lonely sound which the shotgun-mikes picked up, and it made a few tentative steps across the wobbly earth until its instincts took over and it began to graze on the tops of the high grass. The ASPCA would just love this, Steinberg thought as a chill swept between his shoulder blades.

"We've got movement at three-twelve degrees north-west," the Team Colorado researcher watching the comput-ers said. "Downrange two-point-one miles and closing. They're coming in."

"Okay, it's lunchtime." Cooper absently twirled his index finger in the air. "Recorders on, Andy, logon DinoRAM. Look sharp, boys and girls."

As the researchers switched on the camcorders and focused in on the cow, the young man behind the computers tapped codes into one of the Grids which brought a new, map-like display onto one of the screens. Looking over his shoulder, Steinberg recognized the general geography of the Chessier Prairie, with tiny blinking spots denoting the locations of the heifer and the three monsters lurking just out of sight in the far treeline.

"It's called DinoRAM," Cooper quickly said to Chambliss. "It runs off the transceiver in their inhibitors. We use it to mimic the feeding habits of Jason, Michael and Freddie. In the collect mode Andy's running, we can instantly file new data from this day's feeding activity, then rerun it through the computer at our leisure, putting in different stimulae, weather variables and so forth to see what kinds of results emerge, sort of like a simulator. Nice little program."

Chambliss dubiously massaged his chin between his fingers. "Kind of hard on the cows, though, isn't it?" he asked, but Cooper didn't seem to hear him. Denny was about to add his own comeback when one of the researchers spoke up from the camera array.

"Movement on the treeline," she snapped, peering through binoculars at the far side of the clearing. "Three-thirteen degrees northeast and . . . okay, they're out of the trees."

"What type of approach?" Cooper asked, leaning on the back of Andy's chair to watch the computers.

"Walking," Andy replied. "They're bunched together, standard triangle formation." Three blue dots were diagrammed on DinoRAM's screen; he opened a window in the corner of the display and studied a graph. "Seventy-three-point-three percent probability that Freddie's in the lead. Lauren?"

The young woman who had made the sighting chuckled. "Good call. Freddie's still leader of the pack. Guess he won another argument with Jason."

Raising the binoculars to his eyes, Denny watched the prairie. At first he couldn't see the pack. Then they moved, and he could make out three sleek, man-sized shapes at the edge of the trees. "Damn, but they're small," he murmured aloud.

"You were expecting Godzilla?" Gerhardt whispered back. But he nodded in agreement. "Yeah. Cute little fuckers, aren't they?"

Suddenly, the three deinonychi began to sprint forward, running through the high grass towards the cow. "Here they come," Lauren said as the team members operating the camcorders tracked to follow them. "They're beginning to spread out . . ."

"Three-prong attack," Andy murmured, watching his screens. "Michael's heading southwest, Jason's cutting off the southwest, and Fred's going straight in for the kill."

Steinberg's mouth dropped open. "Jesus!" he said aloud. "You mean they're organized?"

"They're not dumb animals," Tiffany said quietly.

Suddenly the deinonychus to the far right changed course, veered in closer to the cow. "Hey!" Andy cried out. "Mikey's going for it! He's going to get that cow first!"

"Keep your voice down," Cooper said calmly. He studied the action through his own field glasses. "Jack, Jeff, keep a camera on Michael but make sure you follow Freddie and Jason. Don't let any of them out of your sight." The grad students behind the camcorders swiveled their instruments to keep all the dinosaurs in their viewfinders.

Now Steinberg could clearly see the deinonychus pack: each was about six feet tall, with light brown skin mottled with dark red tiger stripes, running erect on muscular hind legs, slender forearms tucked in close to their chests. They were somehow smaller than he had expected, but their very weirdness somehow made them look much larger, even from the distance. Although each had a total length of eleven feet, they only stood six feet high; the rest was a long, sinewy tail which lashed about high in the air. He had read that they didn't weigh very much either; an average of 150 pounds, which accounted for their ability to stride across the floating ground without sinking.

In fact, they could have been mistaken as being harmless mini-dinosaurs—surely not as formidable as the ruling carnivorous dinosaurs of their time like the allosaurus or the albertosaurus—were it not for their heads: long and wedge-shaped, with wide, wild eyes under bony ridges and massive jaws which seemed perpetually frozen in a demonic grin, exposing razor-sharp teeth. One look at that face, and all notions of cuteness disappeared: they were creatures which nature had designed to be killers.

Strangely, they somehow seemed more avian than reptilian. Of course they would, he reminded himself. They're ancestors to birds, aren't they? Yet knowledge of that clinical fact didn't help to shake his unease. They were too goddamn alien . . .

By now the pack was close enough that they could be seen without the aid of binoculars. The breeze shifted just then. It was either because of the wind shift, or because it heard the swift approach of its killers, that the cow looked up. Seeing Jason coming in from in front, the cow quickly turned and made a waddling effort to run in the opposite direction—only to find that route cut off by Michael and Freddie. Braying in terror, the heifer clumsily veered again and began to gallop toward the observation platform. "Oh shit, bossie, don't come this way!" one of the camcorder operators hissed.

"Forget about the bait, Jack. Keep your camera on Michael and Freddie." Cooper was intently watching the two deinonychi, who were practically running neck-and-neck now. "Well, now. Let's see if they'd rather fight or feed."

Freddie's massive head suddenly twisted about on its long neck and, in apparent mid-stride, it snapped savagely at Michael. The shotgun-mike picked up the rasping sound of its teeth gnashing together. Daunted, the other deinonychus slowed abruptly and peeled off as Freddie continued to careen forward at full charge.

"Looks like a little bit of both," Andy surmised.

"Did we get that?" Cooper asked Jack. The researcher, his eyes fixed on the viewfinder, gave him the OK sign with his thumb and forefinger. "Well, Freddie, first blood goes to you again," Cooper added softly. He sounded like a dog owner proudly watching his golden retriever bring down a rabbit. Denny looked around at Tiffany to say something, but the naturalist had turned around and was looking in the other direction, away from the killing ground.

Steinberg looked back just in time to see Freddie take down the cow. He almost wished he hadn't . . .

As it reached the fleeing cow, Freddie suddenly leaped into the air, vaulting the last few yards with its hind legs stretched forward. The cow bellowed as Freddie's sharp, curved talons ripped into the soft hide along its belly and ribs; hot red blood jetted from its side as the disemboweled animal, its stomach muscles sliced open, toppled to the ground. Its death scream, hoarse and terrified, was cut short as Freddie's jaw closed around its neck and wrenched upwards to rip the cow's head from its neck. In a swift movement, the dinosaur hurled the head aside, an unwanted bloody morsel which landed near the base of the platform.

"Oh! It's a dunk shot for Fred!" Andy yelled.

"Sign the kid up for the Lakers," Jack replied, shaking his head. "Damn."

"Oh, my God," Chambliss whispered. He had been watching everything through his field glasses; the binoculars fell from his hand and dangled against his chest. The senator was pale; his hand was covering his mouth. Steinberg himself forced down the urge to puke. Like Nixon, he looked away. Gerhardt continued to watch, but even he seemed to be fighting down revulsion.

Cooper seemed unmoved. "Okay, ladies and gentlemen, that's a wrap," he said. As Jason and Michael moved in to wait their turns at the carcass, the researchers began unloading cartridges and discs from the recorders, jotting down notes on their pads, talking quietly among themselves. Steinberg watched Jack pull his wallet from his back pocket and hand a dollar bill to Andy; some sort of continuing wager was being settled for the day. Denny was sure that they had seen this kind of butchery dozens of times in the past several months, yet he doubted that he himself could ever get used to it.

The project leader turned to Pete Chambliss. "Well, Senator, now you've gotten a taste of what we do out here," he said, once more assuming the aloof demeanor of a professional scientist. "Any questions?"

"No . . . no, not right now," Chambliss said quietly. The senator seemed to be recovering his poise, but Steinberg had never seen his boss more at a loss for words. Chambliss glanced over his shoulder at Steinberg and Gerhardt. "I think we'll be wanting to return to the base camp now, if you don't mind," he added stiffly. "We need to get ready for our trip tomorrow."

Cooper nodded. "Certainly. Tiffany will escort you back. I'll be seeing you around suppertime, all right?"

The three of them nodded their heads. Tiffany, still not looking at the grisly scene in the prairie, stepped past them to lead the way to the boardwalk steps. Denny fell into step behind Chambliss and Gerhardt—then stopped, feeling an eerie prickly sensation at his neck, as if someone were watching him.

He gazed back at the researchers. All were busy packing their gear, talking to each other, making notes. But beyond them, on the blood-drenched killing ground a hundred yards away at the edge of the safety zone, one of the dinosaurs was watching them leave. Jason's opaque black eyes were focused on the platform.

Denny took another few steps towards the stairway. Jason's huge head shifted to follow his progress. All at once, Steinberg realized that the deinonychus was watching him . . .

Watching him. Wondering how his blood tasted.

2. Off to See the Lizard

It was light that awoke him this time, a bright shaft of sunlight which hit his eyes as the passenger door of the Osprey was opened. When he awoke this time, he was lying on a stretcher which rested on the floor between the passenger seats. Someone—an older man with a balding forehead and wire-rim glasses—was holding his head steady between his hands, murmuring for him not to move, that he was suffering from a concussion. But he did move his head, just a little, and when he did he saw Tiffany being helped into the aircraft.

She was muddy and soaked; below her shorts her legs were torn with cuts, and her hair was matted with dirt. She looked at him with astonishment as she was guided into a seat just in front of him. "Denny," she breathed. "You got out . . . thank God, you got out of there . . ."

He wanted to say something of the same kind, but instead his eyes drifted from her face to her waist. She was still wearing a gronker on her belt, a yellow plastic box just like his own . . .

His right hand moved, almost involuntarily, to his own belt, and there it was, the inhibitor which should have protected him, yet didn't. A vague memory stirred in his mind; he bent his neck a little to look down at the unit clasped within his hand. The red status light was still on. He wasn't looking for that. Something on the edge of his memory . . .

He turned the little box over in his hand. There, on the side of the case: a strip of white tape, marked with a name: NIXON.

"Don't move your head," the man sitting above him said soothingly. "Just take it easy. We'll get you back in a few minutes."

Someone shut the passenger door and told the police to

take it up again. The Osprey's engines picked up speed; there was a weightless bobbing sensation as the VTOL began to ascend. He laid his head back down, feeling the darkness beginning to come once again—but an unformed thought nagged at him through the fog and the pain. His eyes wandered to Tiffany Nixon.

Someone else was peering at the cuts on her legs, but he could see over his shoulder the gronker on her belt. "Here, move a little to your left," she was told. She put her weight on her left thigh and moved so that a deep cut above her knee could be examined, and when she did, Denny saw the white strip of tape on her unit.

STEINBERG. Isn't that weird? She's got my gronker. I've got hers. STEINBERG . . . NIXON . . . STEINBERG . . . NIXON . . .

"Don't worry," he croaked. "They all work the same."

Tiffany looked down at him then. Her eyes moved first to his gronker, then to her own. Their eyes met and in that briefest of instants just before he passed out again, he realized what had happened down there . . .

From the testimony of Marie Weir; President, WTE Cybernetics Corp.:

SEN. ANTHONY HOFFMAN, D-CA: As you're aware, the Commission would like to know of the details of the reflex inhibitors WTE designed for the project . . . that is, the so-called gronkers . . .

WEIR: Yes, Senator, I understand the importance of this Commission knowing these things. But on advice of our legal counsel, however, I need to inform you that this is proprietary information which, if made public, could be of great benefit to our competitors, so WTE's stance is that we're reluctant to divulge the . . .

KAPLAN: Ms. Weir, I appreciate your reluctance, but you have to remember that you're under federal subpoena to testify to this Commission. Failure to relinquish information which the Commission deems as useful for its investigation could be punishable by you and your company being cited for contempt.

WEIR: My attorney informs me that we can give you general information about our product in this hearing and divulge further information in executive session. I believe this is a fair compromise.

KAPLAN: The chair recognizes Senator Hoffmann.

SEN. HOFFMANN: Ma'am, the only compromise I'm interested in hearing about is whether the inhibitors you built could have compromised the lives of my late colleague and his party. If we have to put you under arrest to get that information, I'll gladly second the motion.

WEIR: Senator, I resent what you're implying. The inhibitors we built for the project were designed according to the University of Colorado research team's own specifications, no more and no less. They were subjected to rigorous field-testing before they were put into actual use, and once they were in operation we monitored their progress. Up until the incident of question, no failures were reported of our equipment. Not one. If you're searching for a smoking gun, I suggest you look elsewhere.

SEN. HOFFMANN: I've studied the report which WTE submitted to the Committee and on the face of it, at least, I have to agree. Under normal circumstances the inhibitors did perform according to the desired standard. I have no wish to start a fight with you on this point. The main question which I have, if your attorney doesn't mind, is whether the gronkers could have been tampered with in such a way to cause their failure.

WEIR: My attorney advises me . . .

SEN. HOFFMANN: The heck with your attorney, Ms. Weir. Just answer a simple damn question for me. Could the inhibitors have been sabotaged in advance? Yes or no?

WEIR: Yes. It's feasible that tampering could have occurred. The inhibitors can be opened with a set of precision screwdrivers.

SEN. HOFFMANN: Fine. I'm glad we're making progress here. Your attorney seems to be fidgeting, Ms. Weir. If he needs to visit the men's room, I think you can let him go now. I believe we can get some straight answers without his advice . . .

There had been three of them: a small pack although maybe much larger once, since the others had been killed by larger predators or simply died from disease or old age. They had been hunting together in a deep valley in a place which, one day, would be known almost mythically as Asiamerica. It was twilight when the rainstorm had begun, but they were still hungry and there was still plenty of prey to be caught before the light vanished from the world. Perhaps they were in pursuit of a larger dinosaur like a lumbering tenontosaurus. Perhaps they had simply become lost on the way back to their den.

Whatever the reason, they had been caught unaware by the flash flood which had suddenly ripped down the valley. The rushing wall of water was on them before they could escape; the walls of the valley were too steep for them to climb, the current too fast for them to swim. Howling their anger at the dark sky, they were torn by branches and battered by stones. In their dying panic, they had clawed and bitten at each other. Finally, one by one, their heads went under the surface for the last time. Their lungs filled with cold water, the fire perished from their eyes, and they died.

Died, and were reborn almost seventy million years later, recalled to life in a sterile white lab by the descendants of the little rodent-like creatures they had once hunted . . .

Pete Chambliss's chair scooted back from the folding table where he had been working, interrupting Denny's reverie. He looked up as the senator picked up his empty beer can. "I'm going in for another one," Chambliss said. "Ready for another round?"

"Umm . . . no thanks, Pete. Still working on this one." He nodded toward the laptop computer on the folding table. "Did you remember to save?"

Chambliss glanced back at his temporary desk, made a self-disgusted grunt, and stepped back across the porch to type a command on the Toshiba's keyboard. Chambliss took the minicomputer with him on all his trips—tonight he was working on a speech for a National Press Club luncheon next week—but he was forever forgetting to save files in memory when he was working on computers. It was one of the little jobs of his aides to foresee this absentminded quirk. "Thanks," Chambliss said.

He walked across the porch and opened the screen door, then quickly stepped aside as Gerhardt came out. "'Scuse me," the senator said as the two men sidestepped each other, then Gerhardt let the door slam shut behind Chambliss. Steinberg fixed his eyes on the darkness beyond the porch as he listened to Gerhardt walk onto the porch, pause, then slowly walk behind him. He heard the rocking chair beside him creak as the Secret Service man settled into it. Then, suddenly, a cold can of Budweiser was dropped in his lap.

Gerhardt laughed as Steinberg started, then popped the top of his own can. "Might as well enjoy yourself," he said. "Tomorrow night we're down to noodles and instant coffee." He took a long tug from his beer and indulged in a resonant belch. "God, I just love the great outdoors," he added sourly, propping his feet up on the rail.

Steinberg picked the can out of his lap and set it down on the floor next to his warm, half-empty beer. "I thought you guys were trained to endure hardship."

"Yeah," Gerhardt replied indifferently. "But I spent two years in the Marines lugging a gun across Central America. Every night down there I sacked out in some rainstorm promising myself that, if I survived this shit, the nearest I would get to wilderness would be mowing the back yard on Sunday." He toasted the night with his beer. "And so what do I do? I join the Secret Service so I can escort some senator on a canoe trip through the Okefenokee. Same job, different swamp. Talk about justice, huh?"

"Maybe you should have been a lawn mower salesman."

"Maybe." Gerhardt took another long sip from his beer. "What's your problem, kid? Still upset because I made you carry the luggage this afternoon?"

"No." He took a deep breath. "I'm just upset because I'm stuck for a weekend with a raving asshole like you."

Gerhardt sighed and shook his head. "Jeez. Try to be nice, and look where it gets you." He looked straight at Steinberg. "Well, if it's any consolation," he said in a lowered voice, "I'd rather be somewhere else than with a brown-nosing little yuppie. I'm here because it's my work and you're here because you want to score points with the boss. Okay?"

Steinberg said nothing, but he felt his face grow hot. Like it or not, Gerhardt had scored a bull's-eye with that remark. He was saved from having to formulate a weak comeback by the screen door opening again and Chambliss swaggering out onto the porch. He held a beer in his right hand and his backpack was slung over his left shoulder. Just behind him was Tiffany Nixon, also carrying a backpack. "Let's go load the canoes, boys," the senator said heartily. "If we do that now, we can shove off a little earlier in the morning."

"Sounds like a right idea." Gerhardt drained his beer, crushed the empty can in his fist, and dropped his feet to the floor. Chambliss tromped across the porch and hopped down the steps. Tiffany threw Denny a quick smile as he stood up to follow, then Gerhardt grabbed his bicep and tugged him toward the stairs. "What's the matter, kid?" he murmured. "'Fraid you might get mud on those expensive designer boots of yours?"

"Fuck off." Steinberg twisted his arm out of Gerhardt's hand, then walked in front of him. Now more than ever, he wished he hadn't volunteered for Pete's spring vacation trip. But then he glanced at Tiffany Nixon's backside as she walked alongside the senator down to the dock and reconsidered. Maybe a little sweet seduction in the swamp would make it all worthwhile. After all, somebody had to share a tent with her tomorrow night, and since Gerhardt himself admitted that he had a job to do . . .

From far away, somewhere out in the moonless dark of the Okefenokee, there came a sound: a *grruuuunngg* from a reptilian throat older than time. Denny stopped on the porch steps as it faintly echoed across the wetlands, feeling an unseasonal chill. On the other hand, he thought, tomorrow night I may want to be sleeping with Gerhardt's MAC-10 instead.

From the testimony of Harlan Lloyd Castle; superintendent, Okefenokee National Wildlife Refuge:

KAPLAN: Mr. Castle, can you tell us a little about the permanent staff of the wildlife refuge? That is, who works there and what do they do?

CASTLE: Well, sir, since the refuge was turned over to the University of Colorado team for their research, the staff was necessarily reduced in number, since we didn't have to maintain the campgrounds and visitors' center and so forth. In fact, we had to let go of most of our resident staff to make way for the team, so . . .

KAPLAN: Pardon me, sir. Your resident staff? What do you mean by that?

CASTLE: Those employees who stayed in the refuge on a full-time basis . . . the ones who lived there year-round. I was able to keep my own residence, of course, and our naturalist Ms. Nixon was able to keep her cabin, but our two full-time rangers and the chief groundskeeper were let go. Fortunately the Interior Department found them other positions within the national park system.

KAPLAN: So there was only Ms. Nixon and yourself living in the park besides the university team. Then who did the maintenance work? Mopping the floors, scrubbing the toilets, cooking for the research staff and so forth?

CASTLE: Well, the science team was responsible for its own cooking. When the changeover occurred, I told Mr. Yamato (*NOTE: Benjamin Yamato, Secretary of the Interior*) that I would be happy to have them in the refuge, but I'd be darned if I'd supply them with a concierge. (*Laughter.*) Was that funny? Well, at any rate, as for the day-to-day maintenance work, we had a number of part-time people who came in each day to do the groundskeeping and cleaning duties. And before you ask, they were brought in each day on the same aircraft which transported the . . . ah, livestock for the dinosaur herd.

KAPLAN: I see. And these part-timers . . . were they official employees of the refuge?

CASTLE: If you mean to ask if they were on the payroll, yes, but I wouldn't characterize them as civil service employees. Since it was rather menial work and part-time at that, we hired whoever we could find in the area who was willing to come in for four hours a day. Typically, we had high school kids, housecleaning staff from nearby motels, locals who wanted to moonlight for a few extra dollars a week . . . that sort of thing. Again, since we were no longer open to the public, we didn't need to have folks who had passed civil service examinations . . . just people who knew how to handle a broom or a toilet brush and who didn't get airsick when they flew in.

KAPLAN: I see. And was there much turnover for these jobs?

CASTLE: Typically, yes, sir, there was. People quit on us all the time. It was dirty work and it didn't pay all that well . . . in fact the Burger King in Folkston paid better wages than we did . . . so we hired who we could get. That's why it wasn't civil service work. There was so much paperwork involved with getting civil service employees that we managed to get an exemption from the Interior Department for these positions.

KAPLAN: Uh-huh. And did these part-timers have access to all the buildings? Including the storage closet in the main building where the reflex inhibitors were kept?

CASTLE: Out of necessity, yes, sir, Mr. Kaplan. Of course, the key rings were given to them when they clocked in at the beginning of the day and they turned them back in when they punched out on the time clock. But . . . ah, yes, they had access to all unrestricted areas of the main compound.

KAPLAN: And that includes the storage closet in the main building?

CASTLE: Yes, sir. There were some cleaning supplies which were kept in that closet, so necessarily they had to . . .

KAPLAN: I understand. One further question, Mr. Castle, and this goes back to what I was asking you about earlier. Just prior to Senator Chambliss's visit to the refuge, did you hire any new part-timers?

CASTLE: Ummm . . . why, yes. One of our cleaning staff, Mary Ann Shorter, suffered a collision with a hit-and-run driver on the highway. She was laid up in the hospital with neck and back injuries, so we had to find a new person to temporarily take her place. A young guy named Jake . . . um, Jacob Adderholt. He answered an ad we had placed in the Folkston newspaper and we hired him. As I recall, that was about a week before the senator came to the refuge.

KAPLAN: And did Mr. Adderholt come to work on the day that Senator Chambliss and his party arrived?

CASTLE: Yes, he did. In fact, he went out with the rest of the part-time staff on the same Osprey that . . . oh, good Lord, Mr. Kaplan, you're not implying . . . ?

KAPLAN: Mr. Castle, did Jake Adderholt reappear for work at the park following Senator Chambliss's death?

CASTLE: Oh, my God . . .

KAPLAN: Mr. Castle, please, did Jake Adderholt come back to work after . . . ?

CASTLE: No, he didn't, he . . . oh, my sweet Lord, how could I have known . . . ?

His paddle dipped again into the dark water. He pulled it straight back to his shoulder, raised it again and absently watched the cool water dribble off the end of the blade, then plunged it forward again into the river. The canal ran straight as a two-lane highway through the low, monotonous swampland; dredged by an industrial explorer in the 1890s in an attempt to form an intracoastal waterway before nature and lack of funds conquered his efforts, the Suwannee Canal was a liquid path through the Okefenokee. Farther downstream it entered the deep bayou of the swamp, a long maze, before it ended at a manmade sill and the mouth of the Suwannee River. But that was a long way from here; they had only travelled the first five miles of the canal, and Denny was already tired.

He pulled the paddle out of the water, rested across the gunnels behind the pointed bow of the Mad River canoe, tipped back his cap and wiped a thin sheen of sweat from his forehead. The early morning fog had long since been burned off by the rising sun; it was close to noon now and the day was getting warmer. An otter had been racing in front of them for a mile or so, occasionally sticking its furry brown head above the water to look back at them as if to say "Nyah nyah nyah, you slow-poke humans" before diving and racing forward again. The little animal had apparently lost interest in them, though, because Denny hadn't spotted him in the past half-hour.

"Out of shape?" Tiffany asked and he looked back over his shoulder at her. She was in the stern seat behind him; he watched as she effortlessly made a J-stroke to keep them in the middle of the narrow canal. "How long has it been since you paddled a canoe?"

"Longer than I care to remember," he admitted. About thirty feet behind them, the second canoe was moving down the river. Joe Gerhardt was doing the muscle work in the bow seat while Pete Chambliss steered from the stern. They had fallen behind because the senator had been constantly pausing to scan the area with his binoculars or to take snapshots of cranes, vultures, otters, and gators. If the Secret Service man had minded, though, he hadn't said anything; like Denny, he had taken off his jacket when the day had become hotter, and now they could all see the Ingram gun slung in the oversized holster under his left armpit. There was also a headset radio slung around his neck; every now and then he had paused to report in, radioing a status report to the compound.

"Catch your breath," Tiffany said. "We'll wait for 'em to catch up." She pulled up her own paddle and laid it across the gunnels, then checked her wristwatch. "We'll be stopping on a little island just up ahead, so you'll get a chance to take a breather."

Denny shifted his butt on the lifejacket; they had long since taken them off and placed them on the hard metal seats. "Lunch?"

"Maybe," she said tersely. She was staring off across the grasslands to their right. Tiffany had been laconic all morning. When they had pushed off from the compound just after sunrise, she had done little more than to make sure everyone's gronker was switched on. Even though the temperature had continued to rise and all the men had stripped down to their undershirts, she hadn't pulled off her own shirt—which was too bad, since Denny would have liked to see what she looked like wearing only shorts and tank-top. Their itinerary called for them to make camp on Bugaboo Island tonight—who the hell had come up with that name?—then to forge their way through the deep swamp tomorrow until they reached the end of the refuge and, just beyond that, Stephen C. Foster State Park, where they would be pulling out of the river for good.

If Denny still hoped to have an amorous adventure with her, it would have to be tonight on Bugaboo Island. Yet, somehow, he was beginning to have his doubts. Tiffany seemed aloof today: her refusal to take off her shirt was a bad omen. Maybe she had come to realize that she was one woman about to spend the night with three men and didn't want to do anything which would seem like a come-on to any of them. But he watched her check her watch again and wondered what sort of schedule she was trying to keep . . .

The second canoe was almost abreast of their own when Pete looked through his binoculars to his right and suddenly pointed. "Over there!" he whispered urgently. "There's the pack!"

Denny looked around. At first he didn't see them . . . then he did, and he involuntarily sucked in his breath. The three long necks of Jason, Freddie and Michael rose above the high yellow grass, about two hundred yards away. It didn't seem as if they had seen the canoeists as they slowly moved across the floating prairie. As Bernie Cooper had pointed out earlier, the dinosaurs seemed to have learned not to stick too closely together lest their combined weight cause them to sink through the peat moss. It was almost a pastoral scene: the bright clear sky, the noonday sun, the high grass wafting in the soft breeze, the distant figures of the dinosaurs. Like a landscape painted by an insane Winslow Homer.

As he watched, one of the deinonychi—Freddie, he reckoned, since it was in the lead—suddenly darted forward, its head snapping downward into the grass. A moment later Freddie reared up again, this time with a small animal caught in its jaws; a raccoon maybe, or perhaps an otter which had not moved fast enough. Freddie's head arced back and they heard the wet leathery snap of its teeth as the unlucky creature was eaten alive. Then the dinosaur kept moving as Michael and Jason caught up with him, their heads slowly swiveling back and forth in search of more prey. The boys were out for a midday stroll. Don't mind us. Just looking for an appetizer or two before we go have a steer for lunch . . .

Denny was distracted by the sudden bump of the bow prodding against the shoreline; while he had been watching the pack, Tiffany had slowly paddled them to the shore. "Get out and pull us up," she said softly, pulling up her paddle and carefully laying it in the canoe.

His eyes widened. "Are you kidding?" he protested. "The pack's right over there!"

"Get out and pull us up, Denny," she repeated. The scornful look in her eyes told him that she wasn't joking, and as the second canoe nosed into the shoreline next to them, Pete Chambliss was already loading a fresh disc into his Nikon. Joe Gerhardt half-stood in the bow, quickly scrambled forward with his hands on the gunnels to keep the canoe steady, and clambered off the front of the canoe onto the ground. He shot a look at Denny which relayed an unspoken admonition: "Kid, I'm not going to shepherd your camera-happy boss all by myself. Get moving."

"I hope you do know how to use that thing," Denny muttered back, meaning Gerhardt's MAC-10. Gerhardt said nothing, but fitted the radio over his head again and murmured something into the mike. Denny laid down his own paddle and carefully stood up to crawl out of the canoe. He managed to get out without tipping the canoe, then he grabbed the prow and hauled the front of the canoe onto the ground.

As Nixon began to crawl across the lashed-down camping gear in the middle of the canoe, Denny tentatively took a few steps forward. The mossy ground squished and rolled under his feet as if he were walking on a feather mattress; it was no wonder that it was called trembling earth. Watching his feet, he took another few steps, then his right boot abruptly sank to his calf in the ground as it found a weak spot in the peat moss. He swore and pitched forward, throwing out his hands to catch himself; the sharp, serrated edges of some weeds cut against his palms, making him cuss and flounder some more before Tiffany grabbed him by the shoulders and hauled him erect.

"Cut it out, willya?" she hissed in his ear. "Test the ground with your foot before you put your weight on it . . . and keep your voice down."

"Not that it matters," Gerhardt said in a slightly louder voice. "They've spotted us."

Denny looked up again and felt his heart freeze. The pack had stopped moving and now they had each looked around, straight in their direction. As he watched, Freddie began to slowly move towards them, followed on either side by

Michael and Jason. Triangle formation, just as Andy the researcher from Team Colorado had said yesterday.

"This is a really stupid idea," he said to no one in particular. "Let's get back in the canoes."

But Pete Chambliss was already stepping past him and Tiffany, holding his camera between his hands as he negotiated his way through the tall grass. Joe Gerhardt moved to his side, pulling the MAC-10 from his shoulder holster and cradling it in his hands. "It's all right," Tiffany said. "The gronkers will keep them at bay. Don't worry about them. Just try to relax."

"Sure. Right." Tiffany was already walking away, following the senator and the Secret Service escort. Steinberg looked back once at the canoes—an office in the White House couldn't be worth this crazy shit—but then he took a deep breath which did little to steady his nerves and stepped into the path made by the naturalist, as the four of them slowly approached the pack.

Five feet away from the canoes, ten feet, twenty . . . the three dinosaurs were still moving toward them, and although they seemed to be keeping their own distance, the gap between them had shrunk to only a few hundred feet. They gradually moved through the high grass like reptilian emissaries from a distant time. It was not at all like yesterday, when they had been separated from the pack by the tall platform and the security fence. This was to be a face-to-face encounter, and Denny was all too aware that Freddie was his own height; just tall enough to snap out and tear his head off. They were man-sized, but their relative lack of stature was not deceptive. These were not men, or even alien lizard-men out of some Hollywood space opera. They were born killers; in their own epoch, they had ganged up on dinosaurs four times their size and ripped them to shreds.

But they'll stay back, he reminded himself. Tiffany's right. That's what the gronkers are for. Team Colorado's gotten closer than this without any problems. Don't worry about it. Yet he found that his feet refused to move any further, that he couldn't look away from the pack as it moved closer, closer . . . Transfixed despite himself by their awful beauty, he barely noticed that Tiffany had paused to let him pass her.

Ahead of him, he heard the click and whirr of Pete's camera as the senator stopped to shoot more pictures. "Absolutely incredible," Chambliss said softly. "Just wonderful. It's like they're just posing for . . ."

Then, all at once, the pack charged.

3. The Smoking Gun

When he awoke again, it was to cool, crisp sheets against his naked skin, to the acrid smell of antiseptics mixed with the foreign yet unmistakable odor of dead flesh, to muffled voices and a strange *pat-pat-pat* of some liquid dripping onto a tiled floor.

"Oh, Christ, there's not much left."

"Do the best you can." He vaguely recognized Bernie Cooper's voice. "When the feds get here they'll want everything in situ that they can get for their . . ."

"Feds? Secret Service? Jesus, Bernie!"

"Secret Service, FBI, Interior, probably the Army and Navy and Air Force too for all I know. . . . I've just been told to keep everyone in the refuge and let nobody leave. It can't be helped, Bob. The shit's hit the fan."

He opened his eyes to harsh fluorescent lights reflecting off formica and stainless steel. The light hurt his eyes and his head felt as if it were encased in taffy-soft cinderblocks; it was hard to think, but he gradually perceived that he was in the compound's clinic. Soft pressure across his forehead and the white edge of gauze just above his brow told him that his head had been treated as well. He moved his head to the right and saw that a screen had been moved into place across one half of the room; the voices came from the other side of the screen.

"If they want us to leave everything alone until they get here, then why are we . . . ?"

"Because I don't want us to look entirely incompetent, that's why. It's going to be bad enough as it is without . . . look, I know they're in bad shape, but I want at least a preliminary autopsy performed before they get here, so just . . ."

"I can't do that, Bernie. You know I can't. I could lose my license." A low intake of breath. The sound of a sheet being pulled back again. "God damn, just look at him. This is one fucking mess we're in. Did we get everything from the site?"

"Everything. Their personal effects are over there . . . the survivors, too, and we're not to touch them under any conditions. Especially not the gronkers, although we could only find the one belonging to the Secret Service guy."

"Where's the . . . no, don't tell me. I'd rather not know."

The slow pattering continued, just under the sound of the voices. He looked down, peering beneath the bottom of the screen. He could see two pairs of shoes on either side of the wheels of a gurney. Blood was pooled at their feet, seeping into the cracks of the white-and-tan tiled floor, dripping from the tabletop above.

"What about the other two? Nixon and . . . aw, what's his name, the senator's flunky?"

"Shaddup. He's right over there. They made it out okay. I thought the kid had a concussion, but it was just a bad cut and shock. She had to be stitched up some but otherwise she's fine. I saw her out in the corridor just a few minutes ago."

Tiffany. He had to tell someone what was going on. He opened his mouth to speak, but all he could manage was a dry, inaudible rasp. As he swallowed, trying to get his voice to work again, he heard the sound of a sheet being pulled forward again.

"Let's get out of here. I haven't seen anything like this

since I interned in an emergency room. Where is everyone, anyway?"

"Down at the dock. We managed to get Freddie's body out of there before the animals got to it. I didn't want it on the landing pad, so that's the only place we can examine it."

"More attention being paid to that damn lizard than . . ."

He heard them walk across the room, then the sound of a door opening and swinging shut. Tiffany. He turned his head again, saw another gurney parked next to his own, but the covers were pushed aside and there was a warm dent in the sheets where she had once lain. She was gone . . . but he had little doubt that she would return. He had seen the look on her face in the Osprey.

He had to get up. Get up, get dressed, go tell someone what he knew before she came for him. Denny sat up, swung his legs over the side of the bed, and stumbled to the sink across the room. He cupped some water in his mouth and swallowed gratefully; his throat was no longer quite so parched, his head a little clearer. He was naked; second order of business to get on some clothes. Didn't the doctor say that his stuff was over there?

He walked across the cold floor to push aside the screen. Two bodies lay side-by-side on adjacent gurneys. He fought back the urge to vomit and was thankful for the sheets that covered them; he could tell that not much was left of either corpse.

There were four large plastic boxes on the counter under the medical cabinets; in them was the clothing he had worn, plus those belonging to the others. As he pawed through one of the boxes, groggily searching for his undershorts, he found the gronker he had been wearing. The one marked NIXON; he picked it up, stared blearily at it, then placed it on the counter and reached into another box. Here, the one Tiffany had worn, marked STEINBERG. Good; he would need to show them to Cooper and the others to convince them of his story.

He placed her gronker back on top of her clothes, then returned his attention to his own clothing. He was about to step into his trousers when he heard the curtain slide back behind him. Denny began to turn around when the hard muzzle of a .22 Beretta was pressed against the side of his head and he heard Tiffany Nixon whisper, "Don't move."

He gasped involuntarily, but froze in place. "Tiffany," he murmured, not daring to even look back at her. "Figured you might be . . ."

"Shut up," she hissed. "Just get dressed."

The barrel of the revolver was removed from his skull and he heard her step away. He glanced across the counter, looking for something nice and lethal to throw at her. "Don't even think about it," Tiffany commanded, her voice raised a little more loudly now. "The building's empty, so no one will hear if I shoot you in the back. Just hurry up and get dressed. We're going for a little walk in the swamp, you and I."

Denny slowly nodded his head. He didn't turn around, but he heard a creak as she bumped against one of the gurneys. As he pulled up his pants, though, he happened to look at the reflective glass of the medical cabinets above the counter and found that he could see her clearly. Tiffany was still behind him, with the gun trained at his back, but with her free hand she had pried open the blinds of the far window and was peering out, undoubtedly watching the people who were gathered around the corpse of the dinosaur by the boat docks. Going for a walk in the swamp. Denny knew exactly what she was implying. "Tiffany," he continued, "you don't want to . . ."

Her face moved away from the window, and he quickly looked away from the medical cabinet. "I'm not kidding, Steinberg. Shut up and put your clothes on." Then she was looking out the window again. "And hurry up."

"Okay, all right." He slowly let out his breath as he zipped his fly. No way out of this. Christ, pal, she's got you dead in her sights. He reached for his shirt, and as he did he glanced down at the counter . . . and spotted the two gronkers he had just found.

Or was there a way out? Holding his breath, studying her reflection in the medical cabinet, Steinberg carefully reached for the gronker with his name written on it.

From the testimony of Alex J. Cardona; Director of Forensic Sciences, Federal Bureau of Investigation:

SEN. HOFFMANN: Mr. Cardona, I think I speak for the rest of the Commission members when I say that we appreciate the hard work the Bureau has done in this case. For the public record, can you summarize the findings of your lab?

CARDONA: Certainly, Senator. We . . .

KAPLAN: Excuse me, Mr. Cardona. I believe Dr. Williams has an important question to ask first before you go on. Fred?

DR. WILLIAMS: Mr. Cardona, the senator from California does not speak for us all, I'm sad to say. I've read your draft report to the Commission and I'm dissatisfied with one of your key findings. There is an unanswered question which interests every American.

CARDONA: I'm sorry to hear that, sir. How may I answer your question?

DR. WILLIAMS: Let me backtrack briefly, so bear with me. According to your draft report, the deaths of Senator Chambliss and his Secret Service escort were caused by tampering with the reflex inhibitors . . . the so-called gronkers . . . which they wore during the trip. It was

found that someone . . . probably this Jacob Adderholt, if
that was indeed his real name . . . had managed to substitute defective Intel 686 microchips into their units, ones
which had been preconfigured to become inoperative at
precisely 1200 hours of the day that the senator's party was
scheduled to be in the refuge. It was because of the failure
of the gronkers that the deinonychus pack was able to make
the fatal attack on Senator Chambliss and Mr. Gerhardt . . .

CARDONA: That's correct, sir, although it should be
pointed out that Mr. Gerhardt managed to open fire and
fatally wound one of the pack before he was . . .

DR. WILLIAMS: I understand, and Mr. Gerhardt will be
receiving posthumous commendation for his bravery, but
that's been pointed out before, so please don't distract me.
Let me continue. Pending the outcome of the final investigation into Jake Adderholt's true identity, it can be safely
assumed that he was a member of the New American
Minutemen Enclave, considering that his fingerprints match
those of a known NAME terrorist. At this point in your draft
report, the FBI seems to imply that Adderholt was solely
responsible for the deaths. Am I correct in inferring this
from the report?

CARDONA: Sir, the FBI has not completed its investigation of the events in the Okefenokee National Wildlife
Refuge. When it has done so, we will be issuing a final
report which will clarify the findings of the draft report.

DR. WILLIAMS: Mr. Cardona, the director of the FBI
has said that the final report will not be issued until at least
a year from now. I'm losing patience with everyone
involved in this investigation hedging their bets, and I think
the public is, too. You found the smoking gun. What I want
to know is, who pulled the trigger?

CARDONA: I beg your pardon, Dr. Williams, but it almost seems certain that Jake Adderholt was the person responsible for . . .

DR. WILLIAMS: I haven't made myself clear and I'm sorry for that. I'll rephrase it as a blunt question. Was Jake Adderholt acting alone, or did he have an accomplice? Was a second person directly involved in the assassination of Senator Petrie Chambliss? Specifically, was it an inside job?

CARDONA: I'm sorry, Dr. Williams, but the FBI isn't prepared to answer that question yet.

Denny stopped the Hummer at the end of the road and looked around over the rear of the vehicle. He could hear the distant aerial chop of a helicopter approaching; the noise grew louder until an olive drab Army Blackhawk helicopter abruptly soared over the treetops, heading for the compound behind them. He turned back around to see Tiffany Nixon climbing out of the front passenger seat, the gun in her hand still trained on him. "Looks like the feds have arrived," he said. "You know you're not going to get away with this, don't you?"

Tiffany winced in disgust. "Did you get that line from a James Bond movie or something?" She gently waved the gun toward the backpack in the back of the vehicle. "Sure I'm going to get away with it. Now pick it up and start walking. I'm going to be behind you . . . and don't even think about trying any 007 shit with me, okay? You've pissed me off enough already as it is."

He sighed as he carefully climbed out of the driver's seat and picked up the backpack—the same one, he noted, that she had in the canoe with them earlier in the day. "No need to knock James Bond, y'know," he grumbled as he put his right arm through the strap and tugged the pack over his shoulder like a rucksack. "Besides, I'm still curious . . . are you working for NAME, or is it someone else?"

"And you're expecting me to play Blofeld and spill the beans." Nixon was keeping her distance; even if he were stupid enough to try attacking her, she could still nail him before he made anything more than a dumb heroic attempt. "Just start walking. Right hand on the shoulder strap, left hand at your side. Now move."

Denny obediently began to march down the raised boardwalk, pushing aside the last gate and heading toward the observation tower in the Chessier Prairie where they had been only yesterday. He didn't have to look over his shoulder to know that Nixon was right behind him. She hadn't said much to him since she had captured him in the infirmary; once he had gotten dressed, she had escorted him out a back door of the lodge to the Hummer. No one had seen them leave the compound; even if the federal agents were looking for them now, it would still take a few minutes before they guessed that the two of them had gone this way—and even then, they might not immediately suspect foul play. As for as Denny knew, he was the only one who had seen through Tiffany Nixon's deception, that the killings of Pete Chambliss and Joe Gerhardt were not accidental.

He swatted aside some growth with his free hand as he strode down the boardwalk. Denny was surprised at how calm he felt, considering that he had little doubt that she intended to kill him. Would she shoot him, or maybe she was counting on the dinosaurs to do the work? Their gronkers were both switched on; she had taken the one she had found among his belongings in the infirmary, the one with STEINBERG written on the tape. If his suspicions had been correct, this fact was probably his only remaining hope for getting out of here alive . . .

"No, I'm not with NAME," she said suddenly.

"Excuse me?" He stopped and started to turn around, but Tiffany waved him forward again with the Beretta. "I thought you didn't want to talk to me."

"It's a long walk," she said tersely. "Might as well fill the time." The unspoken addendum was, "And since I plan to murder you anyway, what's the point in not letting you know?"

"But NAME is involved," Denny added, trying to keep his voice from shaking. "Am I right?"

A pause. "You're right," Tiffany said at last. "They sought me out because they needed a person on the inside . . . but I'm not with them. A bunch of fanatics, if you ask me."

"Uh-huh. I see." Keep her talking, he thought. The longer she talks, the less time she has to think. . . . He remembered something she had said when they had first met yesterday. "Let me guess," he said, "You're doing this for all the gators and deer and rabbits in the . . ."

"Don't tempt me," she hissed angrily. Wrong words; he quickly shut up. They walked in silence for another few yards before she spoke again. "For the gators and the deer and the rabbits, right. They wanted Chambliss out of the way because he would negotiate away the nuclear deterrent if he became president, but that wasn't my objective. Having the pack kill Chambliss would help to ensure that the project would be ended. This ecosystem . . ."

She let out her breath; it came out as a nervous rattle. "The Okefenokee isn't meant to be a stomping ground for dinosaurs," she continued. "The Early Cretaceous should remain where it belongs, seventy million years dead and buried. No one should be trying to graft dinosaurs into this world. Nature can't cope with reincarnation, and if the pack survives the Okefenokee will die."

"But it's research," he argued, if only for the sake of arguing. "It's searching for answers, for . . ."

"For how many ways a new dominant species can destroy an ecological balance? Sorry, Denny, but I can't allow that to happen. I love this land too much. I've given up too much already to . . . don't stop, just keep walking."

"Hey, I love the balance of nature and all that," he babbled, "but this is kind of a drastic measure, don't you think?" She didn't reply. He licked his dry lips and forged on. "So you hoped that, if Peter were killed by a deinony-chus, the public outcry would . . . ?"

"Cancel the project," Tiffany finished. "They'd extermi-nate the pack and leave the Okefenokee alone."

"So you fucked with the gronkers to . . ."

"Not me," she said defensively. "There was another person involved who did that. Look, we're far enough along already, so I'll make it short and give you the rest. They told me that they wanted at least one survivor, someone who could go back and tell a story that would make it look like an accident. I was told that only my gronker would work when the time came, but the more I thought about it later, the more it figured that they were lying. After all, I was the only one who could incriminate NAME. It made sense that you would survive and that I had to die. I wasn't ready to make that sort of sacrifice, if you know what I mean."

They had reached the end of the boardwalk now. The platform was only fifty feet away, devoid of personnel; the vast clearing of the prairie was spread out before them. "Stop here and put down the backpack," she said.

The gate to the enclosure around the platform was locked; he could tell that just by looking, but off in the distance there was something far more unsettling. Denny could see two now-familiar shapes moving in the distance. Jason and Michael, the surviving members of the pack.

"Hurry it up," Tiffany said. She must have spotted Michael and Jason as well. "Get the pack off, Denny."

He unshouldered the North Face pack and carefully laid it down on the boardwalk in front of him. "So you made sure our gronkers were switched," he said. "In fact, you did it yourself, to be certain I had the defective one and you had . . ."

"Right," she interrupted. "You can turn around now. Step over the pack first." Denny stepped over the backpack, then turned around to face her. He absently noticed that her hair was unbraided; the wind blew it around her shoulders and face, which now looked older for some reason. She was not a woman, he decided, who was accustomed to murder. "You got it," she continued. "The problem was, you managed to make it back to the canoe, and Michael and Jason can't swim. The minute I saw you in the Osprey, I knew I was screwed . . ."

"In a manner of speaking," he impulsively replied.

Tiffany smiled despite herself. "Yes, but not by you, my dear." Still keeping her eyes and the Beretta aimed at him, she quickly knelt to pick up the backpack. "I don't like doing this, y'know, but of all the guys on the trip you're the one I personally wanted to see become Dino Chow. I hate it when guys stare at me the way you did." She hoisted the pack and ducked her left arm into the strap. "And I really despise yuppies."

"But you like gators." Forced humor; the final weapon of the doomed. How many yards were they behind them now?

"They're better company than assholes like you." From not so far behind him, he could hear heavy footfalls across the floating marshland. Jason and Michael, the glimmer twins themselves, were coming in for the kill. Tiffany managed to shrug into the backpack without lowering the gun for more than a few moments. "Anyway, it's time to dust off the contingency plan," she went on. "I hike out of here and you get to be a late lunch. I'd shoot you first to put you out of your misery, but someone might dig the bullets out of your carcass and there's no sense in leaving behind any more evidence than I have to. Mikey and Jason are going to have to do the job for me. Sorry."

Denny wanted to make a smartass remark, but his mouth was too dry for him to speak. Tiffany backed up a couple of feet, still pointing the gun at him, then carefully stepped down from the boardwalk onto the mushy ground. The sound of the approaching dinosaurs was growing louder now. Denny could feel his pulse echoing in his ears like aboriginal drums. He glanced at her waist, saw the gronker with his name written on tape on its side, made himself look away. Don't guess, don't guess, please don't guess . . .

Tiffany was staring over his shoulder. "Gotta run," she said. "As they say in the movies, 'Goodbye, Mr. Bond' . . ." She stopped; for a moment there was a look of sympathy in her eyes. "I hope it's quick." Then she was off the boardwalk; turning around, she bolted for the treeline behind them, clumsily running across the trembling earth.

Denny glanced over his shoulder. The deinonychi were hurtling straight toward him; now they seemed to have grown, taking on the dimensions of the fabled tyrannosaurus rex. He saw cold, crazy eyes, dagger-jawed mouths agape and drooling ooze, powerful legs pummeling the peat moss ground like jackhammers, forelegs with razor-sharp claws outstretched to grab, tear—oh god oh god oh god what if I'm wrong—and threw himself flat onto the boardwalk, covering his head with his arms . . .

And howled with what he half-expected to be his last breath, "I SWITCHED THE GRONKERS!"

He kept his head down, even after Jason and Michael leaped across the far end of the boardwalk—completely ignoring him—and hurled themselves toward Tiffany. He shut his eyes and lay still as death even when he heard the futile low-caliber gunshots, her screams, the sound of ripping flesh . . .

From the testimony of Daniel Steinberg:

KAPLAN: In closing, Mr. Steinberg, I would like to extend the appreciation of this Commission for your cooperation. You've been most helpful in resolving some of the unanswered questions of this event.

STEINBERG: Yes, sir. Thank you, sir.

KAPLAN: We realize that you have personally suffered from your ordeal, both in terms of cost to your liberty and your reputation. I'm referring, of course, to the charges of second-degree murder which have been pressed against you by the federal circuit court in Georgia regarding the death of Tiffany Nixon. I cannot give you any guarantees, but I think your testimony here today may have some favorable bearing on your legal case. Frankly, considering the continuing FBI investigation of the matter, I would be rather surprised if the charges aren't dropped in their entirety. In fact, I expect that you will receive vindication for your role in this affair.

STEINBERG: I certainly hope so, sir, and I appreciate your support. Yet before I leave, may I make a final observation?

KAPLAN: Of course.

STEINBERG: I've noticed that, during these hearings, there has been some discussion of terminating the project . . . that, because the deinonychus pack also caused the deaths of Pete Chambliss and Joe Gerhardt, the dinosaurs should be exterminated themselves. I believe this has also become a matter of public debate . . .

KAPLAN: We're aware that the public is interested in the fate of the dinosaurs. Since these hearings have started, this Commission has been deluged with letters defending their right to live, mainly from members of the scientific community and animal rights activists. On the other hand, I happened to catch a radio call-in talk show just last night in which the subject was addressed, and by a three-to-one margin the callers favored exterminating the pack . . .

STEINBERG: I caught that same discussion too, sir, but I'm not certain whether this is an issue which should be decided by the *Larry King Show*. It makes about as much sense as the proposal to rename the refuge as the "Pete

Chambliss Memorial Wetlands" (*Laughter*). I don't think Pete would have appreciated that . . .

KAPLAN: I tend to agree, Mr. Steinberg.

STEINBERG: The point is, Mr. Kaplan, that the dinosaurs were as much pawns in this . . . um, matter as I was. If the pack is exterminated and the research project is discontinued, then in the end Tiffany . . . that is, Ms. Nixon . . . would have succeeded in what she was trying to do. The Colorado project was begun in the name of scientific inquiry. It would be a waste to abandon it because someone tried to turn the dinosaurs into a murder weapon.

KAPLAN: But they did murder two men, Mr. Steinberg. Three people if you count Ms. Nixon. That's the undeniable fact.

STEINBERG: Only because killing is inherent to their nature. They can't help themselves . . . they came from a different world than ours. If the pack is exterminated and the project is discontinued, then the bitter irony is that Tiffany Nixon will have succeeded in the end. The dinosaurs will be lost to an act of terrorism.

KAPLAN: Mr. Steinberg, you may be correct. I can't fault your logic. Yet I'm afraid you're much too late in making your case for the dinosaurs.

STEINBERG: What? . . . I'm sorry, sir, but I don't understand what you're . . .

KAPLAN: This morning the Georgia state legislature decided that the two surviving members of the deinonychus pack should be treated the same way as wild or domesticated animals which have caused the death of a human being. We understand that . . . uh, Jason and Michael were both destroyed at nine o'clock this morning, about the time you began your testimony.

STEINBERG: I wasn't told . . .

KAPLAN: I'm sorry, Mr. Steinberg . . . and I believe Ms. McCaffrey would like to be recognized by the chair. Congresswoman?

McCAFFREY: I'm surprised by your last-minute plea for clemency for the dinosaurs, Mr. Steinberg. You witnessed the horrible deaths of Mr. Gerhardt and your friend and political mentor with your own eyes. If you had not turned the tables on Ms. Nixon, you would have met the same fate yourself. Perhaps you've had a change of mind in the meantime?

STEINBERG: Ummm . . . no, I don't think I've had a change of mind, Ms. McCaffrey. It's just that . . . well, I just don't believe science should be the victim of politics.

McCAFFREY: Mr. Steinberg, we'll have to forgive you for your innocence of youth. That is much too rash a statement. When has science ever been the victim of politics?

STEINBERG: Ma'am, I think you've got it wrong. The question should be, when has science never been the victim of politics?

McCAFFREY: I see . . . Mr. Kaplan, I would like to make a motion for adjournment.

KAPLAN: The motion is seconded and passed. These hearings are adjourned until tomorrow.